STORM SURGE

STEVEN BECKER

THE WHITE MARLIN PRESS, INC.

———

Join my mailing list
and get a free copy of my starter library:
First Bite

Click the image or download here: http://eepurl.com/-obDj

If you're interested in following along with the action or the locations it the book, please check out the Google map here:

https://drive.google.com/open?id=
1aSo_KT3s3b01JP9QmopuotVQdexvC1T&usp=sharing

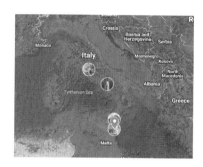

STORM SURGE

PROLOGUE

STEVEN BECKER

STORM SURGE

Syracuse, Sicily, 1969

JOHN STORM STAYED TO THE SHADOWS AT THE BACK OF THE balcony of the church of Santa Lucia. There was no need to check his watch. The slant of the sunlight across the stained-glass windows was now opposite of where it had shone this morning.

Tourists had been streaming in all day to see the church's famous Caravaggio, and most left disappointed. Drop cloths draped over the scaffolding surrounding the painting of the *Burial of Santa Lucia* concealed the master's work from the public eye. The old baroque church was under renovation. The crew's progress was clear as they cleaned the old stone and windows, and they were currently working behind the high altar where the famous painting hung.

From his perch above the altar, John could clearly see the workers on their scaffold. Watching as two men started to remove the painting from its masonry surround, he raised his Minox camera and took several pictures. Checking the advance mechanism, he saw he had a half-dozen shots left. That should be plenty to document the exchange.

Stealing art from a church or a museum was challenging, although in different ways. Both had elaborate security measures in place when the facilities were closed, but they differed during the day. The church offered free admission, collecting what it could from donations. Unlike a museum, there was no daytime security. People roamed in and out at will.

Hidden behind the drop cloth, the men removed the painting from its stretcher, rolling it up and placing it in a tube from which they'd already removed an equally sized canvas. The tube with the priceless original was set aside, as if nothing had happened, while the men installed the forgery as if it were part of their normal workflow.

John Storm had seen enough. As a junior CIA field agent, it was his job to document and report, not police. That was for Interpol, although his superiors had no intention of informing them of the swap. The men working behind the drop cloths were merely the low-hanging fruit. John's picture alone could indict them.

He waited.

An hour later, the workers quit for the day, leaving the protective structure — and the tube — in place. John checked his watch. Four o'clock, and with the church closing to the public in an hour, he expected to soon see who he was really here for: the next link in the chain.

Two priests appeared from a side door. Storm knew both men: Monsignor Albert Maldonado, an American cleric living in Rome, and the resident Sicilian priest. It was the monsignor that he was interested in.

The two men approached the scaffolding and Storm watched as Maldonado graciously swept back the drop cloth to allow the older priest entry to the work area. John now had to make a choice. Remaining in the balcony would allow him to see what the men were doing, but the time it would take to get back downstairs would cripple his ability to tail Maldonado. Since he already knew what was going to happen behind the cloth, having watched the same scene play out in two other churches in the last week, he turned and raced down the stairs.

John ran across the church to the exit, using a group of tourists gawking in the entrance for cover. Seconds later he was across the street, standing by one of the many vendors crowding the sidewalk, browsing through a selection of tourist goods, keeping his eyes on the church door.

With the long tube under his arm, Maldonado exited the church alone, lit a cigarette, and stood by the curb.

John wasn't sure if the monsignor would be recognized as an American by everyone, or if it was just him. From the way Maldonado held his six-foot frame to the Marlboros he smoked, there was no doubt to a sharp-eyed observer.

John snapped two pictures of the cleric and ran for his car, wondering where the monsignor would lead him next.

STORM SURGE

Old Rome

Present Day

MAKO SLAMMED HIS FISTS AGAINST THE TWO LARGE DOORS blocking access to the courtyard, a common feature of the buildings here. As he glanced behind him something small and hard struck his head, and then his shoulder. His first thought was the rain had turned to hail, but a warm trickle of blood running down his face told him otherwise. The skinny sidewalks bordering the narrow street allowed little room for overhangs, forcing him to hug close to the building for protection.

A pair of drones circled overhead, the source of his misery. With his back pressed against the massive, twelve-foot-high wooden doors, he kicked against one. The sound reverberated, although he wasn't sure if it penetrated through the thick wood.

"Hello—" Mako moved his lips, quietly mouthing the word into the bone microphone by his jaw.

"Sorry about that. Had to get some divers out of the water."

The connection was full of static and noise, probably from the boat engines, but there was no mistaking Alicia Phon's nasal voice. She called herself Mako's handler, though they were really partners. Both were cast-offs of the CIA — Alicia due to the greener pastures offered by contract work, Mako when given a shove out the door when another complaint was added to his too-thick personnel file.

"What the hell. Can't you pay someone to do that while I'm out here dying?" Mako muttered.

"Pardon? Who changed the timetable without asking permission?"

He knew she was right. A brilliant analyst, Alicia and her boyfriend, TJ, owned a SCUBA dive shop in Key Largo. It was good cover and paid the bills when the agency's contract work slowed down.

"There are two drones overhead."

"Oh my. Give me a minute."

"Just get the doors open." Another round of pellets flung his way caused several more lacerations to his exposed skin. Mako knew the drones were capable of deadlier firepower, and wondered why they were spraying just buckshot at him. Panicked, he looked around. Alicia had warned him about coming to the compound drop-off site blind. She had sent detailed maps and instructions to help him scout the area. But Mako had found the women of Italy more interesting, making this only the second time he had seen the doors—the first being an hour ago.

"Come on, Alicia. I'm bleeding here." Mako kicked the door again out of frustration, then spied a small cafe across the street and bolted for its door. The sanctuary of the courtyard would have been preferable, but at this point, anything with a roof would stop the incessant pellets from striking him.

"Just a minute," Alicia's voice was in his ear. "I've got, like, zero reception out here."

Mako didn't want to know where they were. He was at least partly responsible for TJ and Alicia's reliance on their dive business to generate additional income—at least in their opinion. Placing the blame for the failure of their last two contracts squarely on his own shoulders, he'd had no choice but to soldier on. Now his life was threatened by his string of bad decisions.

"Hurry."

A stream of static was the only indication they were still connected. Knowing Alicia's distinctive voice would alert him when she was back, he focused on his predicament. He'd accomplished his goal and retrieved the five-hundred-year-old journal penned by Michelangelo Merisi, better known as Caravaggio. The baroque painter had apparently been quite a rogue, always living on the edge, often of his own sword. Constantly broke and on the run from the law, he often created duplicates of his paintings to raise money.

It was common practice at the time for the Master's apprentices to do some if not most of their own work. Caravaggio, because of his nature, did not have the ability to mass produce art.

The journal detailed which ones were original and how to authenticate them. They were all valuable; the difference, though, was substantial, in the tens of millions.

Pulling open the cafe's glass door, it swung back on its hinges. Mako muttered an apology in Italian, grabbing the handle just before a gust of wind took it. He closed the door with a little more finesse and looked around the cafe. Thankfully, it was empty except for a woman behind the counter, allowing him to turn back to the action. Feeling the journal's bulge in his jacket pocket and avoiding the glare of the woman,

Mako studied the sky and the street, looking for any sign of the drones or their operator.

Mako felt the eyes of the matron bore into him. Nothing was free in Rome. With no public restrooms, using a private one required a purchase. Digging into his pocket, he pulled out a wad of euros and handed her a five.

"Espresso."

Snapping up the bill from the countertop, and with his presence now justified, she turned to the machine. While she was occupied, he moved toward the small alcove where he assumed the bathrooms were. Stepping into the men's room, he locked the door behind him. The lights snapped on, revealing a well-appointed bathroom—more lavish than the shop itself.

Looking at his face in the decorative mirror, he angled his tall, lithe frame towards the overhead light and studied his wounds. There was a little blood, but not enough to be worried about. The pellets were more annoyance than dangerous, probably used to decrease the possibility of collateral damage in the small space. Dabbing at the small specks with a damp paper towel, Mako cleaned himself up and, when he deemed he was presentable, slicked back his hair, unlocked the door, and walked out.

His espresso and change were on the counter. Taking the cup to a small table on the back wall, he left the change. The woman said nothing, but as soon as he turned he sensed her swoop in and scoop it up.

The narrow lane was quiet, likely because it didn't go anywhere. The winding maze of side streets was difficult for pedestrians to navigate, and even more so if you were crazy enough to drive here. Most tourists chose to utilize the main avenues.

Raindrops splattered the street and dripped from the shallow awning in front of the shop, another reason for the lack of traffic. The cafe appeared to be the only business. The rest of the street was lined with older buildings, most having the same arrangement of large doors at street level, which were wide enough for a car to enter. Mako knew expansive courtyards lay beyond, but the vertical facades and closed doors gave the street a claustrophobic feel.

The buildings shot straight up. Stone carvings, wood shutters, and several small balconies were the only architectural features. Looking up to see if the drones remained vigilant, from his angle the five-story structures appeared to close off the sky. In order to see if the drones were still overhead, Mako needed to exit the store. And once he did, he knew if he needed refuge it would cost him. If only the woman was younger he could have charmed her for a little leniency, but she was easily old enough to be his mother.

Mako endured the woman's stare, even though it bore into his skin more deeply than the pellets the drones had shot. There was no point leaving the cover of the structure until Alicia was back online. Sitting with his back against the far wall, which allowed him the best, though limited, view of the street, he sipped the strong coffee and waited.

All that was left was to deliver the journal to the client, who was likely the CIA's Rome station chief. It was a fairly transparent arrangement, but only Alicia knew all the details. Taking another sip of the scalding coffee, he asked himself again what the government wanted with an artist's journal, and why they were willing to authorize a mid-six-figure contract for it. If the government was willing to spend that kind of money for the lump in his pocket there was no wonder why the deficit was out of control.

The woman must have sensed the small cup was empty and raised her eyebrows at him. Mako shook his head and rose, heading for the door. Whatever the drones shot at him was better than the daggers the woman threw.

As he stepped out, two black sedans converged from each side of the small street. Passenger and driver doors opened simultaneously, encroaching on the narrow sidewalks.

As the four men approached he could see the barrels of their pistols pointed at him. This was not his first rodeo and Mako knew escape often came from unlikely avenues, but the street was now blocked, and the solid facades of the buildings offered no refuge.

Men approaching from both ends of the street made Mako feel he was in a vice, the gap closing fast. "Alicia!" he yelled into the mic, though it had no effect. Static prevailed as he searched for any means of escape. The massive doors he'd kicked earlier offered sanctuary if only they would open.

The only other option was—again—the cafe.

Dashing toward the door, Mako threw it open and ran past the woman. Recalling a third door by the bathrooms, he ignored her disapproving look and crossed the small room, heading for the alcove. Unmarked, it could have been a closet, but was wider and looked more substantial, either an exterior door or to a back room.

Just as he heard the gunmen enter the cafe, he yanked on the door handle. It resisted his efforts, but didn't feel locked. Hearing the woman talking to the men, he pulled again with the same result.

There was no doubt in his mind she would give him up.

They were halfway across the room when the door finally opened. Instead of finding an avenue of escape, he ran into a woman. Her green eyes met his and an electric charge shot through his body. Wishing the circumstances were different, he pushed her out of the way, knocking over a trash can in the process, and took off down the street.

Behind him everyone was yelling. The confusion increased his safety buffer and he was able to round the corner, removing himself from the gunmen's field of view. Instead of another side street, he found himself in a large plaza. Umbrellas protected the cafe tables on the sidewalks and booths selling tourist trinkets filled the center. With enough cover to avoid the rain, business continued unabated.

Mako ran toward the center of the plaza and looked back. The gunmen had just emerged from the side street and stood together, scanning the scene. Seconds later they split up, each moving in a different direction to enlarge the search area. Thinking that if it worked once, it could work again, and with no apparent hiding places, Mako headed for a bar on the opposite side of the plaza, using the vendor stalls to help obscure him.

He slowed to open the bar door, glancing over his shoulder to see if the men had seen him. For now, the coast looked clear, and he walked through the busy bar, finding a spot near the back with an unobstructed view of the door.

There was nothing to do except wait. With four men in pursuit, any move he made would be noticed. Figuring the best thing he could do was act the part: when in Rome, you know. Catching the bartender's eye, he started to order an Aperol spritz, then changed it to a Glenlivet neat, preferring the taste and power of the aged scotch to the orange spritzes the tourists enjoyed. There was also a rumor that The Glenlivet would render him impervious to bullets. Mako cradled the glass, sipping the single-malt scotch and watching the door.

At one point one of the men poked his head in and glanced around, but Mako saw him first and ducked down, using the bar for cover. He was on his second drink and had struck up a halting conversation with an Italian woman working on her English when Alicia Phon was back in his ear.

"Excuse me for a minute," Mako said to the woman.

"Excuse what?" Alicia asked.

"Not you, but it's about time."

"From your *barstool*, it looks like you're a few minutes away from the compound. What the hell, Mako. We're so close to closing out this deal."

The emphasis on *barstool* was clear. If she could talk to him, she also knew where he was.

"I was waiting for you, my dear," he answered. Mako knew he'd get no sympathy for being pelted by drones or chased by gunmen. The single word that described Alicia was "efficient;" everything else was secondary. He was also aware that the compound was under observation and didn't want her to open the doors too soon.

"We're going to need another way in," Mako said, telling her about the last hour, leaving out his encounters with the two women, judging some things to be irrelevant.

"Head toward the compound. I'll figure it out before you get there."

From anyone other than Alicia, hearing that would have scared the hell out of him, but Mako knew if he had her attention, there was no one better to get him through this.

STEVEN BECKER

STORM SURGE

Key Largo, Florida

ALICIA GRABBED THE DIVER'S TANK VALVE. STANDING ON THE bottom rung of the welded ladder that swung down into the water behind the transom, she helped him remove his gear and guided him into TJ's outstretched arms. One other diver was in the water waiting while they secured the first diver's gear and moved him to the starboard bench.

"You good?" Alicia asked, before turning to the diver in the water.

"Thank you, ma'am," the diver replied in a business-like tone.

Alicia smiled despite the response. She didn't know it was a military thing, but folks were usually way more excited after a dive. Working with adaptive divers had become one of her passions. The other was the future of the reef, currently being decimated by rising water temperatures, sewage outflow, and disease. If things continued to go well today, they had another dive planned the next day for these two veterans, where they would be diving with a local non-profit to plant farmed coral on the reef.

The first diver waited patiently, helping as he could, while Alicia and TJ repeated the procedure. A few minutes later, she left the divers with a cold drink and, ignoring the pile of gear on the deck, climbed the stainless-steel ladder to the flybridge.

"Mako needs you," TJ said, handing her the phone. "I'll square things away down there. Jen also called to ask if we're still on for tomorrow."

The young woman from the Coral Restoration Foundation was scheduled to go out with them and help the disabled veterans replant the reef tomorrow.

"Mako." She spoke softly into the phone, knowing her voice would be relayed to the bud in his ear. While she waited for him to reply, she leaned over the railing to check on the divers, catching their eyes as they looked back at her. Before Mako's voice distracted her, she noticed there was something different about the men. After a successful dive, most of the veterans she worked with were almost euphoric. These two acted as if there was something more important than the dive. Thinking they might be apprehensive about the intricate tasks they were going to perform tomorrow, she turned her attention back to Mako.

STORM SURGE

Old Rome

PELTED BY THE STEADY DOWNPOUR, MAKO MADE HIS WAY BACK TO the compound. Two blocks from the building, he stopped under the small awning of a very expensive shoe store and pulled up a satellite image of the area on his phone. Zooming in lost much of the detail he needed. A birds-eye view didn't help much, either. Unless the picture was taken from directly above, the buildings obscured any alleys or small driveways. Rome was generally not known as a "tall" city. From Mako's point of view, it was a "close" city. With almost a thousand churches, a multitude of museums, and ruins everywhere, real estate available for commercial use was at a premium; every inch of space was utilized.

Putting the phone away, Mako reviewed what he knew of the area: There seemed to be only three ways to reach the double doors guarding the compound: the two ends of the street and the back door of the cafe. The gunmen would likely be watching the street, making the cafe the less dangerous option—even with the deadly stare of the woman behind the counter.

Turning back to the intersection he'd just passed, Mako studied the street before crossing diagonally and darting into the alley behind the cafe.

Finding the overturned trash can he had collided with earlier identified the door, and reaching it, Mako tested the lever. It moved easily, and he was about to open it when he decided to knock instead. He wanted the woman's cooperation. Using his elbow he pounded on the steel door. A minute later the door cracked open and he was momentarily speechless when he found himself staring into those mesmerizing green eyes.

"I need your help," he whispered.

"Saba," she said, holding out her hand and moving to the side to allow him entry.

"Mako." He returned her grasp. "Some men—" he paused— "Thugs. They're in the street. I need to make my way across to number 471. Can I cut through your place?"

She flicked her head at the matronly woman. "Who am I to say no?"

The old woman screeched something in Italian, causing Saba to flinch. Mako looked at Saba, catching her eyes and noticing a strange look passing over her face. Her glance suddenly darted away.

"Don't mind her." Saba looked back at him.

If only I had more time, Mako thought as he moved into the seating area of the cafe. Careful not to meet the eyes of the old woman, he stood to the side of the front door and studied the street. The rain had let up enough for him to see the adjacent intersections where the black sedans had entered the street to let off the gunmen. They were clear now, as was the entire block —almost too clear. The drones were invisible from this angle; all he could hope for was that their batteries had forced them to abort.

The street looked clear, and he placed his hand on the lever.

Pausing for a second, he checked again. Without prior observation of pedestrian and vehicular traffic patterns, he had no way of knowing if this was normal or not.

"Alicia? You there?" he whispered into the bone mic.

"Just a second. I think I have an alternate way in."

Before the words reached his brain he had opened the door. "Don't need it. The street's cool now."

"Don't," she warned.

It was too late. Mako had stepped out onto the sidewalk. The second he did the sedans emerged.

"Open the lock."

"You idiot."

"Just do it." Mako ran across the street. Before he reached the opposite sidewalk, gunshots rang out. Instinctively he headed back toward cover. Had he trusted the doors to be unlocked, he would have gone for it, but if he had found them locked he would be a sitting duck.

The cafe was his only way out. Turning, his course set, he yanked the door open and ran through the cafe. Just before he reached the back door, a hand grasped his elbow.

"Not that way. They saw you come in."

It was Saba. Despite the life or death situation, her grasp felt warm and her green eyes were reassuring. Using his wrong head, Mako blindly followed her lead as she moved him near a table, which she slid several feet to the side, revealing a trapdoor. Taking his hand, she led him down a short flight of stairs that opened to a storeroom. Once he was in, she reached up and pulled a cord, bringing the cover down over the opening and leaving them in the dark. Seconds later, Mako heard the table being pulled into place above. She might not have liked him, but the older woman was protecting Saba.

Darkness surrounded them. Saba had moved several feet

away. He listened but could hear nothing over the blood pounding in his ears. Slowly his heart rate slowed and he heard voices above. It was two men, but they were speaking in Italian. It appeared every man incurred the old woman's ire, as she lashed out at them.

"What are they saying?" Mako whispered.

Just as Saba's finger touched her lips, Alicia's voice was in his ear.

"What the hell are you doing? I opened the door, but you never showed! We're about to lose the contract."

As Alicia continued talking, Mako knew the best course was to wait out her temper. The CIA—at least he assumed it was the agency that had sponsored the contract—would always be there. The small journal in his pocket was gold.

Finally, the connection fell quiet, and he told her, "I'm good. Across the street in a basement."

By this time, his eyes had acclimated to the darkness. He assumed there was a light, but if on, it might have leaked out the cracks around the opening. Saba had chosen to shroud them in darkness, but he could see the outline of her body clearly. It was too dark to see her features, especially those eyes, but he could see her curves. Just as he started to appraise her, she reached out and pulled the bud from his ear. He started to protest, but her finger on his lips quieted him. She held up a single finger and touched her ear, then pointed upstairs.

The only sound Mako could hear was her soft breath, and as they waited, he wondered how it would feel against his skin. Before his imagination got the best of him, Saba pointed to the faint outline of a door in the sidewall of the basement.

Rome was famous for its underground caverns, tunnels, and catacombs. He had been fascinated to learn on a tour earlier this week that most of ancient Rome had been buried over the centuries and only in the last few hundred years had it been excavated. Two millennia of silt, as well as the practice of filling older buildings as foundations for newer ones, had buried the ancient city. With an entire city beneath the ground, the owners of nearly every construction project waited with bated breath through the excavation phase of their jobs; most were affected in some way, and some were halted completely.

Saba opened the slide bolt and cracked the door. As she pulled the door open to creep into the dark passage, a musty breeze surprised Mako.

Heading into the subterranean unknown was not in Mako's comfort zone. As much as he hated having Alicia in his ear, he missed her guidance now.

Mako paused at the threshold. If nothing else, he figured it was safe to talk now. "Where are we going?"

"Where those men can't find you. Rome is filled with secrets, don't worry."

He was afraid of that. Going back was not an option, so Mako ducked his head and followed Saba. He tried to engage her several times, but she ignored him. Moving through what appeared to be a tunnel, Mako walked heel to toe in order to avoid tripping on the rocks and roots scattered along the hard-packed dirt floor, while his hands raked against what felt like stone walls. They were wet, probably from the rain seeping through the ground, but it did give him some comfort that there was a level of engineering to the structure rather than a makeshift mineshaft.

He estimated they had been working their way along for fifteen minutes when he felt the tunnel suddenly start to ascend. Converting the steps he had been counting into an estimate of the distance they had traveled, it seemed they had covered about a half-mile. The pace they moved reconciled with his guess, but still left him clueless as to the direction, although it soon became clear when they reached a grate that overlooked the Tiber River.

Mako glanced at the padlocked gate. Before he could ask, Saba picked up a rock and slammed it against the old mechanism, which fell away, and they stepped out into daylight. It wasn't his first look at the famed waterway, and like the first time he was disappointed. The Tiber, at least from the old Roman accounts, summoned romantic images. Now, graffiti covered the concrete embankments and litter was scattered along the sidewalks. The scene had a barren look to it, but regardless, stepping out of the tunnel he felt relieved.

"Thanks. I owe you for this," Mako said, as he stretched backwards to work the kinks out. Mako's eyes were drawn like a magnet to Saba, who was dusting the dirt from her jeans. Sorting out his thoughts, he knew he needed some answers. Her beautiful veneer might have thrown another man, but Mako had been burnt by beautiful women before. Her appearance and help had been all too convenient.

"Dinner?" He was glad Alicia wasn't in his ear when he asked. She would doubtless have scolded him for his womanizing tendencies, but in this case, it was information that Mako was after.

"I suppose I saved your ass. Probably the least you could do," she said. Her tone implied that this wasn't the first time she had been in this kind of situation. "There's a place I know on the other side of the river."

"Right on. Lead the way."

Side by side, not as close as lovers, nor as far away as strangers, they walked toward the bridge. They moved quickly away from the gate, and Mako looked back at the tunnel entrance to see if they had been followed. It took him several long seconds to find the well-disguised grate. He realized they had traversed the city through a storm drain, or at least a passage disguised as one. Looking at the concrete wall running adjacent to the Tiber, he saw a similar arched opening repeating every hundred yards.

"Are they all like that?" he asked.

Saba followed his gaze and understood. She winked. "Wouldn't you like to know?"

The off-the-cuff comment added to Mako's growing list of questions. He hoped a good bottle of wine with dinner might shed some light on his mysterious savior. The rain was intermittent now, but when a drop landed in the ear his bud had been, he remembered Saba had Alicia in her pocket. It might have been amusing, but it was not a good place for his handler. Adding the recovery of the bud to his list, he followed Saba across the Ponte Umberto.

On the other bank stood a large, cylindrical tower. Looking for a conversation starter, he asked Saba about the fortress.

"It's the Castel Sant'Angelo, otherwise known as Hadrian's tomb. Another relic built with the sweat of slaves. It does have some interesting features, though, like a covered walkway eight hundred meters to Vatican City. Even the pope needs a secret exit."

"Not so secret, though."

"Would you like to see it?"

"Had enough of tunnels for the day, thanks." What he really wanted was a drink, to stare into Saba's green eyes, and see if they were the pathway to her soul—or something else.

STORM SURGE

Trastevere District, Rome

THE FEEL OF COLD, DAMP CONCRETE STARTLED MAKO AWAKE, AND he found himself shivering under the rough material of a threadbare blanket. Sitting up slowly, he cast the worn rag aside. It took a few seconds to get his bearings. He noticed the river stretching in front of him, much the same as it had last night, except this morning he had a blinding headache, no hot babe beside him, and no recollection of how he got here.

Though he suspected the journal was gone, Mako needed to check. He patted the inside pocket of his jacket. Empty. Sticking his finger in his ear, he found the bud had vanished, as well as his phone.

His wallet, however, remained in his pocket. With the journal's contract value well into six figures, whoever had taken it had no need for his money.

Mako sat up and rubbed his eyes, trying to recall how he'd gotten here. As his senses fully returned, he felt movement around him. It turned out he had neighbors—about twenty, from the looks of the sleeping bags and shopping carts nearby.

Then he remembered her eyes. The jade-green eyes that changed with the light. Her face appeared in his mind's eye, and then her name: Saba. As the cobwebs in his mind cleared, he looked around. The graffiti covering the brick embankment across the river looked familiar, as did the bridge. Memories from yesterday started to flood back, none of them good. He had been set up. And with the journal stolen, the contract was lost.

Without the phone and earbud, Alicia was gone as well. His guide, work mom, handler, or whatever she was often irritated him, but her guidance was essential. He was on his own.

Mako was not one to wallow in self-pity. His father, John, a CIA legend, put out to pasture with the last round of budget cuts, had been hard on him. For most of his childhood, it had been just the two of them, but with John often away on "business," Mako was raised by doting grandparents. His mother was nothing but a fond memory, one that he had probably fabricated. She had died when he was young; a car accident, he was told at the time. It wasn't until he had joined the agency himself that his father had told him the truth—she had been killed by a Russian assassin.

Rising to his feet, Mako staggered for several steps. Glancing around to see if his neighbors had noticed, he figured he could have fallen into the river for all the attention it got him. The other vagrants assumed he was probably high, a condition they were familiar with.

After several ungainly steps, Mako got his bearings and started walking more normally. The appearance of the Castel Sant'Angelo gave him the landmark he needed. Turning to the south, he started following the river. Without his phone, trying to make his way through the city would be impossible. His father would chide him if he knew, but the old man was the only one he knew that still used paper maps. At least he recognized several landmarks and decided, with the fortress behind him, to continue along the banks of the Tiber until he found the Vittorio Emanuel II Monument, built in honor of the first king of a unified Italy. The twentieth-century neoclassical building loomed large over the city. It might have been gaudy, but was easy to find. From there he could make his way back to what he hoped was still his safe house, an apartment in the Monti district.

Mako followed the straight section of the river for a few miles, passing several other homeless camps. The city was starting to come to life by the time he reached the first bend in the river that told him he was getting close. Groups of bicycle riders and joggers invaded the sidewalk, forcing him to the side. Then, an island appeared mid-stream. Mako remembered the landmark. To his left, a steep staircase broke the expanse of the concrete embankment. After ascending the old stone stairs, Mako looked to the left and saw the monument. It was a simple matter now. Once he reached the Piazza Venezia, he followed the Via dei Fori Imperiali toward the Colosseum.

Halfway to the iconic ruin, he found the street, and turned left. A block removed from the main avenue, the neighborhood took over. Walking past the shuttered wine bars and restaurants, the street had a quiet feel, though that would change later. There was no traffic. It was too narrow for a thoroughfare. In the death maze of the city's layout, unless you owned or rented a garage or were looking for an elusive parking spot, there was no reason to travel the cobblestone street.

Finding the building, Mako reached into his pocket. Relieved when he felt the shape of the keys, he pulled them out. Finding them was the first thing that had gone right in two days. Then he noticed the main entry door was ajar, and worried that someone had penetrated his upper-floor safe house. Removing a wad of paper that had been stuck in the door jamb to stop the bolt from engaging, Mako pushed open the door. Aware that the apartment could have been compromised, he crept up the uneven stone stairs, stopping at each floor to listen. Reaching the third-floor landing, he moved toward the wooden apartment door and ran his fingers around the jamb, checking for the tell-tale hair he had placed on top of the door.

Convinced he was safe, Mako unlocked the door, and entered the sanctuary. In no rush to incur Alicia's wrath, he walked past the phone, and entered the bathroom. A steaming hot shower, shave, and change of clothes later, Mako brewed a cup of coffee, sat down, and reviewed what had happened.

There was no point belaboring his foolishness in trusting Saba. What he needed to do was to find her, and to do that, he needed Alicia. Crossing the room to the phone, he lifted the handset, and punched in a six-digit code. There were several messages—all from her. Deleting them, Mako dialed her number, sat down, and prepared himself for the browbeating he knew was coming.

STORM SURGE

Vatican City

AFTER ALL THE TIME HE HAD SPENT ABROAD, THE ESPRESSO CUP still felt like a child's tea set to John Storm. He didn't know what to do with it, and finally just drained it and set it on the small metal table. Coffee had supplanted scotch years ago as his drink of choice, and he reveled in the brew; it was the demitasse cups he couldn't deal with.

"The journal was not delivered." The man sitting with him paused. "But you already know that."

John studied the bishop across the table, thinking how things had changed over the years. Dressed in plain black clerical clothing, Bishop Maldonado's eyes locked onto his. It was a game of chicken now, and John pursed his lips to hold back the smile.

Finally, a well-dressed woman walked past, giving both the men, priest and spy, an excuse to end the contest.

"We'll get it back." John tried to instill a confidence he didn't feel in the words. Unknown to Mako, he had been watching the street yesterday. He'd seen Mako try to gain access to the compound, fail, then take harbor in the cafe when the gunmen blocked the street. From his perch in the choir of the church across the back street, he had lost sight of him after that and was forced to leave his observation spot to call Alicia.

At first, she had been angry and it took a few minutes of venting for her to clarify she was not mad at him. This was not the first time he had tailed his son, nor probably the last. It had been a proud day when Mako entered the agency, but his hopes for his son had been shattered by the boy's reckless behavior. Now, forced into retirement, John's purpose was to keep his son alive. It wasn't hard to follow him; his tradecraft was as sloppy as his personal relationships.

John's agency contacts kept him apprised of the contracts Mako worked on. And in this case, for John it was just a matter of connecting the dots. It wasn't hard to figure out the buyer, and he had called Maldonado. With the journal now missing, he needed the bishop to extend the time limit on the contract.

"If it were you, my friend, I would believe it, but the contract is with your son's group."

"I'll take care of it," John said, harshly. He wasn't sure if it was the coffee or Maldonado's smug attitude that was gnawing at his gut.

"Twenty-four hours, my old friend. And that is only because you're involved. The authentication is scheduled for Saturday evening in Sicily. Without the journal...."

John didn't need him to complete the sentence. After fifty years, there were rumors that Caravaggio's *Nativity with Saint Francis and Saint Lawrence* had resurfaced—if it was the original. The timing was no surprise, after another of the painter's long-lost works had just sold for almost two hundred million dollars. Most thought the Church had been the hero in recovering the painting; John knew otherwise—it was involved in the theft.

"The journal will be delivered before then." John accepted the reprieve, adding a degree of vagueness at the same time.

"See that it is." The bishop rose, and extended his hand.

John half-rose and reluctantly took Maldonado's hand. He sat back down, and waited until the bishop was out of sight before signaling the waitress for his check. Dropping a twenty-euro note on the bill, John thought about his predicament while he waited for his change.

He didn't need to be told the Church wanted the journal, though he did wonder what they held over the CIA to force the agency to authorize the contract. The tactics weren't unusual, though. J. Edgar Hoover wouldn't have made it past choir-boy status in the Church's clandestine and brutish web. You didn't stay as powerful as it had for two millennium without brokering secrets.

Rome was familiar to John. His area of expertise with the agency had been the Roman Catholic Church. He knew Vatican politics, knew the players, and most of all understood how Vatican, Inc., worked. He also knew how the holy veneer of the Church hid the evil inside many of the men behind its trappings; John could easily see through it. Once John discovered the contract was antiquity related, the involvement of the Church was his first guess. The Vatican had the largest collection of stolen art on the planet, and most of it was hidden below the Sistine Chapel.

With the deadline extended, it was time to talk to Alicia. Across the small plaza from where he sat was one of Rome's many fountains. John cared little about the provenance of the horse spitting out water; what he liked was the privacy the sound of the cascading flow gave him.

"Sorry to bother you so early," John said, after a sleepy voice came over the phone.

"Do you know where he is?" Alicia asked.

Their relationship was stilted; neither John nor Alicia was able to bridge the generation gap, or in this case, the technological chasm that separated the old school from the new.

"I lost sight of him last night. I do have some good news for you. Bishop Maldonado has extended your contract."

"How do you know?" she asked.

John sensed that she was going on the defensive. "I've been at this game since you and my boy were in diapers. I know a few things." He tried for a little self-deprecation to ease the tension. "Listen. You know I'm looking out for you guys."

"Fair enough. What do you plan on doing?"

"Find the boy and get the journal back." Though their methods were opposite, their goal was the same.

"He's back in the safe house. I just got a notification that he picked up his messages. Do you need the address?"

"Your safe house was pretty easy to find." John decided this was not the time for a lesson in tradecraft. "That'll be my next stop, then."

John put the odds at fifty-fifty that if Mako knew his father was on the way, he would bolt to avoid him. John was also one-hundred percent certain that Mako wouldn't answer Alicia's call. He wouldn't suspect John was coming until he walked in the door.

STEVEN BECKER

STORM SURGE

Vatican City

ALBERT MALDONADO WAS A DIFFERENT KIND OF BISHOP. FOR starters, he was American, which put him in an exclusive group. For years, the dioceses in the U.S. were treated like red-headed stepchildren—until the money they contributed to the Vatican could no longer be ignored. Still, even after pouring millions into the Vatican coffers, Americans were not well represented in the Holy See. Maldonado had broken the mold—he had power, as well as a unique position.

Maldonado's mentor was another unique American: Archbishop Paul Marcinkus, president of the Vatican bank from 1971-89. Maldonado had acted as the right-hand to the man who answered to the pope alone. But several financial scandals had brought down Marcinkus and temporarily dimmed Maldonado's hopes to eventually fill his shoes.

Growing up on the South Side of Chicago in the sixties, and surrounded by gangs and violence, Maldonado had learned to protect himself both physically and mentally. Survival on the streets or in the boardroom was a skill and even now, with his esteemed position, he still worked at it.

For a man in his seventies, Maldonado's lithe and muscular frame was incongruous with the stereotypical clergyman, and to keep it that way his workout was demanding. Counting in his head, he reached ten and set the barbell on the rack. Trembling, he lay back on the bench to recover. Over the years, he'd watched his strength slowly decline, but he was still a powerful man. His mind was sharp as ever, but it was his physical prowess that separated him from his peers and had endeared him to two popes.

It had been a surprise to many when a much younger Albert Maldonado had chosen the seminary over a football scholarship, but to those who knew him best, it was his natural course. Putting aside the talk about his potential on the gridiron was hard and several times he had wavered in his decision. But the Church had always been something special for him; a refuge from a drunken father and a mother who did whatever she could to rationalize her husband's behavior. There were many reasons that other young men stayed clear of the Church. Some left after being exposed to the deviant nature of some clergy. Albert had heard stories, but no priest had ever touched him, probably out of fear.

Maldonado sat up and checked his phone before moving to the squat rack. There he added two thirty-five-pound plates to the forty-five-pound bar, each of which he suspected held only his fingerprints. The meek might inherit the earth, but it was the strong who would rule it. Maldonado had learned early on that he could achieve his goals by subtle intimidation. His superiors recognized it as well, and were happy to distance themselves from him. There was no question he was too restless to pastor a parish, and on graduation, Albert, who was fluent in a half-dozen languages, was assigned as an interpreter to the Vatican.

Larger than life, he quickly made both friends and enemies.

His phone had rung after the first rep. Sneaking a glance, he saw it wasn't the pontiff's secretary, the only person he would have stopped his workout for. Five reps later, the bar was back on the rack and Maldonado grabbed a towel and his phone. The call had been from a local number, one he didn't recognize. A notification for a voicemail came through and, listening to it recognized the voice of John Storm.

"Well?" he asked, after returning the call.

"We need to meet," Storm said.

He forgave the brusqueness. Few men could dictate terms to him; John Storm was one of those men. Because of Storm, he was still here. The two men had first met longer ago than either would admit, and each had quickly realized the worth of the other. Maldonado had been knee-deep in the security fraud scandal that brought down his mentor. He knew it was John Storm who had concealed evidence linking him to the crimes. In doing so, John had made a powerful friend.

They agreed on a time and place. Maldonado already knew what the meeting was about. He had personally authorized the contract to retrieve the journal, and had been waiting inside the compound to receive it last night. The key to authenticating Caravaggio's works could not fall into his enemies' hands. He was well aware that Storm could bring good news as well as bad. His paranoia had kept him in power through several scandals, so he assumed the worst.

Making a quick calculation, he decided to complete his workout, and eased himself under the bar for another set.

7

STEVEN BECKER

STORM SURGE

Rome

PULLING ON A PAIR OF NITRILE GLOVES, SABA STUDIED THE COVER of the journal, and with a tinge of guilt, gently flipped through the pages. Written in Latin in hard-to-decipher handwriting, it would take a specialist to decode the clues Caravaggio had left, but as an artist, he had clarified his words with line drawings.

Known as an arrogant brawler, Michelangelo Merisi da Caravaggio was an anomaly. Had he been born in the present day, he would likely have been an L.A. rapper. Known and licensed to carry a sword, he was not afraid to use it, and several bodies lay in his wake as he moved from Rome to Malta to Sicily to Naples, each time to escape his deeds. His renown as a painter afforded him second, third, and even fourth chances. Living a life on the run had its pitfalls and Caravaggio, unlike his contemporaries with their "art factories," rarely profited from his work.

As a painter he was a unique talent. Known to paint directly on the canvas without layout or sketches, his work was difficult to authenticate. In only one case was his signature apparent. *The*

Beheading of Saint John the Baptist had been painted to garner the favor of the Grandmaster of the Knights of Malta. Caravaggio had sought refuge on the island in an attempt to be knighted, which would allow him to return to Rome, which he had been forced to flee after being accused of murder. Yet another body, this time in Malta, had foiled that plan, forcing Caravaggio to escape to Sicily. The *Beheading* remains unique as the only work that he admitted to signing outright. Known to have produced several "duplicates" opened the door for forgeries.

These were the clues that the journal held.

After two years of nonstop effort, the journal sat in front of her. Saba knew that if she turned it over to her superiors at Interpol it would be the pinnacle of her career. However, her conscience would not allow it. Over the course of her investigation she had discovered many things, chief among them the Vatican's stolen art collection. Maldonado had lobbied hard that the journal, when it was found, should revert to the Church. As an additional measure that showed just how important Caravaggio's clues were, Maldonado had included the CIA, along with Interpol, in his effort to retrieve the journal. To outsiders the redundant contracts looked much like Caravaggio's own paranoia, but Saba knew the bishop must have a reason.

Should the journal go public, the Vatican would be faced with another scandal. With Pope Francis trying to clean up the financial mess he had inherited, the revelation that the Holy See was also involved in an art forgery scam would rock the foundation of the Church.

Saba respected the new pontiff's goals, but she didn't trust the Church. Her childhood in Croatia had been filled with stories of the atrocities perpetuated during World War II by the Nazis' puppet government—all financed and run by the Church. The Church had played both sides of the fence during the war.

She understood their greater enemy was communism, not the Nazis, but what they had allowed was unforgivable.

The journal sucked her in. Though she couldn't make out every word, it was all here, not that it was a total secret—excerpts had been circulating for years. But without the original, the excerpts were discounted as forgers' attempts to authenticate more forgery.

Saba had been tracking Mako Storm for weeks, in some cases even providing him clues. It had taken all her patience to allow the CIA operatives to retrieve the journal, but now they had lost it, and only one man, left with a limited memory after the injection she had given him last night, knew she had it.

Recovering it herself would have endangered her plans. Leading Mako Storm to it had been her only play. This bothered her, but the end had justified the means. He was unharmed and she had the journal. What played on her conscience was the "leak" she'd made to the Mafia that Mako had the journal—and where to find him.

La Cosa Nostra had as much to lose as did the Church if the journal turned up. The Church and the Mafia had been partners in crime for years, but the new pope's willingness to unravel the tangled web of Vatican, Inc., and expose the players placed their relationship in jeopardy.

But here it was, lying on the table in front of her. The key to taking down the Church, and with it, she hoped, retribution for all who had suffered by its decision to support the Nazis.

8

STORM SURGE

Monti District, Rome

MAKO KNEW HIS INSTINCTS HAD BEEN DULLED BY THE DRUG. A brief examination of his body while the water heated for the shower showed a small bump on his neck, standing out from the multiple pellet wounds from the drones. A more thorough examination in the mirror after showed not only the bump but a red circle where the drug had been administered. He'd likely never know exactly what it was. It didn't matter. The journal was gone.

Memories weren't exactly flooding back, either. As much as he didn't want it to be true, Saba was the only suspect. Spreading antibiotic ointment on the pellet wounds, he wondered if she was responsible for them as well. She had clearly set him up. He now had a fair recollection of the few hours they had spent together. The details were sketchy—all except her green eyes. The orbs were embedded in his brain.

Finished doctoring his wounds, he heard a soft knock on the door. At first he ignored it and started to dress, but the cordial knock turned into a pounding.

"Mako." John stood in the doorway.

"What do you want, an invitation to come in?" Mako asked, trying to hide his surprise. He stood with a towel wrapped around his waist.

"It was locked, if it makes you feel any better."

"You always know the right thing to say. Don't just freaking stand there."

John Storm's unexpected appearance was not a coincidence. Mako had to admit his father, even in his mid-seventies, was one crafty dude. Closing on thirty-five himself, half his parent's age, Mako suspected he had less than half of John's skillset. But what had made his father a legend, to the few who had security clearances high enough to know of his exploits, had also made him obsolete. What John Storm had once used his body and mind for, Mako now accomplished with technology—or rather, as the human conduit for Alicia's work.

John stepped awkwardly into the room, clearly not comfortable with his son's state of undress, or being here at all. "How about I make some coffee while you finish?"

"Great, Dad. Coffee fixes everything."

"Better than women and booze."

With the niceties out of the way, Mako walked back to the bathroom, purposefully dropping the towel to the floor before he entered. He closed the door and stared in the mirror, scolding himself for his attack on his father. The elder Storm's appearance had been unexpected, but if Mako was honest with himself, a blessing. After spending more of Mako's childhood in Rome than at home, few knew the inner workings of the city better than his father.

Dressing in skinny jeans and a button-down shirt, Mako decided to leave the shirt untucked. He knew the latest style would solicit a reaction from his father, but this wasn't the time. After losing his connection with Alicia he needed John's help.

John had opened the French doors in the kitchen, allowing the activity from the waking street to enter the apartment. There were no windows here; the kitchen, living room, and bedroom each had a set of doors, making the process of getting fresh air an all-or-nothing affair. Unique to the area, the apartment had a ductless air-conditioning system, but he doubted John knew it was there. John sat at the small, round café table, which he had moved for a better view of the street.

Filling two cups from the espresso pot on the stove, Mako turned off the gas, and brought the cups to the table. Hoping the caffeine would clear some of the cobwebs, he drank half the cup, sans cream and sugar, before starting the conversation. Any additives to coffee, even to make café Cubano, would send his father on a rant.

"What do you know?" Mako asked.

"What makes you think this isn't a social call?"

"Just happened to be in Rome the day after my contract fell apart?"

"Okay. I do have friends here, though. I saw most of it—"

"What the hell?"

John cut him off. "It's not the way you think. I was working on something different and happened to see what happened, though it appears our contracts are related."

"You're still working?"

"I've developed some *special* relationships over the years."

"What does that mean?"

John studied the street. "Why don't you call your boss? Make sure my cooperation won't void your contract."

Mako looked down at his cup. Picking it up, he finished the remaining espresso. "It's already done. As you probably already know, the journal is gone."

"There's more than one way to skin a cat without getting scratched."

Mako nodded to John's cup. It was merely a courtesy; his father drank coffee like a hipster. It was the quantity of their consumption, not the "latte" this or that which was probably the only similarity between the generations. He felt like he needed another few cups himself. Moving back to the stove, he refilled the pot with water. After topping off the filter with grounds, he scraped the excess off, screwed on the top, then turned on the burner. While the coffee brewed Mako stepped to the side and called Alicia from the house phone.

Out of habit he spoke in generalities, only clarifying something when she insisted. It was a safe house, and he was fairly certain the phone was clear as well, but someone outside of Alicia, TJ, and their contact had known the meet was set. Mako knew the leak could have come from the CIA, but not the timing. Working on contract, the means to the end were entirely up to the contractor. Plausible deniability had become a catchphrase outside of the Oval Office

Thankfully, Alicia didn't dwell on the loss of the journal. It was one of the things he liked about her—she moved on. Now, her focus was on retrieving it. When the conversation turned to the future, Mako brought up John's involvement.

Motioning to his ear, John signaled to Mako to turn on the phone's speaker. After clearing it with Alicia, the three were soon connected. This was not the first time they had worked together; in fact, somehow it happened more often than not.

"Why are you there, John?" Alicia asked.

Mako could tell by her voice she was on the defensive, and studied her tone for the deception he expected. He interceded, not wanting the conversation to head in that direction. "John knows someone." They'd worked together enough that Mako had quit using the "father" or "dad" title long ago.

"Bishop Maldonado, actually," John said.

Alicia was quiet for a long second, probably doing a quick

Google search. "Really. That's impressive, but what bearing does it have on our contract?"

"Back in the day, when he was still a monsignor, Maldonado engineered the replacement of several paintings with forgeries."

"Caravaggio's?" An optimistic tone came through the line.

"And others."

"Your monsignor friend would probably not be interested in helping us prove the painting is a forgery. It would be more likely he would want the journal himself to protect the Church."

"Exactly, but he knows where the bones are buried."

"There are rumors the *Nativity* has surfaced."

It felt strange, talking about multi-million dollar works with his father. Despite a rather detailed orientation of the art world, Mako didn't really understand how the paintings fetched the prices they did. The last Caravaggio sold at auction had gone for almost two hundred million dollars. With those kinds of price tags, there was little wonder the CIA, Interpol, and the Vatican were involved. Silence fell over the apartment as they thought through the implications. Mako took the opportunity to turn off the coffee pot and pour them each a cup.

"Give me a little time, and I'll run it up the flagpole. And, Mako. Get a burner." The line fell dead.

"It was easier before all this crap. Smartphones, burners, even the internet." John shook his head and drank.

Mako placed the cup to his lips, but didn't drink. He used the movement more to think. Waiting on an answer from Alicia, he was faced with a father and son activity. Bringing your father along to buy a burner phone didn't sound like a whole lot of fun.

The sound of a motorcycle speeding down the street interrupted his thoughts. When the brakes squealed, both Storms instinctively dropped to the floor. Bullets flew through the open doors, ricocheting off the masonry walls. Mako moved to the far side of the room to cut down on the shooter's angle, but his father did the opposite. Drawing a Colt 1911 from his shoulder holster, John crept toward the open doors. Using the thick walls for protection, he returned fire. Backing away when a stray bullet shattered a pane of glass, he kicked the door shut and waited.

9

STEVEN BECKER

STORM SURGE

Key Largo, Florida

ALICIA WAS PAST BEING UPSET WHEN MAKO CALLED WITH HIS NEW number. Key Largo was in its busy season. Charters were booked solid and after losing the journal—and the contract—she and TJ needed to work all they could. Their custom-blend dive charters were unique and allowed them to charge a premium for their trips, but the added science came with an additional labor cost—unless they did the fill work themselves. TJ as captain already had a full plate, leaving the divemasters to fill tanks. With standard gas mixes it was relatively simple, but their unique combinations were not. Blended specifically for the dive profiles, their fills covered a broad spectrum, and a mistake in the filling process could prove deadly. The dive geeks loved it for the nerdiness and science of the whole thing; spearfishermen got more time on the less-frequented sections of the reef; and the adventurous divers and photographers found it more appealing than the typical charter. Both were willing to pay a premium for the additional bottom time.

Typically, Nitrox, a breathing gas with a higher oxygen

content than air, was blended to either thirty-two or thirty-six percent oxygen, as compared to the atmosphere, at just under twenty-one percent The added oxygen allowed divers longer bottom times. It did come at a cost, though: oxygen toxicity. Standard-air fills were safe at any depth, though recreational divers generally called 130 feet their limit. The downside was that bottom time was short and decompression stops, long. Nitrox fills capped the dive depth at 112 feet at the thirty-two percent blend and ninety-five feet at thirty-six percent but by mitigating nitrogen buildup allowed for considerably longer dives, with shorter decompression stops.

The Keys were famous for their reefs. Running from Biscayne National Park in Miami to beyond Key West, and marked by a string of iconic steel lighthouses set at intervals down the chain, standing sentinel over the shallower sections. Fish life was abundant in the sanctuaries by the lighthouses, but experienced divers craved depth and solitude. Diving was like a drug, and in some cases, with nitrogen narcosis, it was. Nitrox allowed the adventurous longer bottom times with shorter surface intervals. Typical charter operations included two dives. The first one deep, followed by a surface interval of about an hour, then a shallow dive. TJ and Alicia's charters, using their custom blends, allowed three deep-water dives in the same timeframe.

In a highly competitive market, their business plan was solid and had differentiated them from the companies running twice-a-day cattle-cars out to the reef. Missing the two charters today to babysit Mako was going to cost the couple hundreds of dollars which, with the theft of the journal, they badly needed. Hurricane Irma had put a damper on last season's tourist business as well as their resources. Although Key Largo had been sixty miles away from the eye and suffered only minor damage, the perception was that the Keys got slammed—all of them.

She and TJ had talked late into the night about the loss of the journal and if her being on the charter had contributed to the bad outcome. To some degree it probably had, but they agreed that Mako had been set up by someone who knew the effect women had on him. Alicia's voice in his ear would probably have had little effect on Mako's decision-making.

It was three a.m., and she had been awake for what she guessed was an hour. With their charter at eight, she got up to try to see if she could get Mako back on track before going to her day job. Easing herself out of bed, trying not to wake TJ, she slid across the room, and closed the door.

In the kitchen, she brewed a pot of coffee and took the decanter into the war room. Behind what looked like double doors leading to a closet was a living-room-sized computer paradise. TJ, a skilled gamer, had his own work area highlighted by a captain's chair that could have come from the deck of the *Starship Enterprise*. Alicia's area was more modest, with a standard chair and desk. The centerpiece of the room was not the workstations, but the twenty-five-foot-long wall entirely covered in monitors.

Setting the coffee decanter down on her desk, she poured herself a cup, adjusted her chair, and pressed the space bar on her keyboard. Nothing happened for two long seconds, then the entire wall lit up. Acting as one display, the forty-odd monitors showed a replica of her desktop. TJ had configured the monitors to act independently, or together, or in any grouping the user desired. Blinded by the harsh light, Alicia scaled it back to a grouping of four monitors.

The first thing she saw was a motorcycle stopping in front of the safe house. Her training kicked in, and she picked up the headset on her desk, but then realized there would be no one on the other end.

10

Monti District, Rome

MAKO CRAWLED TO THE BEDROOM, WHERE HE REMOVED HIS backup weapon, a Sig Sauer P320, from the safe in the closet and moved toward the door. His favorite, a Glock 43, was another casualty from last night. He got John's attention, and put his index and middle finger to his eyes. John nodded, then squeezed off two more rounds from his trusty Colt 1911. Swinging the gun in the direction of the front door, he covered Mako, who slowly opened it and peered into the hallway.

Finding it empty, Mako started down the stairs, pausing at each landing to listen for anyone coming up. On the second floor he froze, and focused on the apartment's door. It appeared closed, but Mako had heard something inside. With his body pressed against the adjacent wall, he slid closer. The door cracked an inch, and he instinctively moved, placing his back to the wall adjacent to the door. This was no time for safety and his finger slid toward the trigger. His gun hand was almost fully extended when he realized it was only the resident, whose curiosity had almost gotten him killed. Mako waved the gun at the man, and he disappeared back inside.

With John behind him, Mako dropped down to the main floor. They walked out the propped-open entry door and, looking in opposite directions, surveyed the street. To the left Mako saw one of the thousand *arches de* something. With no threat there he looked at John who shook his head. The gunman had fled. Or at least that's what Mako thought. The only sign of the attack was the pockmarked stucco and the sound of sirens coming towards them.

"We're good. He split."

"Guess it's not much of a safe house." John stated the obvious, but his head was on a swivel, still very aware of his surroundings.

The last thing Mako wanted to do was bunk with his father, but he couldn't stay here. "Where are you staying?"

"Got a flat near Vatican City."

"Company house?"

John ignored the question and walked toward a small wine bar occupying the ground floor of the building next door. He took a table just inside the open roll-up door and watched the street while Mako grabbed his things from upstairs. Just as Mako appeared with a backpack and a small bag, several police cars with their sirens blaring made a high-speed turn into the street, then slowed. Mako motioned to John to meet him on the next block and, with the police cars slowly cruising past, he started walking toward the Via Cavour. In the few minutes it took to reach the main boulevard, the sirens had faded into the distance, probably chasing an anonymous tip called in by one of the assassins.

Once on the main avenue, Mako relaxed slightly, as they blended in with the hundreds of other tourists. The street, the most direct route to the ruins of the Colosseum and Forum, was crowded. Vendors broke the flow of traffic hawking roses, blankets, and selfie sticks, while the maître d's and waiters of the street-side cafes accosted pedestrians in a mostly futile attempt to seduce them to dine in their restaurants. Mako, with his duffle bag and backpack, fit right in with the couples and groups of people carrying, pulling, and pushing luggage.

Stepping past groups of tourists, John appeared anxious as he worked his way through the crowd. Mako tried to slow him, to no avail. For the old man to be nervous meant he expected the threat was not over.

"We're good, right?" Mako asked, struggling with the extra weight and bulk of his bags to catch up.

"Like hell we are." John jerked his head up the street.

Mako followed his father's gaze to the next intersection, where he saw not one, but three, crotch-rockets. The high-speed motorcycles revved their engines, waiting for the light to turn. Seeing that John's instincts were still right-on, Mako followed his lead.

The light changed, releasing the pent-up energy in the bikes. As they screamed down the avenue, John pulled Mako into a doorway.

"In here," John yelled over the roar of the motorcycles. "Get a phone and get Alicia on the line." Mako knew right away that John's choice of refuge was not a random move. It couldn't have been chance that he had pulled him into an electronics store, a rarity between the restaurants and souvenir stores.

"How do you know it's them? There're a dozen of those things on any street here."

"Zero - eight - six - zero - nine."

"You got the plate number."

John didn't bother answering. With one eye on the shelf stocked with phones behind the counter, and the other on the street, he guided Mako to the counter.

"Get two, and an extra couple of prepaid SIM cards."

Mako didn't question his reason, though he was surprised that his father knew what a SIM card was. John moved back to the door to watch the road while Mako purchased two identical phones and the cards. With the purchase complete, he opened one of the boxes.

"Dude says they're usually at least half-charged." Mako handed a phone to John.

"I don't need one," John said.

"They're both for me?" Again, Mako wasn't about to question his father's motives. With one phone in his pocket, he stuffed the boxes in his backpack and slung it over his shoulder.

"Get Alicia on the line. We need her help to get us out of here."

Mako slid the phone out and punched in the emergency number. Doing some quick math, he thought he'd be waking her up, but the phone barely rang before she picked up.

"What's going on? I saw the motorcycle."

"I've got a tag number, but we need to get out of here. There's three of them, and they just cruised by."

"Right. Getting your location from the phone. Hold."

Mako often wondered if she had a human side, but right now he was happy if she didn't. He waited while she worked, and was again thankful when he heard her yell for TJ.

"All right, we've got your location: 841 Via Cavour."

"Right. We need to get to Vatican City. John says he has a place there."

Mako was surprised that Alicia didn't comment about their destination, but when the motorcycles screamed by, making another pass, the thought was gone in the flash—the flash of a bullet leaving the barrel of a gun.

The storefront window exploded.

John pulled his pistol from the holster, grabbed the duffle

bag from Mako. Using it to conceal the weapon, he held the pistol pointed at the ground. From that position, in an instant it would be ready to discharge.

"Was that a gunshot?" Alicia asked.

"Yes, ma'am. We'll be needing a route." Mako looked out the window. Two of the bikes were pulled up on the sidewalk. He couldn't tell if they were men or women from their bulky leathers and helmets, but from what he could see of their bodies, he suspected one of each. The third rider was nowhere in sight.

John worked his way to the side of the door and, between a gap in the stream of pedestrians who hadn't quite figured out what was going on, fired a shot.

"It's no use. There're too many people out there. We need another exit. Now!"

"The metro would be the best place to ditch them," Alicia said. "Checking stations."

Squeezing the phone with his shoulder in order to keep his hands free, Mako only caught every other word, but it was enough. "Where's the closest metro?" They both looked at the clerk.

He pointed toward the ruins at the end of the street running perpendicular to the Via Cavour. "We're going to head to the Colosseum. See if we can get onto the metro."

"I've got several traffic cameras streaming."

Mako recognized TJ's voice, and imagined him sitting in the captain's chair manipulating the wall of monitors lighting up with information.

"We don't have time for this, Mako," John said.

Mako looked up and saw the two bikers, guns drawn, approaching the door. The few pedestrians that the broken window hadn't scared away now ran, and the sirens that had faded into the distance became clearer.

The clerk rose from the protection of the counter, shrugged, and ran to the back of the shop. Mako and John followed, hoping for a back door. A minute later they found themselves in an alley, and turned toward the Colosseum.

"You'll do better by heading to the central station. The Colosseum is a massive logjam," TJ said.

Mako relayed TJ's advice to John, who quickly switched directions. Once they were underway TJ's logic became apparent. Like salmon fighting their way upstream, the two men moved against the flow of traffic toward the terminal. Fighting through the crowds moving toward the Colosseum and Forum hindered their ability to flee, but for now it provided them cover.

Staying close to the storefronts in case they needed to duck into one for cover, Mako and John dodged café tables as they moved up the slight incline toward the station. With each block, the area became less touristy and quieter. There was still a steady stream of traffic heading toward the tourist attractions, but with no stores or cafes to stop it, it moved like a river, stopping only for red lights.

The change was marginally reassuring for the Storms. The quieter streets would make it easier for them to be spotted, but at least they could maneuver.

"Got them coming up the street. All three together," TJ's voice came over the phone, surprising them.

Mako had put the phone on speaker and stuck it in his pocket. "Roger," Mako responded. He could just make out the roar of the engines. It sounded like the bikes were only a few blocks away. "Make a run for it?"

"Think you can keep up?"

They took off toward a line of buses blocking the entrance to the terminal. Mako's long legs made it easy work to keep up with his surprisingly fit father. He thought about challenging him, to see what the old man still had, but it was the bullets he needed to outrun, not dear old dad. One struck a streetlamp just beyond them. The two men didn't need TJ, who was coaching them from Key Largo, to tell them to pick up the pace. They cut between two buses and found themselves staring at a line of cabs where the avenue dead ended.

The bikes paused, then accelerated again. Chancing a look back, Mako saw them blast through a gap between the buses. They jumped the sidewalk, and skidded to a stop at the entrance to the station. Mako and John were barely through the doors before the engines died.

"Escalator dead ahead. Take it up to the trains."

"We want the metro." Mako pulled the phone from his pocket so TJ could hear over the noise of the crowded terminal.

"You want out, so listen!" TJ said.

There was no one better at this. A master gamer who, until Alicia had straightened him out, spent more time online than running his business. This was like a video game to him. And he rarely lost.

"Okay," Mako said, heading for the escalator.

TJ was working at a disadvantage, looking at the scene through the two-dimensional cameras. Upon entering the station, the three gunmen had instinctively looked up. They'd removed their helmets and Mako confirmed it was two men and a woman. In some kind of twisted way, he was glad the woman had blond hair and didn't have green eyes. The escalator was packed, but at two abreast it was easy to see who was on it.

There was nowhere to go as they waited for the escalator to ascend. The gunmen were heading up now too, but it was only the woman and one of the men. "Is there another way up? They've split," Mako spoke to TJ.

Finally, the escalator dropped them at the second floor. A glance behind showed the woman pushing up the escalator in an attempt to reach them. John took the lead and headed toward the back of the station. With their pursuers still waiting to disembark, the gap opened. John steered Mako around a fat column, then through a large passageway with a string of shops.

"Stairs are just past the stores," TJ said.

Near the last store stood the third man with his pistol held low, but clearly visible, in front of him. The Storms skidded to a stop, sensing the other two pursuers moving behind them.

STEVEN BECKER

STORM SURGE

The Colosseum, Rome

"This was a bad idea," Mako spoke into the speaker to let TJ and Alicia know they were in trouble, then put the phone back into his pocket.

John turned to evaluate the threat from behind while Mako looked ahead for an escape. A busy coffee bar with a cluster of people gathered around the pickup area caught his attention. From his travels, Mako knew that individual countries had distinguishing traits. In Italy, orderly lines were nonexistent. Thinking he could take advantage of the confusion around the counter, he moved in that direction.

"What the hell are you doing?" John asked.

"Just watch." The disorder around the counter allowed him to push straight into the mix. Obscured by the crowd, he turned to John. "They're not terrorists. They won't shoot with all these people here." When the gunmen had removed their helmets, Mako had noticed they looked just like the locals.

"You would hope not. What now?"

It wasn't only the presence of innocents that prevented the

pursuers from shooting. There was a strong military presence throughout the public areas of Rome. Armed with submachine guns, they wouldn't hesitate to shoot. That effectively neutralized both parties' weapons.

"The Carabinieri over there will give us our out. Keep an eye on our friends."

Mako slid sideways between several people. This was no Starbucks. There were no handwritten names on the cups set on the counter or numbered receipts for the customers to claim their coffee. It was a total free-for-all. When a barista approached with two cups, Mako shoved forward, moving an older couple to the side, and with his long arms reached over them to grab the cups. The man turned back to Mako with a disapproving look, but Mako countered with a shrug, hoping his apparent ineptitude for the local customs would get him a pass. He couldn't afford for the man to make a scene.

Cups in hand, Mako pushed his way out of the crowd and approached the soldiers. Clutching their coffees, the backpack slung over Mako's shoulder, and John carrying the duffle bag, he hoped they looked like unassuming tourists.

"English?" Mako asked. "We're lost."

The soldiers smiled. "Where are you going?"

"The metro to Vatican City?"

One of the soldiers pointed back toward the escalator. "The bottom floor." He said it with a smirk, probably wondering how anyone would lack the common sense to look for an underground train on the upper level of the station.

"Thanks," Mako said, and started walking away. Once out of earshot of the soldiers he turned to John. "We should be good until we're out of sight." He noticed the soldiers watching the wayward Americans. He also saw their pursuers follow, careful to keep enough distance to not appear threatening.

"Well done. That bought us some time."

There was no time to revel in his father's rare compliment. The escalator was nearing the ground floor. "We need to get out of here."

John looked at the herd moving out of the station and down the Via Corvo. "When in Rome ... "

With their pursuit so close, the tourists who had initially hindered them were now their best chance to evade their pursuers. Stepping off the escalator, Mako risked a glance back. All three were there, but about halfway down. "Let's go." He tossed his coffee cup in a nearby trash can and bolted through the exit doors.

Deciding to avoid the Via Cavour, Mako and John headed into the backstreets of the Monti district and Esquiline Hill. Making their way through the neighborhood, the drop in background noise allowed Alicia's voice to come through. Mako ignored it at first, but she was persistent. They were moving as fast as they felt they could without attracting attention. Settling into a lope, a half-run of sorts, Mako pulled the phone from his pocket.

"We're here," he panted.

"We see you. TJ's plotting from the phone's location."

"Any ideas?"

"It's up to you to lose them, but I wanted to let you know, I ran a facial recognition search from the surveillance cameras we tapped into in the train station and got a hit."

It wasn't relevant to their current situation, but Mako knew he wasn't going to stop her.

"Carlota Burga."

The name meant nothing to Mako, but it did to John, who reached for the phone.

"What the hell is she doing coming after us?"

"I'm working on that. Check in once you get somewhere safe." She disconnected.

Mako looked at John.

"She's Mafia. Runs their art division."

Typical CIA, Mako thought. Thinking of the Mafia like a corporation.

The conversation was muffled by the roar of a motorcycle. Turning back, Mako noticed the bike was yellow and had two riders. It blazed by without incident, but reminded them how easily they could be found. Just a block ahead a cast-iron gate stood open; beyond it was the entrance to what appeared to be a park. "We can cut through there."

"It's as good an option as we've got," John said.

The steep incline slowed their pace, but they caught a break when a light turned red. Dancing through the oncoming traffic, Mako glanced behind them. It appeared they had temporarily lost their pursuers.

"We can cross the hill and come out by the Domus Aurea. Across the street is the metro station." John said, leading the way onto a grassy area. Though it was a green space, there were still roads running through the park. The hill was once the site of Nero's palace, covered over long ago to erase his name from history. It was originally filled to create public baths, then when those decayed, was turned into the current hill to create the modern-day park. It was surprising to see how much of Rome's history could be seen by cutting a cross-section through the terrain.

They reached the top, allowing them a nice view of the surrounding area, but neither stopped to enjoy it, although they were able to orient themselves with the Colosseum and the metro station. Taking a path in the direction of the ancient stadium, itself built over the site of an ancient lake, they found a set of concrete stairs that took them past the entrance to the Domus Aurea, then down to street level. Once through another open gate, they were back in the press of tourists, buses, and hawkers.

Late morning marked the start of prime tourist time and the streets reflected the influx of people. Gridlocked with both traffic and people making their way to the Colosseum, the Forum, and Palatine Hill, the Storms' progress was stymied.

They had just started to cross the street to enter the safety of the metro station when two motorcycles converged on them. One stopped directly in the entrance, effectively blocking their way. The driver wasn't showing a weapon, but the threat was implied. The other bike appeared behind them, blocking their other avenue of escape. There was only one direction open to them and in this case safety was in numbers. Blending in with a tour group, they ran across the street to the Colosseum.

Groups of tourists, all following their guides, who hoisted flags and other symbols for their followers to locate them, moved towards the entrances. John and Mako stayed with the group they had crossed the street with, picking up a few words of German along the way. Standing toward the center of the group, they waited while the guide passed out tickets. Someone toward the back would likely not get one, as the woman handed a pair to John and Mako.

The group moved forward, slowing as the line passed through the recently installed metal detectors. Armed, neither Storm could afford the scrutiny of an alarm and the sure reaction of the military standing by. There was no choice but to ditch their weapons in a nearby trash can. Unfortunately, the next group they saw was Burga and the two men.

"Shit," John said.

The odd number of their pursuers had allowed one man to remain behind by the gate. Burga and the other man followed the group inside. Mako and John both searched for a way out. They had stepped out of line, but a move to leave through the entrance would attract the attention of the waiting man. They were still upstream of the metal detectors when they saw a gate open and a small UTV carrying trash drove through, pulling onto the sidewalk. Sprinting across the walkway, they reached the gate, making it inside before it slammed shut and the electronic lock engaged.

They were on the first level now, and despite the tension of the chase, neither man could take their eyes away from the venerable ruin. The sound of running feet on the old pavement pulled them back to the present and, looking toward the source, Mako saw they had been spotted.

Pushing their way through tour groups, the Storms sought an exit. An alcove with a set of stairs appeared ahead. John tore down the curved corridor hoping the oval shape of the Colosseum would conceal them. With Mako on his heels, he yanked his son into the alcove and up several steps, only to find a set of steel bars blocking their path. It wasn't a way out, but at least they weren't visible. Making a move back to the main corridor would put them in plain view of their pursuers.

"Against the wall."

With their bodies deep in the shadows, they waited, hoping Burga and the man would miss them. It worked, at least for a moment. John stepped out, seeing the backs of their pursuers moving away from him. But turning the other way to make an escape, he found himself staring down the barrel of a pistol.

"Back in there," the man said. He withdrew his cell phone to call his partners back.

There was no time to question how the man had evaded the security protocols and entered the Colosseum. Mako knew they had to act now, while the odds were in their favor. If they waited until the assailants reversed course and reached them, the tables would flip.

Straight across from the alcove was one of the regularly

spaced openings to the arena floor. Between the half-dozen steps they had climbed, and Mako's own height, he could see the labyrinth of cells and corridors that at one time had been hidden below the sand-covered wooden floor. If they could get there, they could probably escape, but the man with the gun stood in their way.

Turning back, he caught a look from John. It wasn't much, not even a wink, just the tick of his eye. If it wasn't his father standing across from him, he would have missed it. The gunman's attention was focused on the elder Storm, allowing Mako to respond. He knew what his father wanted, and strolled out into the corridor as if there were no threat at his back.

Immediately, without evaluating her, he reached for the first woman he saw, hoping the gunman would resist the urge to injure a woman. Even if he chose to, there would be a split-second that he would think about it—that was all they needed. The man turned toward him, and before Mako knew what the outcome was going to be, he saw John wind up and slam his rigid hand into the man's neck.

Both men took off at a run without waiting for the man to crumple to the ground. Not knowing where Burga and her accomplice were, they took the next stairway down a level and entered the space Mako had seen from above. Two millenniums removed from its purpose, there was still a morbid feel to it. Thousands of men and beasts had been led down this corridor to one of only two possible outcomes: fame or death.

Mako felt a tug on his arm and turned to John. To the side was a triangular-shaped opening at the base of a stone wall. A small stream of water ran across the bottom. It wasn't going to be pretty, but they had found their way out. He followed John into what he guessed was the old sewer.

The chamber was high enough they could walk if they stooped, though Mako, six inches taller, was more exaggerated than John's. As they walked deeper into the tunnel, the air chilled. Despite the gloominess of their surroundings they felt safe. Their only problem now was finding the exit. One memory in particular stood out from last night—there had been a gate at the end of the tunnel. Mako realized they could very well be facing the same obstacle at the end of the drain.

12

STORM SURGE

Old Rome

ONCE THEY WERE WELL INTO THE PASSAGE, JOHN STOPPED AND turned back to Mako. "Call Alicia and see if she can get us out of here."

Mako glanced back into the dark passageway. Their footsteps echoing off the stone surfaces of the triangular space were the only sound they heard. That didn't mean they were alone. The acoustics of the pipe would make it difficult to hear any pursuit. An intersection was just ahead. Knowing they could easily get lost, they needed help.

"Alicia?" Mako whispered.

"Here, but where the hell are you guys?"

"Can you get a sewer layout?"

"It looks like you're by the Arch of Constantine."

"You'd never know it from here. We're actually in some ancient sewer system." Thankfully it wasn't active.

"Hold on. I trust I'll get the story once I get you out of there."

Mako tuned her out, and stuck his head into the tunnel running perpendicular to the one they were in. It all looked the same. They would need her help. The line was quiet for a few minutes.

"Take a right there. It should bring you out in a park."

A hundred yards later they could see daylight and, after what he guessed was a quarter mile, a pinpoint of light appeared. As they approached they saw it was an old gate. The exit was indeed locked.

John fished around in his pocket.

Mako reached for his wallet and extracted a black card from which he removed several embossed lockpick tools. "I got this," Mako said, pushing past John, he easily handled the old mechanism. They stepped out into a low pool of water.

"Where are we?"

"By the Circus Maximus. There's a metro station there."

Mako could see the grassy outline of the old chariot track.

Vatican City

After traveling a half-dozen miles, Mako stepped off the metro, climbed the stairs and found himself in a neighborhood resembling the one where the safe house had been. The only indication of their location was the wall to his left delineating the border of Vatican City. John appeared behind him, and led the way to a small four-story walkup.

Mako was surprised about the apparent lack of tradecraft his father displayed. It was almost as if he knew it was safe. Maybe it was age creeping up on the old man; it was hard to tell. He had seemed fine earlier. As he studied the street a security camera caught his eye and he wondered if John Storm had someone like Alicia watching over him—or maybe it was her.

To Mako, his father was a bellwether of what he had to look forward to. In many ways it wasn't bad. Mako didn't expect many seventy-five-year-olds could have managed the last few hours like his father had. Aside from the glasses, which he had always worn, and the recent addition of a hearing aid, the older Storm was doing pretty well.

Approaching the entrance, John punched a four-digit code into the security panel. The lock buzzed and he opened the door. Remembering the wad of paper jammed into the door jamb of his safe house, Mako was relieved that the security lock actually worked. Once the smoke cleared, he would have to talk to Alicia about their un-safe house.

John's, or likely his benefactor's, apartment was on the second floor, well-placed for both observation and escape. Mako walked through the one-bedroom apartment, finding it much like the safe house where he had been staying.

13

STEVEN BECKER

STORM SURGE

Key Largo, Florida

WHEN THE DOOR OPENED AND THE STORMS WALKED INTO THE safe house, Alicia leaned back and took a deep breath. Turning her attention back to the face on the screen, she studied Carlota Burga. On another screen, she could see her facial recognition algorithm continue to plow through the faces in the databases she had tapped into, still searching for a match. While it worked, she got up, grabbed her empty coffee carafe, and went to the kitchen thinking about the Mafia boss.

The woman in the picture on the monitors looked more like an attractive business woman than who she really was. In a male-dominated organization, it took a very special woman to rise as she had. Part of her success was her background in art. The other was her inborn meanness. Her temper and sadistic tendencies were well known, and incurring her wrath was to be avoided. Carlota Burga was no gun moll.

"You sure you're okay if I go?" TJ asked.

Alicia looked up. "They're in the Vatican City safe house

now. Hopefully they'll stay put for a while. Did you get Jen to give you a hand?"

"She's good. If you need me just call in with a fake thunderstorm or something." TJ grabbed the cooler from the counter, kissed Alicia on the cheek, and headed down to the boat.

Alicia looked out the window at the clouds, thinking she might not have to manufacture a fake storm. She felt guilty about staying back, but though the charter business provided day-to-day income, the contracts were their future. While she waited for the coffee to brew, she checked both the forecast and radar apps on her phone. TJ might have been joking about the thunderstorm, but this time of year in the Keys, they could be deadly. Every resident had their own go-to websites or apps to divine the weather here. Living on the thin strand of islands in the middle of the ocean instilled an awareness of the weather that to the residents became instinct.

Looking out the window, she watched TJ check the tanks. At least they'd had the forethought to fill them last night while the action across the pond was at a minimum. Sometimes the time change worked in their favor; mostly it didn't. Alicia leaned back, realizing how tired she was.

The divers started to trickle in, and TJ was ready to greet them. Alicia always found the meet-and greet-interesting, later comparing her first impressions of how people talked about themselves and their experience against what actually happened. Most times she was able to tell the pretenders from the real deals, a trait that separated the good divemasters from those who just went through the motions.

Alicia heard a *ding* from the war room. Taking the fresh pot of coffee with her, she entered the sanctuary for round two. Juggling the two Storms when they were separate was problematic; when they were together, impossible. Sooner rather than later, if they hadn't already figured it out, she'd have to tell them she was working with both of them. It had been a necessary evil to enlist the stable John to counteract the mercurial Mako. This was not the first time Alicia had used them both for the same contract. Having John around was an additional expense, but good insurance wasn't cheap.

Two previously dark monitors had come to life while she had stepped away. Each showed the face of one of the other assailants and their records. It was a small victory, and Alicia allowed herself a smile. With rare exceptions, she worked as an analyst. Field agents got the glory; the backroom agents, who the agency couldn't do without, had to take their accolades in smaller doses.

Alicia had always been a star. Driven hard by her mother, she matriculated Stanford in just three years on a full-ride scholarship. Even before she graduated, she had several offers, including grad school. In the post-9/11 atmosphere of her graduation, wanting to do something for her country made the decision easy for her. At least at that point in her career, the excitement of top-secret work and international intrigue appealed to her more than the six-figure salaries the private companies were tossing around. It was a good thing that Langley, Virginia, was thousands of miles from her mother, who thought turning down the big payday was a bad move. Alicia stayed the course. She always knew the money would come.

She had risen quickly through the ranks, garnering notice from many supervisors. One in particular adopted her, but he turned out to be a rogue agent. To clear her name, she had gone into the field. Thinking about it, she smiled. Alicia and TJ had met on that case, through fishing guide/diver Mac Travis and his wayward deckhand, Trufante. Alicia wasn't charged or even disciplined, but the association with the man was enough to derail her career. Instead of slugging it out in the trenches trying to reestablish herself, she chose the island life and the occasional contract.

Even during the hard times, most notably post-Irma, she had never regretted her decision. Through her childhood and early adult life she had been buried in books, both by her mother's insistence and her own inclination. After getting a taste of the field and becoming an accomplished diver, she relished her time away from the wall of monitors.

She put aside thoughts of TJ and the reef and focused on the bios of the three faces on the screen. All morning she'd been searching for an explanation of how they knew about the safe house. It was a CIA property, and she laid the blame at its feet. She would deal with that later, and turned her attention to the half-dozen screens on the upper-right section of the wall showing the Vatican City property. The video was in real time, all taken from public or easily accessible private feeds. Between the advent of facial recognition software and the proliferation of surveillance cameras, there was a distinct possibility that someone was sitting in a room just like this—sans Captain Kirk's chair—looking at the same information, but with different intent. The parallel spy universe.

Situational awareness was an attribute that separated the good analysts from the great ones. Alicia redirected her attention to what was important. If she was going down a rabbit hole, it would be one that directly affected their case, not just because she could. Sipping her coffee, she read the bios of the men. There was no question they were Mafia.

Beside both being headquartered in Italy, she wondered about the connection between the Church and La Cosa Nostra. Five minutes later, she had just scratched the surface of the two entities' involvement. Shocked, she sat back and tried to digest the scope of the conspiracies that linked them together. Seeing Burga and the men on one screen and the Vatican in the background put an idea in Alicia's head.

14

STORM SURGE

Outside Vatican City

WITH THE BURNER PHONE LAYING ON THE TABLE BETWEEN THEM, Mako and John sat by the window, watching the street and debating what their next move should be. Alicia had passed on the information about their assailants; now the question was what to do about it.

"With two groups after us, it would make sense to split up," John said.

Mako had no problem with that. The fact that they had gotten through the morning without a fight was not lost on him.

"John should stay here and work the Vatican angle. I'll head to Sicily," he spoke into the phone.

"We've got to find the journal first. My suggestion would be for you both to stay put and work together."

"Looks like the boss has spoken," John said quietly. "You're right."

Mako nodded.

"Mako?"

At least she didn't have cameras in here. "Yes, I'm good with that. The burner phones are fine for general communication, but I lost the earbud."

"John, can you handle that? Once you have it, I'll sync it up."

They disconnected and John headed to the bedroom. He returned a minute later with an old-school phone book, leafed through the worn pages, and dialed a number on the house phone. A brief conversation ensued, from which a meet was set.

"You think James Bond's got cool shit. Wait till you meet my guy."

"A regular father-son outing to the arms dealer, very nice," Mako said, without a trace of sarcasm.

Castel Sant'Angelo, Rome

As they walked up to the entrance of the Castel Sant'Angelo, Mako looked up at the cylindrical building. "A museum? Looks more like a castle to me."

"It's been everything from Hadrian's family tomb to a prison. The curator here is an old friend." John led the way through a side door marked as an employee entrance.

They climbed a circular stairway that rose into the heart of the old fortress. Near what Mako assumed was the top, John pulled a door open and they entered a room with a display of armaments. Tourists crowded the fronts of the glass-lined cases, but Mako was able to see some old, yet pretty impressive weaponry. They passed through the room and stopped at an unmarked door. This time John knocked.

Several minutes later, the door cracked open and they entered. Mako had expected an "old friend" of his father's to be, well, old. That was not the case at all; the woman hugging his father was closer to Mako's age—and very attractive.

"Juliet, this is Mako."

While they exchanged pleasantries Mako studied the woman. She was indeed his contemporary. Standing about his father's height, six inches shorter than he himself stood, she was a stunning woman with wavy auburn hair and classic Italian features. Her sleeveless blouse showed her toned arms. They, at least, were bare of tattoos, something he really liked about Italian women.

"Come, let me see if I can help you." She led them into a small room.

James Bond had been one of Mako's heroes, and now he was standing in what looked like Q's lab, but Juliet looked a whole lot different than the bookish scientist.

"Here." Juliet held out two earbuds.

Mako reached for one and placed it in his ear, half expecting Alicia to know it was there and to start talking. Not surprisingly, John declined one.

"What other goodies have you got?" John asked. "We had to ditch our weapons."

"Most are above your pay grade, but I can give you a quick tour."

Mako followed John and Juliet into a dark room. The flick of a switch turned on a bank of overhead lights illuminating another weapons collection. Laid out on tables was an assortment of modern-day weaponry. There were no glass cases protecting the weapons, and Mako reached for a Glock 43, a very familiar weapon.

"Ghost Rocket Connector for a 3.5lb trigger pull and fiberoptic sights," she said, leading them past the tables to another door.

"Take what you need. I know where to send the bill," Juliet said.

"You might want something with a little more power," John said.

Mako lifted his shirt tail and stuck the weapon in his waist-band. After replacing his shirt, the pistol was barely noticeable.

John picked up a .45, similar to the Colt 1911 he usually carried. "This'll do the trick."

"That's got an 8-pound trigger pull. Might be a little heavy," Juliet said.

"It'll work," John said.

Mako turned back to the display. "We should at least both get something chambered for 9-millimeter," Mako said. Sooner or later having weapons with different ammunition would get them into trouble.

Juliet raised her eyebrows in agreement, but John shook his head.

Agreeing to disagree, they each reached for a box of bullets and two spare magazines.

"You Americans are so boring," Juliet said, lifting a miniature version of a submachine gun.

"Trust what you know," John said, removing his gun and sliding the pistol into his shoulder holster, checking that it fit neatly underneath his jacket. He turned and hugged Juliet.

Thanking Juliet, Mako could only hope to find an excuse and come back alone.

Piazza Novona, Rome

With phones in hand, Carlota Burga and her two henchmen sat within view of each other, but at separate cafés. Using a proven tactic to communicate without attracting suspicion, they texted each other. With security cameras now mounted every-where and tied into facial recognition software, Burga was constantly vigilant about who she was seen with. Rather than risk being overheard on their phones, they used SnapChat, knowing in twenty-four hours their conversation would be deleted.

There was no finger-pointing. It wasn't particularly their

fault the two Americans had escaped. They were working on limited intelligence; their targets being handed to them from an anonymous source just last night. Considering the circumstances, they had come close to their goal.

Even in failure, Carlota now knew the journal existed. Working from a tip that the journal was about to be brought to light, Burga and her associates had worked nonstop, tracking down the man she now knew as Mako Storm.

Her search led her to believe the men were CIA. It wasn't from any particular piece of evidence, but rather the amount of subterfuge involved. Clandestine agencies liked to hide behind shills and paperwork. Burga was very good at tearing down their fronts. Banking and laziness often provided the clues. The tip that the journal was about to change hands had been accurate, although it failed to bear fruit. In the past twenty-four hours, she had dug into Mako Storm's background. Once she knew who he was, the rest had been easy. Knowing what bank the CIA checks were drawn on, she had discovered a monthly payment to an apartment in the Monti district. Her prey had proven elusive so far, but she knew persistence paid off, and had every expectation of recovering the journal.

15

STORM SURGE

Vatican City

ALBERT MALDONADO HAD BEEN WAITING IN THE SHADOWS OF THE complex when the drop was supposed to take place. He knew firsthand something had gone wrong, and now he had no choice but to wait by his phone for John Storm or the CIA to make it right. He was grateful, at least to this point, that no one knew the drop had gone awry. If word had gotten out, one of his many enemies in the Vatican would be relishing his loss.

Maldonado knew the playing field—he had been the one to set the pieces in place. Waiting on the CIA, he had called Interpol, which also had an investigator looking for the journal. He knew who she was. If there was anyone who knew what had happened to the CIA operative last night it was Saba, though that wasn't particularly good news. He knew the woman could hold a grudge.

Offering a visit to the warehouses of the Vatican as a lure, he called Saba and invited her to come by his office. She accepted, and surprised the bishop when she said it would take her less than an hour to reach his office. After alerting the guards at the

Piazza del Sant'Uffizio, one of the Vatican entrances accessible by vehicle, he waited, trying not to let his paranoia get the best of him.

Behind the Institute of Works for Religion was a small parking lot where she would have been directed to park. Maldonado glanced at the six-foot-tall tube leaning innocently in the corner of his office. Leaving it, he exited the room and walked to the parking lot. He was standing by the entrance to greet her when she arrived. These visits required all the pomp and circumstance he could gather.

Saba parked her car, got out, and looked around. Maldonado could tell from the direction of her gaze that she was looking at the dome over St. Peter's just behind the office building. He enjoyed her apparent awe for a moment before moving toward her. As he approached, she came back to earth, and accepted a kiss on each cheek. Arm in arm, like a father and daughter, they walked across the parking lot to the entrance to the Institute of Works for Religion.

His office was a shrine of sorts as well, built to impress visitors. Doctors, lawyers, and businessmen all had their wall of achievements. There were no diplomas on Maldonado's, only multiple pictures of the bishop alongside the two popes he had worked for. Each was taken in a different location and there were enough to let the visitor know that he and the popes were more than casual acquaintances.

"Saba, my dear, how are you?"

"I'm fine, Bishop Maldonado. What can I do for you?"

He liked the woman sitting across from him. It wasn't sexual, although he did have an eye for beauty. With a reputation for employing the hottest secretaries in Vatican City, there were many who sought to find the scandal that would oust him from power, but Albert Maldonado was a careful man.

"As well as can be expected," he said, giving her an inquiring look. Maldonado had found his collar was often more intimidating than his size. "Come, let's talk where we have more privacy." Few outsiders had been allowed to visit the vault under the Sistine Chapel. Considering the circumstances, and her position with Interpol, he found it appropriate to show her exactly how much power the Church had. Although the contents were concealed, the countless boxes and tubes stacked on the shelves in the vault were awe-inspiring—and worth more than the pieces displayed in the museum.

Leaving the offices of the Institute of Works for Religion, commonly known as the Vatican Bank, Maldonado gave Saba a quick insider's tour as they skirted St. Peter's and walked up to an unmarked door on the side of the Sistine Chapel, stopping by the two colorfully attired Swiss Guards. The bishop was immediately recognized and, without a word, one of the armed men opened the door.

They walked down the short hallway to an elevator, where Maldonado slid his access card into a slot. A whooshing sound came from the shaft as the car climbed to the main floor. The doors opened, Maldonado waved a gracious hand allowing Saba to board first, stepped in, then pressed the button marked "2."

He looked over at Saba, and got the expected surprise when the cab went down instead of up. A few seconds later they left the elevator, where they were greeted by another guard, who unlocked a steel cage. This was the end of the physical security, although he knew there were cameras hidden everywhere. The temperature-controlled room was lined with shelves as far as the eye could see. They were full of crates, boxes, and tubes, each with a handwritten tag on it.

There was no computer inventory of the world's largest collection of stolen art.

Walking toward the rear of the vault, the bishop found the row of shelves he was looking for and stepped into the close quarters. There was no need to check if Saba was behind him. He could sense she was tripping over her dropped jaw—the expected reaction.

Stopping by an area labeled "Caravaggio," he looked at her sternly. "I understand the journal was lost," Maldonado said, templing his fingers into a church steeple. The gesture was crafted to provide a level of solemnness, but he often thought about inverting his hands and "showing the people."

"Unfortunate, but I have every reason to believe we will recover it."

"Any leads?"

"You know that is classified."

He knew she was trying to maintain eye contact, but her attention was diverted to the contents of the vault. Even the most sophisticated people were intimidated here.

"Of course, but you will let me know the minute you have anything you can release," he said.

"Of course," she said. "Do you mind?" she asked, moving closer to study the contents of the shelves.

Maldonado ignored the request. Using his body, he started to guide her away from the racks. Being here was enough; even a casual examination of the tags and labels would reveal more than he had intended her—or anyone—to see.

"Ouch," Saba exclaimed, dropping to one knee.

Maldonado turned.

"Sorry, just stubbed my toe. I should have worn sturdier shoes."

He turned back toward the main aisle. Noticing Saba lagging behind, he stopped, and turned to see what was wrong.

"I'm okay. These sandals ... " She shrugged, and rose to her full height.

Leading her back through to the elevator, he hoped the visit would serve its purpose to show his control over the wealth and power of the church. He signaled the guard, who opened the gate. The elevator was waiting for them, and they stepped in together.

"I have every confidence we will recover the journal," she said.

Maldonado wasn't sure it would be coming from her, but he would get it. He had other irons in the fire. With all the scandals surrounding the Vatican—and more specifically the IOR, the Institute for Works of Religion, where he was positioned at the right hand of the bank's president—it was important to do a little politicking with Interpol and the CIA. He'd already talked to John Storm, his connection there. Meeting with Saba was just checking another box.

Until the most recent pope took office, the IOR was one of the most secretive—and wealthy—institutions in the world. Formed in 1942 by Pope Pius XII, the bank had slipped through every fiducial, political, and moral loophole in turning the Vatican away from the doorstep of bankruptcy to being one of the wealthiest corporations on the planet. They accomplished this by faceless control. As a sovereign nation, the Vatican Bank avoided the restrictions placed on private institutions. With no paper trail, investigators had been stymied in proving what they knew to be true: The Vatican Bank excelled at transferring wealth, otherwise known as money laundering.

The elevator reached the main floor, where they exited and crossed the small foyer to the exit.

"If that's everything, I'd like to get back to work," Saba said.

Maldonado was relieved, and he walked her to her car, then watched her drive away.

16

STORM SURGE

Piazza Navona, Rome

WITH THE REASSURING BULK OF THEIR NEW WEAPONS—MAKO'S IN the small of his back, and John's in a shoulder holster under his jacket—the two men walked confidently across the Ponte' Umberto. Leaving Castel Sant'Angelo behind, John and Mako had no immediate destination. Juliet had synced the earbud before they left and Mako had Alicia back in his head.

"She's got a hit on the woman who had taken the journal through a camera at the Vatican." Mako relayed the conversation to John, explained her name was Saba Dragovich, and an Interpol agent. He was still processing that last bit when John interrupted.

"Woman scares me," John said, meaning Alicia. He was curious how the analyst had found Saba, but didn't want to bog down the discussion. Thinking about how much computer power it would take to run facial recognition software on every surveillance camera in Rome, he realized that nerds really did rule the earth.

"Is she still there?" He stopped; Vatican City was behind them now.

Mako relayed the question. "No, Alicia caught her on the way out. Found the car she's driving on a traffic camera. She's headed out of town, toward A90."

The beltway around Rome could be taking her anywhere, but John had an idea where she was going. If his assumption was correct, she would head south until reaching A90 which would intersect with A91, and take her to the airport. Even if they left immediately, they were too far behind to catch her.

"No point wasting energy chasing our tails. You hungry? We can grab a bite and wait till she gets where she's going." John had learned long ago that time, even during critical stages of an operation, fell into a different continuum. They would lose nothing by getting a bite and recharging. "You might want to have Alicia book us flights to Sicily—Palermo and Catania, near Syracuse."

"Right on. The extra tickets'll put her over the edge." With a smile on his face, Mako paused. "There's a plaza up there with a couple of fountains and some cafes."

John didn't care about the financial arrangements. He was sure Saba was headed to Sicily. Buying tickets to the two cities was well worth the cancellation fee for one. He let Mako take the lead until they reached the Piazza Navona. Stopping by the Egyptian obelisk the Romans had been so fond of collecting, he studied the square. Location was just as important to John as the menu or food. He sought out a position with clear sight lines and an easy exit. His experience had taught him that there seemed to be a universal pull between adversaries, often bringing them together when they least expected it. There was also the fact that Burga had found them before—she could do it again.

Something unusual caught his eye. At first, he wasn't sure

what it was. Even someone with clandestine skills in their blood, like John Storm, would have had trouble identifying as suspect any of the people sitting in the café across the piazza. To most, they just looked like customers—some drinking coffee, others not, with their faces buried in their phones. Anomalies were what he was trained to notice. Instinctively, his eyes tracked back and forth, comparing the customers. He was not sure what was bothering him. It wasn't unusual for someone to be alone, enjoying drinks in the afternoon.

Most of the patrons were enjoying Aperol spritzes or wine, but what John had noticed was an attractive woman and two men all sitting alone, drinking coffee. He had no reason to hide his suspicions from Mako.

"Those two men over there, and that woman ..." He was curious to see if Mako picked up on anything. "Did you get a good look at them earlier?" His son looked up from his own phone.

"That's them."

While Mako relayed the information to Alicia, John continued his observation. It took a few minutes to realize what had eluded him, but after Mako had confirmed their identities, he picked up a pattern. The three were clearly texting each other. If they had been sitting together, John would have noticed it immediately. Very clever, John thought, as he revised his estimate of his adversaries' capabilities. He knew their escape in the Colosseum had been as much luck as skill. If they hadn't found the old drainage pipe they would have been discovered.

Without any acknowledgment to the other two, the woman got up and left the café. John thought for a second about splitting up and following her, while Mako watched the men. He decided against it.

"What about that other woman, Saba?" John asked.

Mako asked Alicia. "Still in transit. What do you want to do? Split up?"

John Storm preferred to work alone, but he knew in this case it wasn't a good idea. "We watch these guys until Alicia has a location for your girlfriend." Mako's face reddened at the barb. John hadn't meant to get under his skin. He knew his presence was enough to do that on its own. Moving to an open area, he sat on the lip of the fountain, where the flow of water from a stallion's mouth concealed them from the assailants.

The woman ran to a black Ford Focus, which John suspected to be an Uber. Cursing the service and their endless stream of anonymous vehicles, they made the old "follow that cab" routine obsolete. The car pulled into traffic. As one of the most popular models in Rome, it instantly blended in with a half-dozen similar vehicles. Straining his eyes, it was soon too far away for him to see the license plate.

"Get the plate on that car," John said, pointing out the vehicle to Mako, who had been talking to Alicia and missed the woman's exit.

Mako started to rise. John grabbed him, pulling him back. A quick glance confirmed the two men were still sitting in the cafe. At six feet, Mako stood out in a crowd.

"Too far," Mako said.

"Give her the description of the Uber to pass along in case she gets lucky with the traffic cameras."

Mako relayed the information. "She's on it. We've also got the plane tickets."

John never doubted Alicia's efficiency. He glanced at his old analogue watch. "Just under an hour until the first flight." Having seen Alicia and TJ's war room in Key Largo firsthand, he was well aware she had both the mind and the tools to multitask.

"Let's keep an eye on our friends here for a bit until we know her destination." As they sat watching, John was starting to feel like the gears around them were all turning, but the cog that represented him and Mako was missing.

It was disheartening, but he knew he needed to be patient. Feeling his stomach grumble, he scanned the outdoor cafés. Lag times needed to be utilized and food was important. "Let's grab a bite over there." He pointed at a café across the plaza with another fountain between them.

Mako rose, but John grabbed his arm. Again. "The other two are leaving."

The Storms watched as the men left the café and started across the plaza, moving directly toward them. They again spaced themselves far enough apart that they wouldn't appear together, but their direction was clear. Just before they reached the fountain, John let out a breath he hadn't known he was holding. The men separated. One walked toward the plaza's far end, but the other man was still coming directly toward them. John reached into his jacket, securing a grip on the 1911 and waiting for the inevitable.

17

STORM SURGE

Outside Rome

SABA TRIED TO RELAX HER FOOT ON THE GAS PEDAL. FOCUSING ON her goal, she slowed for a red light and started to breath deeply. Inhaling for four seconds, she held her breath for four seconds, exhaled for four seconds, and held again. It took several cycles for the rhythm to relax her. With her "monkey mind" on hold, her thoughts clarified. Maldonado's charisma had almost sucked her in; fortunately, she'd had nothing to give him at the time, and her feigned stumble had actually revealed something that might be useful.

In hindsight, taking the meeting had been a mistake, but she felt she had to see what cards the bishop held. Now that she knew, as she followed the signs toward A12 and the airport, she relaxed. In a few days she would produce the journal and expose the Vatican's charade. It would be the tip of a very large iceberg and, once dislodged, she hoped the house of cards would fall and expose the Church for what it was. She couldn't wait for Maldonado's press conference to explain his way out of this. She expected the statement was already written, explaining to the art world how the Church's motive was to protect the artwork, not enrich themselves.

As she closed on the airport, she accelerated. Timing was crucial. One of the hindrances to being with Interpol was being accountable to her superiors, and she couldn't travel under an assumed name—unless she wanted to cover her own expenses. There was a trade-off, the benefit being that she was allowed to travel with her firearm. In this case, knowing what was involved, she chose protection over anonymity.

Saba had been ruthless in her pursuit of art thefts and forgeries. So much so that she had cultivated an image of being a lone wolf. Allowed to work without a partner, she had freedom. Though she could do what and go where she wanted—as long as results followed—she lacked the resources having a partner provided. In this case it would have been to keep an eye on Mako Storm. He might have been an easy mark last night, but he was sure to be after her now—with the resources of the CIA and Alicia Phon behind him.

She hadn't checked in with her office since last night, and it was past time for an update. To her superiors this trip had to look like the natural progression of a case and not a witch hunt. As she started to think about a plausible reason for her trip to Syracuse, the bumper of the car in front of her came up quickly —almost too quickly. The flash of brake lights barely gave warning of the accident ahead. Grabbing the wheel, she pulled onto the shoulder to avoid the entangled vehicles, and coasted to a stop behind the collision.

Several bystanders pulled over near the accident, many with the intention of being good Samaritans. Trying to merge back into traffic, she noticed a black Ford Focus pull in behind her. There was no reason to expect the driver was doing anything except trying to help, until she saw the Uber sign stuck to the windshield, and the barrel of a gun emerge from the rear window.

Saba was conflicted, but there was no time to sort through the impressions racing through her mind. Her instincts as a criminal investigator screamed "shooter." Then, as the gun swung in her direction, she realized it wasn't a random occurrence. Accelerating into an opening between the rubberneckers, she was able to dodge the first bullet, but the driver compensated for her action. Leaning out the window the passenger fired again. Caught in the traffic gridlock, there was no way for Saba to avoid the next shot. The back windshield shattered, spraying glass into the front seat. Something warm and sticky started running down the back of her neck.

With her head on a swivel, Saba sought for an escape from the stopped traffic. Sirens could be heard in the background. They weren't for her situation, though. A glance in her mirror told her the shooter, a woman, had exited the Uber. As the shooter approached the car she locked the doors and reached for her purse. Dragging the bag from the passenger side toward her, she rummaged through it, looking for her pistol. Traffic was now moving at a snail's pace, allowing the woman to easily overtake the vehicle. She grabbed the grip of the pistol, but before she could aim it, the glass from the passenger window shattered and the barrel of the gun encroached on her space. The woman used the weapon to clear away the broken glass and pointed it directly at her.

"You will remove your hand from the bag, move it out of reach, and place both hands on the wheel," the woman said as she entered the vehicle.

"What do you want? I am an officer with Interpol. This will not end well for you." Saba sat back, startled when she realized it was Carlotta Burga holding the gun on her.

"I am fully aware of who you are— and what you took from the American agent."

Saba's mind raced. The sirens were close now. Traffic was still at a standstill. In her rearview mirror she could see the lights of a fire truck and an ambulance trying to penetrate the logjam to reach the accident. Looking over at the Mafia boss pointing a gun at her head, Saba desperately tried to figure out how to play the traffic jam to her advantage. Her first instinct was to get out, but her weapon was in her bag set behind her, just out of reach. There was little doubt Burga would shoot her in the back. Saba held her breath.

Dying was not going to bring down the Church. If the journal was lost, the Church would win, and that was not acceptable. Thinking through her options, she glanced at her cellphone in the cup holder. As if reading her mind, Burga reached for it and tossed it out the shattered window. There was nothing she could do now except drive—and think.

"Where are we going?" she asked. Saba's training had taught her to engage her captor. She'd long known her strength was in research, and was one of the reasons she had ended up in the art world, where the investigations tended to be detail oriented. Taking the journal was a first for her. She'd worked on her own before, but never with her own agenda overriding the mission. Though her captor didn't know it, this mess was Saba's own fault. She cursed herself for tipping off the woman across from her. She was well aware that using her good looks plus a little charm—never mind having a prearranged escape route—had made Mako Storm an easy target. Calling in the anonymous tip to a Mafia connection to flush him out had been her choice, though a necessary means to flush out Mako before he could complete the contract.

She'd never been in this situation before. The woman who had overtaken the passenger's seat would not be fazed by looks or wit. The best Saba could do was to keep her talking in the hope it would humanize her if it came to a life or death choice.

Burga didn't respond to her question, only motioned with the barrel of the gun for her to continue. Saba considered her actions, knowing she was in the hands of a sociopath.

It was hard to plan not knowing their destination. A91 ran to the coast, as well as to Leonardo da Vinci Airport, where Saba had been headed. If their destination was still the airport, she had no idea how Burga was going to get her on a plane. As an Interpol agent, Saba had to identify herself prior to security. Another option was to take her by boat. The third, and least preferable, was to an unmarked grave somewhere in the scenic countryside. That thought alone made her even more vigilant for any opportunity for escape.

They had been driving for about fifteen minutes when Burga finally spoke. Since abducting Saba, Burga had searched her bag and the front-seat area of the vehicle, then had spoken in hushed tones with someone over the phone. Burga was clearly frustrated, and Saba wondered how long it would take her to figure out the journal was hidden in her apartment back in the city. Saba had painstakingly photographed each aged page, some several times under different light. To a buyer, the authenticity of the journal was critical; Saba already knew it was the real thing. Her goal was to use Caravaggio's own words to crack the window of doubt. As paranoid as art collectors were, that would be enough. Then, she would show the art world how they had been duped.

"Take the next exit."

They were still twenty minutes from the airport. There was little point speculating where Burga was taking her. Saba had learned early in her career that it was useless to waste energy on things beyond your control, especially trying to anticipate the criminal mind. Even after a dozen years she still had trouble understanding their actions.

Precious little space separated the vehicles as the traffic speed finally climbed to the 131 kilometer per hour speed limit. The woman, still on the phone, motioned with the gun at the exit sign, a not-so-subtle reminder of what she had previously ordered.

With the exit approaching, Saba could see Burga glancing frequently toward it. Saba started to panic, as the blinker seemed to have no effect on the drivers to her right. She glanced over her shoulder, making eye contact with the driver beside her. Fortunately, it was a man, who graciously waved her across. Glancing back at the road, she found herself in the same predicament with two more lanes to cross. The turn signal was again ignored and, wanting to use the same ploy, Saba took one more look ahead to confirm the spacing of the cars in front of and beside her. A brake light two cars up kept her attention forward for a few seconds—long enough to catch the eye of a man in the passenger seat of an adjacent car. She thought she recognized the man, but before she could get another look, the cars were separated.

The driver ahead released the brakes, and the contact was quickly forgotten, as Saba noticed that Burga seemed more nervous as the exit approached. Becoming more aggressive, Saba willed the car across the two lanes of traffic separating her from the exit. With less than a hundred feet to spare, she pulled into the exit lane and prepared for the inevitable. With her phone lost miles back and probably shattered, she feared for her life.

18

STORM SURGE

Old Rome

FOR NO APPARENT REASON, THE MAN COMING DIRECTLY TOWARD them veered away at the last second. Neither Mako nor John had expected it, and each eased their grip on their weapon as he passed without a glance. It was a strange encounter, to say the least. Maybe it was because his head was down, looking at his phone screen, but the man should have recognized them. Just another sign of sloppy tradecraft.

"We need to split up," John said. "You take the airport, I'll follow our friend here." John was more familiar with Rome, and felt he had a better chance of tailing the man.

"Sounds good." Mako pulled out his phone.

"What the hell are you doing?"

"Uber, Pops. Ever try it? Works for the good guys, too."

John regarded the rideshare service as just another technological complication. "Whatever. Keep in touch."

"Sure thing." Mako took off for an adjacent street.

John didn't wait to see what kind of ride Mako had arranged for himself. His eyes hadn't left the man from the café since he had moved past them. In the moment, he studied his adversary. From a hundred feet away, the guy towered over the other tourists, who parted to allow him to pass. If he'd had "THUG" tattooed on his forehead it couldn't be any more apparent what he was. His lips were tightly pursed as he studied the street as if he didn't have a plan. John took that as a blessing and, glancing each way to evaluate his surroundings, he took off after the man.

The man headed toward Old Rome, which worked to the elder Storm's benefit. With each block, pedestrian and vehicular traffic increased until both were near a standstill at the traffic circle in front of the Victor Emanuel II monument. From John's experience, it held the standard afternoon fair: pedestrians, bicycles, scooters, street vendors, horns, sirens, and drivers flipping each other off. The only things that had changed over the years were the goods the vendors shoved in front of the pedestrians.

John eased sideways through the crowd, thankful for the height of the man he followed. It worked in his favor, and he felt the reassuring bulk of the 1911 in its holster. Knowing, if it came to a face-off, he would likely need it.

Taking up the entire horizon, the massive monument loomed large behind the gridlocked traffic creeping around the Piazza Venezia. Just before crossing the street to the green space in the center of the oval, the man instead turned right onto Via Plebiscito. John followed, allowing a little more space between them to compensate for the thinning foot traffic. After one long block, taken up by the National Museum, and several shorter ones, John found himself looking down at another set of ruins. The Largo di Torre Argentina encompassed an entire city block. It was one of a few sites where visitors were allowed to descend to the level of the ancient city and walk through the ancient columns surrounding a decayed circular foundation.

The site of Julius Caesar's murder was one of the "undiscovered" ruins of Rome, frequented more by the local cat population, which were protected inside its boundaries, than by tourists. John became suspicious, as the man descended a set of stone stairs from the street to the ruins. With the amount of tourist traffic at the old sites, they were perfect for clandestine meetings and dead drops, though John wondered why the man had chosen this less-frequented place.

Moving to the metal railing outlining the perimeter of the excavation, John looked down at the ruins of the Curia de Pompey, where Caesar had been stabbed to death over two thousand years ago. From this perspective, there was no sign of the man, but there were many blind spots scattered throughout the old site, leaving John no choice but to climb down the staircase.

John hurried down the stairs, knowing he was exposed and vulnerable as he descended ten feet to the level of the ancient city. Reaching the old paving stones, he glanced around, drawing a deep breath when he saw no sign of the man. Staying tight to the crumbling walls, he started moving around the perimeter searching for the man. From his position he had been able to observe the other three staircases. They remained vacant. The man was still down here.

He felt something, gasped and jumped forward, then realizing it was only one of the feral cats brushing against his legs, tried to calm down. John had felt his age in the last few years. It had been all good through his fifties and sixties, but the next decade had started to take its toll. From his early years, starting as an intelligence officer in charge of a reconnaissance team in Vietnam, John had believed that over everything else, including luck, it was discipline and attention to detail that had kept him alive. It was not lost on him that the Roman Empire was built on the same trait, and though a fierce patriot, there was something in this city's Stoic roots that drew him like a magnet.

Staying in the shadows as much as possible, he passed the old foundation of the theater, trying to look into the dark arches ahead. He was certain the man was not behind him—he had to be inside one of the openings. A brief inspection told him that these were newer, built as a retaining wall to hold the street above. The arches were shallow, mere decoration, but a clandestine conversation or exchange could easily occur in the three-foot-deep recess.

The first opening was bricked up. Sliding along the wall, John approached the next opening, listening as he moved. Stepping past the archway was a bit like walking off a cliff, but the recess was empty, as was the next. John took a second to scan the rest of the ruins. There was no sign of the man. He had to be in one of the three openings ahead.

Knowing he was close, John reached into his jacket for his pistol, removed it from the holster and, with his right hand shielded from view by the brick wall, dropped the weapon to his side. His hand remained on the stock and his finger on the trigger guard as he approached the second-to-last archway.

Something flashed past him just as he stepped into the opening, but after the last encounter he was ready and stepped aside as two cats bolted from the cover of the archway and ran across the ruins. He was prepared for them, but in the split second that they had drawn his attention, a hand reached around his neck, grabbing his nose and mouth. Before he could react, he could feel the man's forearm and bicep squeezing his carotid artery.

Everything went black.

When his eyes fluttered open, squinting at the bright light, he had no idea how long he had been out, and it took a few seconds for his memory to reboot and come fully back to consciousness. Seated on the old stone floor of the archway, the man hovered over him. There was no need to check his pocket for his pistol—the man had it pointed at him.

19

STEVEN BECKER

STORM
SURGE

Outside Rome

MAKO KNEW USING UBER WAS A CRAPSHOOT, AND THE DRIVER OF the compact didn't disappoint. As he snatched the twenty-euro note from Mako's fingertips, he simultaneously slammed his foot on the accelerator. With a smile on his face, he wove in and out of traffic, navigating the busy streets. Several times, even before reaching the highway, the G-forces had pulled Mako back into the small seat. Having to jam his body into the the tiny car had seemed like getting into a clown car, but as the driver skillfully fit the ultra-compact into spaces even a small sedan couldn't enter, he appreciated the vehicle.

Reaching A91, the driver took the entry ramp marked for the airport and accelerated onto the highway, the gravitational pull as he accelerated strong enough to shove Mako against the door. Traffic was still heavy, causing Mako to calculate the time he had until the first flight. Sitting back, he felt a tingling in his legs. Trying to find a comfortable position, finally, his body and the car reached a compromise and he relaxed. With the driver's propensity for speed, they should reach the airport in plenty of time.

That was true until they crested a small rise and looked down on a long line of brake lights ahead. In the distance Mako could see the flashing lights of several emergency vehicles working an accident. Before he could come up with a plan "B," the car was wedged between a truck on one side, and even larger vehicles on the other three. With the small space of the car closing in on him, Mako had to make a decision.

According to the last sign they had passed, they were still forty kilometers from the airport. His flight left in ninety minutes. There was no way, even if the accident were cleared in the next few minutes—and with the ambulance still on site, it didn't seem likely—that he would make the flight.

Trying not to feel like he was reporting to, but rather simply checking in with his partner, he pressed John's number in the short contact list he had entered in the burner phone. The call went to voicemail. Mako left a brief but innocuous message, in case anyone was listening, that he was stuck in traffic, and disconnected.

"Any idea how long?" Mako peered across at the driver's phone, set into a holder attached to the windshield. The estimated time to their destination now read over an hour. If that was correct, he would miss the second flight as well. The driver shrugged in response. There had been no indication that he spoke English.

"It looks bad," Alicia's voice penetrated his skull.

Mako had forgotten about the earbud. Instead of responding immediately, which would surely have elicited a response from the driver, he raised the phone to his ear.

"Hello," he started, trying to make it sound like an ordinary phone call.

"What are you doing?" Alicia asked.

The proximity of the smartphone to the earpiece shot a screaming feedback noise through his head. Alicia must have heard it as well.

"Oh, got it. Good idea. I see you're stopped. What's going on?"

Mako gave her an update on the traffic and waited for a response. The logical move would be to take the next exit and work the surface streets, something Alicia was more than competent enough to guide them through. Unfortunately, they had just passed an exit, and had not even reached a sign for the next.

"No way we can exit anytime soon," Mako said, anticipating her next question.

Stuck in the passenger seat with his knees jammed in his chest, Mako was in no mood to spar. Instead of responding, he turned his head, watching the traffic speeding by in the other direction. Suddenly a pair of green eyes met his. Moving at the speed limit in the next lane, she was gone in a flash, but Mako was sure.

"Black Ford Focus, couldn't get the plate," he told Alicia.

"We've got to spin this around," he pleaded with the driver, making a swirling motion with his hand, and pulling a hundred euros from his pocket. From the way the driver grabbed the bills, Mako suspected the man did speak some English. Certain he had seen the green-eyed woman in the car, he didn't care either way.

Outside Rome

The exit ramp ended abruptly at a stop signal, forcing Saba to look at her captor for directions. The respite gave her a chance to study Carlota Burga for the first time. Her face was well known, at least to those in international law enforcement, but seeing her in person cast her in a different light than the mug shots plastered around the internet. She looked like a glamorous woman, though from only a foot away Saba could see the careful use of foundation hid several scars. Still, Burga was someone—though probably closing on fifty—might at one time have been a model. There was nothing about her look, including her toned, slim build that said "Mafia boss." Rock climbing, Krav Maga, and countless kettlebell swings had given Saba's muscles the same tone. Saba had learned long ago not to make assumptions based on looks, not that it mattered here: Burga looked fit and able. Saba might have an advantage with her martial arts training, which had her looking for any opening. Still, the weapon in Burga's hand precluded any opportunity.

For a brief second, Burga seemed unsure of herself. Her inspection of the car and Saba's purse had failed to produce the journal. She had to be wondering what to do. Sensing this, a thought occurred to Saba that might help gain her freedom.

"The journal. I gave it to Maldonado earlier." She wasn't sure how long Burga had been following her. A touch of the truth never hurt, and if Burga knew Saba's mission, she might accept it had been completed.

"Then you'll have to get it back, won't you?" Burga said.

Saba started to turn toward her, but the sight of the weapon trained on her stopped her. Burga appeared to have bought the lie, though there was no way to really know. Ending Saba's speculation, Burga signaled her to make a left turn and re-enter the freeway going the other direction—back to Rome.

The car fell silent as they retraced their path, allowing Saba to think about her next step. The Vatican would be a natural place to lose Burga, and Maldonado would likely cooperate if Saba hinted that turning over the journal to him would be the result. It might be worth a try, although there was little chance

Burga would follow her into the Vatican, even to retrieve the journal.

"We'll need to go to Vatican City, then," Saba said. Cooperation at this point would keep her alive. The gun overrode any physical advantage Saba might have over the woman. If she had any hope of escape she had to crawl into Burga's mind, and knowing her opponent, that was not going to be easy.

Burga had made no comment on her proposed destination, allowing her what seemed to be the freedom to plan her next move. Maldonado would have to cooperate—he had no reason not to if he thought the prize was in reach. Pitting the two villains against each other might allow her to find a crack to extricate herself.

"You'll need to draw him out," Burga said.

Her poorly conceived plot to lose Burga in Vatican City fell apart. "What if he won't? He already has what he wants. Maldonado has no reason to endanger the journal."

"You're a smart woman," she said.

"And he's a smart man. I'd bet that journal is buried deep in the vault below the Sistine Chapel."

Saba's stomach dropped when Burga's finger moved from the guard to the trigger. "Maybe you should call him?"

"You tossed my phone on the highway."

Burga pulled an old-style flip phone from an interior pocket of the leather jacket she wore. From the corner of her eye, Saba watched as Burga did a quick search on her smartphone, found a number, and entered it into the flip phone.

Placing the phone in speaker mode, she laid it on the console between them.

The best-case scenario was that the call didn't get picked up or went to voicemail, but God's minions always answered the phone, and after four rings, a man answered.

The pistol moving back toward Saba's head ended the pause.

"Bishop Maldonado, please," she said,

"Who may I ask is calling?"

"Inspector Saba Dragovich. We are acquainted."

"Please hold the line."

A piped-in choir filled the dead air while the call was transferred.

"Miss Dragovich?"

"Yes." It wasn't the bishop, but she recognized the voice.

"Bishop Maldonado is out of the office right now. Can I take a message?"

Saba gripped the wheel tighter, trying to come up with some kind of cryptic message that would let Maldonado know she was in trouble. "Please tell him that I have found a way to authenticate the painting. Please let him know. I think he would be grateful to be informed immediately." That much was true and she expected his aid would find him directly.

"Where can he reach you?"

Saba glanced over at Burga, who shook her head.

"We'll call back when we're closer."

20

STORM SURGE

Old Rome

JOHN SHOOK HIS HEAD LIKE A FIGHTER WOOZY FROM A HAYMAKER. The man loomed above him with the recently acquired pistol trained at his head.

"The journal. Where is it?"

"I don't know what you're talking about," John responded.

The butt of the pistol slammed into John's temple, knocking him onto his side. John had to wonder if the man was that quick or if the previous blow had dulled his senses. Whichever, the harsh look on the man's face left no doubt that he had done this before. John took his time recovering from the blow, feinting as if he was hurt worse than he actually was, though the act was pretty close to his current condition. He had to regain his senses. Playing this game with half-a-deck could be fatal.

"Again. The journal."

Knowing another blow would either add his suspected concussion, John tried to buy some time. Using his hands, he rose to his knees and shook his head in an attempt to clear it.

The thug's question was forgotten when fireworks exploded in front of his open eyes. Carefully, John held his hands palm up in front of him. The gesture not only communicated that he didn't know, but also placed his arms where he could use them to block another blow.

"Where is your son?"

Mako was traveling under his own name. There was little point in lying when the truth could be easily verified. "Heading to Sicily. You have to know that he lost the journal last night."

"Foolish man, falling for a woman like that."

"We've got that in common, anyway," John said, using the interlude to slowly gain his feet. The man stood back in case John fell, but his aim never left John's head. John used the brick wall behind him to maintain his balance. Thankfully, the tinge of double vision faded slowly.

"I don't have the journal, but I do have an idea who does," John said.

The man lifted his eyebrows, signaling him to continue.

"That woman who seduced my son has it."

As it echoed off the walls of the alcove, the sudden shrillness of a cell phone ring almost put John back on his knees. The man pulled the phone from his pocket and glanced at the screen. After accepting the call, he stepped backwards and held the phone to his ear with his left hand, while maintaining his aim on John with the gun in his right.

John had spent enough time in the country that he had a fair command of Italian. He could make out fragments of the conversation and had ascertained a woman had been taken. Then, an anglicized word stood out: Vatican.

Maldonado held the key to whatever was going on, but with a gun trained at his head John would never know unless he escaped. While the man talked, his attention moved away from

John, though his aim remained true. John took the opportunity to scan his surroundings. Ten feet below street level and hidden by the alcove, he doubted anyone would be able to react to a call for help before the man either shot or crippled him. Standing was an effort; John had no illusions that he could take the man, even if he had the element of surprise.

A dozen or so people were spread out over the block-sized excavation. He noticed some were feeding and petting the local cats. Looking around, he saw the site was infested with them. Never a feline lover, he jerked back when he felt one brush against his legs. The man continued to talk, not seeing the cat at John's feet.

John took a chance, thinking it was the only one he was going to get. Slowly, while maintaining eye contact with his assailant, he bent over and petted the cat. Gauging the man's interest, he saw nothing to warn him off his next move.

Trying to hide his face, he grabbed the cat by the scruff of its neck and with a swift motion flung the feline at the man. Claws extended, the cat let out a vicious scream as it latched onto the man's face. His phone dropped, but for a long second the gun remained pointed at John. The man's efforts to free himself of the animal seemed to have no effect on his gun hand. Then, instead of releasing, the terrified cat dug its claws deeper.

The gun hand dropped, and John was on the man in an instant. Grabbing the man's gun hand, knowing very well that the trigger could inadvertently be pulled, John slammed the man's wrist into his raised knee. Still plagued by the cat, the man was disoriented, every ounce of his focus intent on dislodging the claws before they gouged his eyes out. With every attempt to dislodge the animal, its claws cut deeper. Finally, the man's hand reflexively opened and the gun dropped to the old stone floor. John reached down and grabbed it a millisecond before he saw the cat flung against the brick wall. There was no time to find out if it still had any lives left—the cat had served its purpose.

John pointed the gun at the man, who raised his hands. Backing out of the alcove, he stumbled into the waiting hands of two gendarmes.

21

STEVEN BECKER

STORM SURGE

Outside Rome

THERE ARE CERTAIN ELEMENTS OF A SITUATION THAT MAKE IT difficult to notice something right in front of your face. Having seen the green-eyed woman in a black car, as he peered ahead every other car on the road seemed to be black, too. So many of the cars looked identical to each other that it was almost impossible to locate the one with the woman.

It turned out the driver knew a fair amount of English and was more than willing to practice on Mako, who had little more than a spattering of Italian. What he'd found was that whenever he attempted to practice his Italian, he was waved off by the enthusiasm of the Italians wanting to practice their English.

The driver was babbling to the point of distraction, but Mako was reluctant to silence him. He had already shown both a willingness and aptitude to flex the traffic laws. In fact, a glance at the speedometer revealed they were traveling at 140 kilometers per hour. Mako did the math in his head that this was somewhere north of eighty-five miles per hour. This driver checked every one of the boxes of the stereotypical Italian driver, driving the Focus like a Ferrari and gesturing wildly as he wove in and out of traffic.

"Up ahead," Mako said, pointing to another black sedan.

"I'm on it, boss."

The car lurched forward as the driver accelerated. They quickly reached the slower-moving car and Mako turned away. It wasn't her. What he needed was a bird's-eye view. Touching his earpiece, he woke the connection. "Alicia?"

"No, my name is Lucia," the driver said.

After giving him plenty of euros, now stuffed in Lucia's pocket, Mako was already in deep enough. He turned his head and pointed to the flesh-colored bud in his ear.

"You some CIA spy or something?"

Mako couldn't resist. "Bond. James Bond."

Both men chuckled at the reference to the iconic spy. Without directly answering the question, Mako had answered. "We could use some help." He said Alicia's name again.

"I'm here. Just helping TJ on the dock."

She sounded out of breath and Mako pictured the diminutive woman hauling dive tanks. "I need you." He hated to say the words.

"Let me get upstairs."

He could hear her breathing as he imagined her walking down the dock and taking the single flight of stairs up to the apartment located over the dive shop.

"Almost there. What do you have?" Alicia asked.

Mako could see Lucia straining to hear the conversation. He shrugged and ignored him.

"Okay, I've got your location. What the hell are you doing? Last I heard you were flying to Sicily."

"I saw the woman."

"Vehicle?" Alicia was all business now.

"Black Focus. And don't say it, I know, half the cars in the country look like that."

"It'll take a minute to load the traffic cameras, but we should be able to track her. What are you driving?"

"I took an Uber to the airport. The driver's cool." Mako saw Lucia smile. Whatever happened, short of violence, the driver was all-in.

"I'm gonna grab TJ. He's better at this than I am."

Mako continued to check out each black car they passed, but there was no sign of her. Estimating it had cost them five minutes to exit and return to the freeway, he really didn't expect a hit yet. Assuming they were traveling at the speed limit, for every minute the black Focus had on them, it would take five minutes to make up the time. Plus, there was always the chance the Focus had exited already.

"Yo, Mako."

"Hey, TJ. Did Alicia fill you in?"

"Right on, brother. I'm on it. Okay, I've got you now. Tracking the cameras ahead of you. Black cars over there are like grunts on the reef, man. You'll have to check them one at a time." He paused.

Mako imagined TJ sitting in his captain's chair, populating his monitors using the double joysticks built into the arms. "Roger, that."

"Two coming up on your right."

"Got 'em."

Mako leaned forward to confirm what he expected, that neither car was the one. Without any kind of breadcrumbs to follow, this was futile. To Mako, patience and perseverance seemed like weaknesses; things had always come naturally to him.

Several more black cars came and went, and then he saw her.

Their eyes met, but something was different. She clearly recognized him. There was no smile or frown; she didn't turn away, as he had expected. Instead her eyes bore into him. He could see fear on her face.

"Pace that car. That's the one."

"Cool," Lucia said, slowing slightly to maintain spacing.

"We've got her," Mako said into the mic.

"Right on. I'll grab the plate at the next camera and run a trace."

"Ten to one it's an Uber like this one," Mako said.

A hurt look came over Lucia's face. "There is no other Uber like this one."

Dealing with an Uber driver's fragile ego was low on Mako's priorities, but the driver had been an asset. "You the man." He reached over and fist-bumped him.

The smile returned, and Lucia leaned forward, concentrating on the car in the left lane.

Mako wasn't sure what to make of her. Ducking slightly to avoid a direct line of sight, he looked back at the green-eyed driver. Her glance darted back and forth, as if she were looking for something. It was then that Mako glanced at the passenger, realizing it was the woman who had chased him and John earlier.

Just as he made the identification, his phone rang. There were only two people who had the number, and he was already connected to one.

"Dad?"

"Listen, Mako. I'm in jail. I'll text you the info. Get Alicia to hook me up with a local lawyer and get me out."

The call disconnected, as if someone had taken the phone from the older Storm's hand. *Shit*, Mako thought. Just as he finally caught a break, the old man ends up in jail. Relaying the information to TJ, he waited for the text.

Outside Rome

Saba had spotted Mako before he saw her. With her low opinion of Storm, it would have been a disappointment if she hadn't. Instead of looking away, as if he had caught her doing something wrong, she held his gaze. Forced to choose between Carlota Burga, who sat in the passenger seat pointing a gun at her, and Mako Storm, who had to have figured out it was she who had stolen the journal, Mako was her only ally.

Using eye movements, she tried to signal him that she was in trouble. Then his car slid away, and she thought her attempt had failed. But when she looked across at the traffic in the adjacent lane, he was still there, his car keeping pace with her's.

For the last few miles, since Burga had ordered her to turn around and head back to Rome, she had wracked her brain for anything in her power to free herself. There were few options when driving with a gun pointed at you. The vehicle, of course, was a weapon, but anything she did with it would affect her as well.

Once they had reentered the highway, she slowly increased the speed to ten, then twenty, kilometers over the limit, but Burga had caught her ploy to try to get pulled over, and she was now cruising at the speed limit. Until she actually saw a police car, there was nothing she could do—until Mako had appeared.

This was the only time she could recall where, instead of trying to avoid another vehicle, she was praying that one would follow. Whatever happened, she needed to facilitate the other car's effort, not a simple task if Mako's tradecraft was as bad as she had observed last night.

Still, there was something about him that intrigued her.

Putting those thoughts on hold, her immediate priority was getting Maldonado out of the Vatican. The journal was hidden in Rome—not that she would just hand it over. Her phone was gone, but the pictures she had taken were accessible through the cloud. *Know your enemy* had been beaten into her since the first days of Interpol training, and she had done her homework on Mako's group. The tech-savvy couple in Key Largo had the resources to bring the journal back to life—at least electronically. In order to do that, she had to make amends with the tall, dark man, who was now peering at her across traffic lanes like a teenager.

Carlotta Burga was a different problem. That enemy had slipped under her radar. Stereotyping was generally a bad idea, but when it looked like a duck, and quacked like a duck.... The Mafia was still the Mafia, and extortion was one of their prime tactics. Saba knew their relationship with the Church went back decades. As the Church had decided to back, or at least aid, the Nazis in a fight against communism, brushing all the group's monstrous sins under the rug for the greater cause, so had they allied with La Cosa Nostra to keep the communists out of Italy. And like every storekeeper who paid for "protection," the Church had found that once you became intertwined with the Mafia, it was near impossible to extricate yourself from their clutches.

Saba set those thoughts aside, too. Somehow she needed to turn what she had done to Mako last night to her advantage, but first, she needed Maldonado. From her initial scan of the journal she had noticed that Caravaggio had made reference to several paintings whose providence were not in question. One in particular came to mind, and it was close at hand. The *Fortune Teller*, whose fraternal twin was on display in the Louvre, hung in the Capitoline Museums. Set behind the Vittorio Emmanuel II monument, the site was perfect for her purposes. If she could arrange a meeting there, it might be possible to escape.

"I need to try Maldonado again."

"Be my guest." Burga went to her recent call log and pressed the number for the Vatican offices, then handed her the phone.

Burga was so preoccupied with something that she forgot to put the call on speaker, Saba noticed, as she took the phone from her captor's hand. With Burga listening to only one side of the conversation, she might be able to arrange the meeting without Maldonado ruining the party.

The same voice she had spoken to earlier picked up the call. He clearly remembered her, and transferred her to the bishop.

"Ah, my dear. I hope this is good news."

"Indeed, Bishop. Can you meet me at the Capitoline, near the *Fortune Teller*?"

"I'm assuming that you have the journal?"

"A question of authenticity has come up. I think it would be wise to compare the journal against a known painting." It wasn't an unusual request. The journal's value came in its ability to authenticate the paintings in Sicily. There were notes about several others in it as well. If the journal were a forgery, there might be errors. It had always amazed Saba that even with the stakes so high how lazy forgers and criminals could be.

"This is unusual, but if you have it, I will meet you. An hour?"

"That would be fine. I'll see you then." When she heard the call disconnect, she added, "Bring the original, not copies."

She handed the phone back to Burga, tentatively glancing at her face. There was no sign she had sensed the deception. That problem handled, as Saba drove toward the city, she concentrated on moving her two pawns, Mako Storm and Bishop Maldonado, into place.

22

STORM SURGE

Key Largo, Florida

AFTER SHE FINISHED SAYING GOODBYE TO THE LAST OF THEIR charter clients, Alicia ran up the stairs to their apartment. She hoped she hadn't appeared impatient with them. Some tip money had surely been lost with TJ already upstairs guiding Mako through the streets of Rome. Return customers and their goodwill in recommending their shop were critical to the business's survival. Though her mind was racing ahead to the problems in Italy, Alicia tried to concentrate on the people who regularly paid their bills. Glancing back at the gear strewn across the deck of the boat and the dock, she continued to the front door. People were important; the boat and gear could wait.

"What have you got?" she asked TJ, while sliding in front of her own computer. About two-thirds of the wall monitors were lit, displaying an assortment of traffic cameras and maps.

"We found her. They're heading back to the city."

"That takes care of Mako and the woman. What about John Storm?"

"Jail."

"Get the hell out. John Storm's in jail?" Alicia was stunned. Of all the players least likely to get locked up, it was the senior Storm. "What happened?"

"Not much for details, but Mako sent me a text with some information. Sending it to you now."

Alicia's phone pinged, alerting her to the text from TJ. It was pretty straightforward, just the address and phone number of the *questura* where John was being held. "I've got this angle. Let me know if anything changes on your end."

"Will do. As soon as they hit the city center, all hell's probably going to break loose."

TJ's attention had never left the screens. Wearing a long sleeved dry-fit shirt and boardshorts, he sat in his captain's chair, totally engaged in the action in front of him. "Divers said they had a good trip. Got some tip money, and they all said they'd be back."

"Awesome."

Alicia realized that TJ probably hadn't had anything to eat or drink. Hydration in the Florida heat was a big issue. After spending less than a half-hour outside with their charter guests, her own throat was dry. She knew TJ's level of dedication and decided to grab some drinks and food before digging in to figure out what had happened to John.

With two Diet Cokes for each of them and a bag of chips for TJ, she sat back down at her station, thinking TJ must have been ravenous by the way he dug into the chips. Diving had that effect on her as well. It didn't appear to be a whole lot of work, but it sucked your energy. Some of it was the ordeal of gearing up in the sun and heat. Once you were in the water, though, movement was effortless, unless there was a strong current. What sapped your strength, even in these warmer waters, was maintaining body temperature. Although lately the tropical waters had been hovering in the low eighties, that was a big difference from the ninety-eight point six degrees of a human body. The energy required to maintain warmth burned more calories than running.

"Thanks, babe. The lead car just stopped. Mako's in an Uber, the woman appears to be driving her own car. Got time to crack their database and see what you can get on the passenger?"

Finding the woman's identity trumped getting John out of jail. "On it."

23

STEVEN BECKER

STORM
SURGE

Rome

SABA FELT A WAVE OF RELIEF AS THEY CROSSED THE TIBER AND entered the old city. Burga had made it clear the journal was more important than Saba's life, an attitude that worried Saba. The knowledge that she was the only one who knew the location should make her indispensable. The problem lay in the lie she'd told her captor that Maldonado had the journal. Maldonado had agreed to meet her, but he was expecting the journal as well. Implicating Maldonado could go either way. She'd had no choice, figuring the only way to decrease the odds of her death was to add another party.

Burga was becoming frustrated as Saba cruised the streets. Parking was always an issue here, and Burga's frustration was quickly becoming hers. She stubbornly drove the side streets surrounding Capitoline Hill looking for a space. The only options open were the half-spaces that Smart cars could fit into by parking perpendicular to the street—about the only thing justifying their existence. Glancing at her watch, she started to worry that they would be late.

"We're going to miss him. I'll use a garage." She hadn't wanted to push Burga, but Maldonado was not likely to wait. Saba was counting on help from Alicia, a woman she'd never talked to, to figure out her own identity and put the pieces together. Finally, Saba found a couple preparing to exit a space and pulled behind them. On the single-lane cobblestoned streets this in itself caused a bit of a spectacle, as traffic was forced to wait behind them.

Once they parked, Saba led the way to the Cordonata Capitolina. Saba had no time to pause and admire Michelangelo's architectural feat. The famous stairway was more of a ramp with steps every dozen or so feet, allowing horses, donkeys, and carts the ability to climb to the Piazza del Campidoglio, where the museum was located. Passing the twin statues of a man leading a horse at the top of the stairway, Saba turned to the right. Tourists milled around, studying a statue of Marcus Aurelius in the center, and the design of the stone paving. Laid out by the master, the elliptical pattern gave the illusion that the trapezoidal layout of the buildings were square.

Through the crowd, Saba saw Maldonado standing in the entrance. She was thankful he appeared without his usual entourage. Saba knew the appearance was a deception. He wouldn't come alone, and she quickly scanned the plaza for at least the bodyguard or driver she suspected was nearby.

Burga had agreed to linger behind, allowing her to "retrieve" the journal without raising an alarm. Greeting the bishop at the entrance, he followed her inside toward the alcove containing Caravaggio's *Fortune Teller*. Graciously he extended his arm for her and together they walked the corridors of the famed museum looking like a father and daughter.

Her mind was spinning as the renowned art collection slipped past her, as did Maldonado's running commentary. As they approached the room where the *Fortune Teller* hung, she still had no answers. They reached the alcove dedicated to the painting. Maldonado had a smile on his face, and stood quiet for a minute as he gazed at the painting.

Finally, he turned to her. "The journal, my dear."

Piazza del Campidoglio, Rome

"Mako? Are you there?" Alicia's voice came through the earbud. "I know who she is."

That got his attention. "Right on."

"Saba Dragovich. Get this, she's an Interpol agent specializing in art. I got a hit on a still from the traffic cameras and used facial recognition software to identify her."

Mako didn't know what to think. "She drugged me and stole the journal. What the hell? Interpol, really?"

"I'm certain. So, now the question is what to do with the information."

"Call her boss for starters. She drugged me and stole the journal." Mako stopped, realizing that repeating himself made it appear that he was whining.

"If we do that, she'll likely be recalled. We need to figure out what her game is. Is she working on or off the books, for starters."

"She looked like she was in trouble." The black Focus was still ahead. A change in tactics would be needed as they reached the inner city. As the traffic steadily built, the chances of them continuing their surveillance without being seen were getting slimmer.

"They park. There." Lucia pointed to a black car blocking the street.

"I need to follow them. You can drop me at the corner."

"And miss the action?" The driver pulled a pad from the

console and wrote down his name and phone number. "You follow on foot. I'll see if I can track them from the road."

Mako wasn't about to turn down the help. Without being in the car himself, the driver would be able to follow much closer. "Thanks, man," Mako said, pulling a couple of wadded-up twenty-euro notes from his pocket. With the road blocked, there was no need for the driver to pull over. Mako exited the car in the middle of the street and slid into the alcove of a building close by. He turned to face the wall when he saw Saba and a woman approach. They passed without incident, and he followed.

"You there, Alicia?" He updated her on his situation, not that she hadn't heard most of it anyway.

"We're tracking you."

Until a few years ago, anyone walking down the street seeming to talk to themselves would have drawn stares and hushed whispers. Now, with the advent of smartphones and earbuds, there was nothing unusual about it, allowing Mako to keep a running dialogue with Alicia as he followed.

Ahead was a steep ramp leading up to a plaza. Mako stayed a good hundred feet behind Saba and the woman. His gut was telling him that she would be glad to see him; the other woman, not so much. As he reached the last landing, he saw a tall priest wave to Saba from the entry to one of the buildings, which Mako guessed was another museum. Plazas, statues, museums, and churches—these summed up Rome.

The trio entered the museum with the woman a few paces behind. Mako waited a minute and followed. Focused on finding Saba and not on the art lining the walls, he quickly caught up to them. Ducking into an alcove, he studied the crowd, looking for the other woman. Mako caught sight of her a minute later as she tried to blend in with a tour group. She was clearly not looking

at what the guide was talking about; rather, her focus
Saba and the priest.

They stood in front of a painting set off by itself, its position
telling Mako it was valuable. It was an oil painting of a person
who he would describe as a dandy, complete with a feather in
his hat, who was having his palm read—and his ring stolen—by
a smiling woman. Mako was far from an art aficionado, but even
he could recognize something special about the piece.

His silent critique was interrupted by the raised voice and exaggerated hand gestures of the man talking to Saba. Understanding
the conversation was impossible, as they were speaking in Italian.
His own grasp of the language was barely enough to order dinner.

"Get closer," Alicia's voice came through the ear piece.

Mako wondered how she knew what was going on, then saw
a surveillance camera discreetly hidden in a corner and could
imagine the scene being cast on the screens in the war room.
Stepping to the side of the painting to appear to look at another
work, the conversation became louder.

"Can you hear me now?" Mako joked.

"Shhh. I'm getting it. Running through a translation
program."

The voices had died down, the conversation ending with
Saba extending both hands and shrugging.

"You've got to help her," Alicia said in his ear. "I couldn't get
the whole gist of it, but she apparently promised the man, who
facial recognition tells me is Bishop Albert Maldonado, the journal. He was expecting it."

"But she has it." Saba and the bishop were talking again,
lower this time, and Mako moved a few feet closer hoping Alicia
could pick up on the conversation.

"You have the pictures on your phone?" Alicia asked.

It took Mako a second to realize she was asking about the

pictures he had taken of the journal before the transfer. "Yeah, but she took it, remember?"

"Shit. Hold on. I've got them in the cloud. Downloading to your new phone now."

The phone vibrated in Mako's hand, telling him that an attachment had been received. He glanced down, waiting for the small clock symbol to tell him it was downloaded. When it finished, he tapped the icon and saw the ancient pages in front of him.

Stepping into the open, he walked toward Saba and the bishop. "Maybe this will help. We wouldn't want to expose the journal to any risk before authenticating it." Mako handed Saba his phone.

"And you are?" the man asked.

"Mako Storm, at your service." He loved the James Bond inference.

"John Storm's son?" the bishop asked.

"Yes, you know him?"

Instead of answering, the bishop took the phone from Saba's hand and started scrolling through the photographed pages. While his head was down, Mako and Saba made eye contact. Mako was surprised as their eyes locked. Knowing the power she had lorded over him before, he was wary. His only response was a flush to his face.

"It seems this is an accurate copy," the bishop said, handing the phone to Saba. "Can you find the passages about the *Fortune Teller*? That should tell us if this is the real deal."

Saba scrolled through the document on Mako's phone, pausing every few seconds to glance at Mako. Every time she did, his eyes were fixed on her. While she had expected a hostile response, what she saw instead was caring. Trying not to let her emotions conflict with her work, she pulled her eyes back to the screen. It took a long minute until she found the passage, and handed the phone back to Maldonado.

"I suspect your Italian is better than mine," she said.

The bishop's head was buried in the text. Satisfied that he had found what he was looking for, he moved closer to the painting, looking at the phone, then the canvas. He did this several times before handing the phone back to Saba.

"It appears to be authentic. Now, let's make arrangements for the real journal."

Saba had reached the point of no return. She had to tell someone the truth.

"I felt I had to keep it safe until I knew whether it was real or not," she said.

"Now we know," Maldonado said. "When can we expect the original?"

"We have a small problem there. She glanced toward a nearby tour group. Mako followed her eyes. If her face hadn't been etched into his memory from the chase earlier, he would never have recognized Burga in the low, ambient light. He wondered if Maldonado would be able to identify her too.

"Jesus Christ. They are relentless," Mako muttered.

"I think it would be better if you disappeared now," Saba told Maldonado. "As soon we can shake her, I'll call you."

Capitoline Museum, Rome

Carlota Burga stood at the fringe of a nearby tour group watching Saba and the bishop. It was as good a cover as she could ask for, and allowed her to place others in the group in front of her when they passed the surveillance cameras.

She almost blew her cover when Mako Storm appeared. Fortunately, she was dragged along with the group when they moved to the next painting. From her current position she could still see the *Fortune Teller*, and she could tell that something was wrong.

The priest was holding a phone, not the journal, comparing what she guessed was a copy of Caravaggio's notes to the painting instead of the real thing. With tens of millions at stake, she knew the journal itself had to be authenticated, and she studied the man's frame, looking for any bulges in his jacket that might alert her of the real journal's location.

Maldonado handed the phone back to Saba, who in turn passed it to Mako. Someone backed into Burga, forcing her to take her eyes off the trio around the *Fortune Teller*. The tour group started to push her forward again. This time she resisted, as she would lose her line of sight, and made a comment about finding a restroom. After the camouflage the group had provided, she felt like she was on an island now. Seeking any cover she could find, she left the group and darted into a hallway from where she could barely see the painting.

Something was wrong. She couldn't hear the words, but she could read body language. From the way Saba opened her arms to the bishop, it looked certain that the woman had misled her. The bishop didn't have the journal. It almost looked like he was expecting it from her. Burga thought back to Saba's conversation with Maldonado, and had to scold herself for being preoccupied and not having the call on speaker. Saba was no rookie, and had used Burga's momentary lapse of tradecraft to her own advantage. Now, Burga would seek revenge.

It was clear the bishop didn't have the journal. Saba or Mako or the pair together were playing some kind of game—that was about to end. Reaching into her jacket pocket, her hand felt the comforting grip of the Glock. With the pistol ready, she took several long strides across the polished stone floor, planning how to reach them discreetly to avoid the cameras which would alert security if she tried a full frontal assault. She had to be careful, knowing that with the value of the collection housed there every security guard on duty—and that might be quite a few—would converge on the scene in seconds if she showed her intent.

As she crossed the room, she circled around the group standing in front of the painting. Each move brought her one step closer to the trio. Finally, Burga had moved into position behind Saba and played the best card she had—she stuck the barrel of the gun in her back.

"Enough of your games. One sound, one move, and you're dead."

STORM SURGE

Old Rome

MAKO INSTANTLY KNEW SOMETHING WAS WRONG. HE GLANCED around and saw Burga behind Saba. He scolded himself for allowing the woman to reach them without his noticing.

He tried to decipher the words spoken in Italian. It wasn't necessary when he saw the bulge in the assailant's pocket pressed against Saba's back. Saba's eyes met his again, this time with an altogether different look—fear. Mako wasn't sure what Saba's game was, but it was clear she had overplayed her hand.

"Let's all walk out of here nice and calm." The woman used the barrel of the gun to push Saba away from the *Fortune Teller*, and toward the exit. "You too." Her cold eyes bore into Mako, letting him know if he ran Saba would pay for it.

Fate is a strange animal. Whether an individualistic theory, such as karma, or a religious belief, where God or the gods issued decrees for disciples to follow, it doesn't matter. Most people will tell you it exists in one form or another. Mako was in the karma camp. He was probably the only one in the room who knew that Saba had the journal. Karma had nudged them together the other night; now fate had given him a push forward. He realized he had no choice but to ally himself with a woman who had seduced him, drugged him, then stolen from him less than twenty-four hours ago. He felt Saba's eyes on him as she walked toward the exit, and nodded in acceptance of his fate, saying a quick prayer to the goddess Fortuna.

They reached the exit doors without incident. Mako scanned the courtyard. Not sure what he was looking for, he didn't see anything that might help free Saba and lead to the eventual recovery of the journal.

The earbud he wore was a standard wireless device. Without the more sensitive bone mic, Alicia was more or less worthless. If he talked, the woman with the gun pressed against Saba's back would hear it.

Once they reached the plaza, Mako tried to separate himself enough to talk to Alicia, but the woman would have none of it, warning him off with a vicous stare at him while jamming the gun into Saba's back.

The pistol tucked into the small of his back reminded Mako that he had options. The courtyard of the plaza was too crowded to take the woman out without collateral damage, but if he was patient, he would likely get an opportunity. As they approached the bronze statue of Marcus Aurelius, Mako realized there was another way to play this, one that should have been his first priority. Both Saba and the woman were his enemy. Forget about the alluring green eyes and smooth curves. An idea occurred to him that if he sided with the other woman, forcing Saba to retrieve the journal, he might be able to take it from her.

The idea intrigued him, but setting Saba up to take the fall or worse, especially now that he knew she was an Interpol agent, didn't sit right with him. There was good and bad, and though she had taken advantage of him last night, she hadn't killed him. If Saba was Interpol, she was most certainly one of the good guys. That knowledge placed the woman with the gun on the other side of the spectrum.

Alicia had been intermittently asking if he was all right for several minutes. If he tried to respond either verbally or with a text, the woman would see or hear. By not answering, Alicia would assume he either had tech problems or was in trouble. Unfortunately, tech savviness was not in the Storms genes and she might assume his phone had gone dead. Either way, he knew Burga would be alert.

Burga pushed Saba toward one of the statues situated on either side of the steps. It was as out of the way as any other space in the crowded plaza. Moving Saba toward the horse's back end, Burga gestured for Mako to move closer.

The three of them closed into a tight circle and when she was so close that Mako could smell the breath of the woman, she stated her demand.

Surprising him, she looked right at Mako instead of Saba. "The journal ... where is it?"

A quick risk-benefit analysis told Mako that he needed to make his move now. For whatever reason, and it was highly possible that Saba had thrown him under the bus, the woman believed Mako had the journal. In her mind Saba was disposable. Mako couldn't risk that.

People often have a hard time knowing what to do with their hands in a stressful situation. Crossing your arms or leaving your hands at your sides is viewed as an aggressive posture. Placing his hands behind his back in a non-threatening pose allowed Mako's right hand to reach for the pistol.

His casual body language relaxed the woman just enough for him to make his move. Separating his hands, which had been interlocked in an "at-ease" stance, he slowly lifted his right hand under his shirt and removed the Glock. Using his leg to shield it from the woman, he shrugged in response to her question.

Mako got the reaction he had wanted. Frustrated with the non-answer, the woman turned the gun on Mako. At the same instant Mako's hand flew around his body. Oblivious to the screams of the bystanders, he trained the sights on the woman.

"Run. I'll be right behind you." Now that he had found her, Mako was not letting Saba out of his sight.

Saba executed a perfectly placed side kick to the woman's midsection, causing her to hinge at the waist, then slammed her elbow into her back. Despite the velocity of the strike, the woman remained standing. Mako would have liked to make a play to disarm her, but Saba was already crossing the plaza. Mako saw an opening beside the building that Saba was running toward. From his vantage point, he could see a steep, narrow road leading down to the old Forum. Michelangelo had, by order of his patron, purposefully designed the plaza to face away from old Rome and directly toward the Vatican. The stairs leading up to the plaza had been built for horses and donkeys, not vehicles, necessitating the need for a service road.

Mako could run. From grade school on, he'd been in the top three of every class, including Langley. In a half-dozen long paces, he caught up to Saba. Together they ran down to street level, not risking the time it would take to see if the woman was behind. They just assumed she would be.

"Take the lead," Mako said to Saba as they reached the street. "Alicia? We've got trouble."

"I assumed so from the radio silence. The phone's too new for you to have burned up the battery already."

"If that's Alicia Phon you're talking to ... " Saba paused to breath. "We need to get to Syracuse."

"I heard. Get to the airport. I'll have flights booked," Alicia responded.

The stairs ended at a main thoroughfare, where Saba turned right. Mako risked a look back and saw the woman about fifty feet back. Saba's attack had slowed Burga, but the distance allowed for a shot if she wanted to take it. Mako could only hope the woman didn't want to attract the attention that a gunshot would bring and be satisfied to follow. She too wanted the journal, and with either or both Mako and Saba dead, she would lose her chance to recover it.

"Where are we going?" Mako asked, slightly out of breath. Saba was in an all-out sprint, dodging the tourists and souvenir vendors as she bolted down the street. Mako loped behind her, hoping she could hold the pace until they lost the woman.

"The Palatine. I could lose myself there."

It made sense. Crowds of people were their friends. Staying to the outside of the rectangular Forum, they sprinted toward Palatine Hill.

Piazza del Campidoglio, Rome

Maldonado heard Saba's warning and immediately scanned the room for any threats. It took only a second to see the woman moving toward them—a woman he unfortunately recognized—and another second to locate the closest exit. It was his situational awareness, ingrained into him from his youth on the streets of Chicago, again saved him.

These same instincts were partly responsible for his surprising rise in the hierarchy of the Church. He was intent on gaining power not in the day-to-day business of a parish or diocese. It was Rome and the power in Vatican City that he was drawn to. Because of his aptitude for languages, as well as the relationships he had nurtured, he was assigned to the position he wanted: Vatican translator.

Before the twentieth century, popes rarely traveled. Until the 1980s, some never even left the protection of the walls of Vatican City at all. Security was an issue on the first overseas visits by the papal entourage, an area Maldonado had a knack for. He had helped with the complicated arrangements, working on his own and with Vatican security and, in one case, physically intervened in a bad situation.

That was how he had originally gotten noticed and endeared himself to two pontiffs Along with his relationship with Archbishop Marcinkus, a fellow American, Maldonado was able to bypass the heavily Italian-centric Roman Curia. Once elevated to a position of trust, it was his shrewdness that had kept him there. Anything but the stereotypical bishop, Maldonado played golf, a rarity for a clergyman and, despite his vow of chastity, he had a reputation as a womanizer. His offices always had the best-looking secretaries.

Subverting the power structure as he had, as well as his tastes for "real world" indulgences, had made many enemies along the way, which in his current situation might hurt him. In Rome, especially within the art circles, he was a well-known figure. Being seen exiting through the side door of a museum would surely ignite the wrong kind of gossip. But a quick threat assessment told him that being caught inside a museum with both an Interpol agent and a Mafia boss would have worse consequences than a quick exit.

Pushing past a tour group, he hit the bar on the steel door, hoping it wouldn't trigger an alarm. Raising the collar on his jacket to hide his face, he lowered his head as he stepped onto the stone pavers.

Two figures running caught his eye as they ran down the winding access road caught his eye: Saba Dragovich and Mako Storm. Following them was out of the question. He smiled for the first time since receiving the mysterious call from Saba. With John Storm's son involved, he expected his old friend would help him out. Instead, he turned to the plaza and started walking at a brisk pace down the Cordonata. Upon reaching the street he waved to his waiting driver, who quickly pulled up the car and, with a glance around, ducked down into the backseat.

"Back to the office?" the driver asked.

Maldonado thought for a second. "No. Swing by my apartment and then the airport."

25

STORM SURGE

Rome

JOHN HELD HIS TEMPER. IT WAS ALL HE COULD DO TO MAKE IT through processing without incident. Frustrated that after disarming and escaping from the gunman he had walked right into the arms of two policeman, he stomped around the small cell. At least, for now, he was alone. He'd made his one phone call, regretting now that he hadn't called the Embassy or State Department. Unaware of the Italian procedures, he slammed his open palms against the concrete block wall, and sat down on the spartan bed.

He knew Alicia had the resources to free him, but time was of the essence. For all he knew the journal was already in Sicily. He glanced around. The cell had no windows, and his watch and other personal effects had been taken when he was processed. At this point, knowing the exact time didn't matter. It was later than he expected the magistrates or judges worked, anyway. A night in prison was not on his agenda. Somehow, he needed to secure his release. Alicia could pull a rabbit out of a hat, but he wasn't sure she could get him out of jail without a lawyer and hearing.

The State Department was his best bet.

With forty years of CIA operations on his resume, John was no stranger to jails. Having had to perform less-than-legal "jobs" on every continent save Antarctica, he could write a travel guide on foreign prisons. There were a whole lot of countries less accommodating than the Italians. At least that was in his favor.

Most "modern" governments were cautious with their international detainees. By now, his identity would surely have been checked, verified, and with any luck, flagged. He could only hope that his status hadn't been deleted when he "retired." Even if it had been, that was something Alicia could fix.

Through years of dealing with undesirables, prison guards had developed a talent where they could look at you without looking at you. For the majority of guards who hadn't chosen the occupation to satisfy their masochistic tendencies, face-to-face confrontations with the dregs of society were not desirable. John knew a breakout wasn't on the table. That would only get him killed. Still, out of habit, he studied the guards and, after a few hours in the cell, he knew their routines.

Without any interactions to base his bias on, John had to use his gut to decide which guard to approach. Hearing the now familiar sound of rubber-soled boots on the concrete floor, John rose from the bunk and moved to the bars. It was the guard he wanted.

"English?" John asked as the man walked by.

Imperceptibly, the man changed the angle of his head just enough to see John out of the corner of his eye. He evaluated the threat and responded, "Some."

"I'm American, working for the State Department. Someone should have been here already."

"I have no idea of the procedures of the administrators."

At least he was honest. "How can I arrange to make a phone call?"

The man rubbed his thumb against his fore and middle fingers leaving no doubt what it would take.

John stuck his hands in his pockets, pulled them out, and shrugged. The cell block was mostly full, making gestures safer than talking on the off-chance that another inmate within earshot knew English.

The guard held up two fingers. John nodded. Two hundred euros to get out tonight would be well worth it.

26

Palatine Hill

EARLIER, BURGA HAD INSISTED, AT GUNPOINT, THAT SABA LEAVE her bag in the car. Understanding the value of her Interpol credentials and passport, she carried a money belt around her waist. Bags got lost or stolen; for someone to liberate her of the belt would take the knowledge that it was there and the will to take it.

Entering the grounds of the ancient Forum, the crowds forced them to slow their pace to what she called the tourist shuffle. Negotiating the paths between the ruins to avoid the tour groups, Saba risked a glance behind to insure Burga was in the same predicament. Unless she wanted a shootout, the woman's firearm had been neutralized when Mako had shown his. Now, it was a strategic game of cat and mouse, with the airport the immediate goal.

Ahead was the Arch of Titus, near the end of the Forum. The Colosseum rose above the rest of the ruins in the background. To the right was the gate allowing access to Palatine Hill. Reaching inside her clothes to swing the belt around to face her front, Saba continued pushing through the crowds. Once the pouch was accessible, she removed the slim, bifold wallet holding her credentials and continued toward the entrance. While Rome had a surprising number of free venues, mainly churches, the ruins of Palatine Hill were not one.

"Interpol, please step aside," Saba called out when they were still fifty feet from the gates. The crowd parted, allowing her and Mako to reach the entrance.

Flicking the wallet open, Saba subverted the line, directing Mako toward the handicap entry, where she flashed her credentials. The attendant made an attempt to verify the ID, but Saba continued unabated. If there was a security force here, it was minimal, and she doubted, even if she was trying to get in for free, it was enough of a breach to call for reinforcements.

"Come on. This is our chance."

"You know your way around here?" Mako asked, snagging a map from a holder mounted on a pole. "All looks the same to me."

Saba glanced back, "She's going to have to wait in line. Hurry up," she said, and bolted up a series of steps. The ruins here were of the wealthy neighborhood from Rome's glory days. Now, all that was left of the residents' power was the size of the foundations they passed. Otherwise the hill looked like many other urban parks, cut up by paths and heavily treed, rather than landscaped.

Mako had shown that he was in shape, at least to run, but by the time they climbed two more steep flights of uneven steps he was winded. Standing with his hands on his knees, his body language told Saba to take a breather.

She climbed one more set of steps at a brisk walk instead of a sprint, allowing them a short respite to catch their breath. The stakes were too high for a full-fledged rest. They looked back at the stairs. There were few straight lines in the park, outside of the decrepit foundation walls, leaving no clear line of sight to the entrance. Burga could be stuck in line, or one landing below. Saba guessed somewhere in the middle, leaving no time to waste.

"That's it for the stairs." Saba pointed to the Colosseum. "We'll work our way over there and grab a cab." The park was bordered by a black cast-iron fence. The vertical spindles in between the larger posts were smooth and, with only a top and bottom rail running horizontally, would be near impossible to climb.

"Ask Alicia to find us a way out."

"We can just wander out the gate down there," Mako said, pointing to an exit.

She had overlooked the simple solution, something Mako appeared adept at finding. Throughout her career, if there was one trait that had held her back, it had been her knack of making things complicated. In her defense, working in the world of stolen art, few things were cut and dried.

"Sounds good." She left the well-worn path, taking off cross-country in the direction of the gate. They were descending now, and after catching her breath, she started to move faster. The only problem was the hillsides, which were barren of vegetation, leaving Saba and Mako exposed. It wasn't a full minute after she realized their predicament that her eyes locked onto Burga's.

She was making her way up a stairway they had ascended just a few minutes ago. Stopping with her hands on her hips, the woman surveyed the area. They ducked into a copse of trees. Saba's choice to leave the trail system left her and Mako only a hundred feet from Burga. The advantage they had gained was now lost. Saba could tell from Burga's body language that she was heavily winded, but looking at Mako, she decided he wasn't in much better shape.

Mako had his Glock drawn, and was about to swing into a

shooter's stance when Saba grabbed his arm and pulled the weapon out of sight. "That's going to cause more problems than it'll solve. A gunman out of uniform here is going to start a panic." She thought about that for a second, realizing maybe it wasn't such a bad idea. The park was lightly patrolled, and even if they were subdued by the security guards, as long as there were no casualties, her credentials would be enough to walk away.

"Fire a few shots at that hill."

Mako raised his brows in a questioning look. There was no time to explain. Burga had left the trail. The only thing in their favor was the uneven terrain that had her picking her way toward them, forcing her to use all four appendages. Until she reached better ground, she would be forced to come to a complete stop to shoot. Saba lost her patience. Grabbing the gun from Mako, Saba fired three shots at the grass embankment.

Screams followed the gunshots. Turning back to the hill, with the gun extended in front of her, Saba started running for the cover of the trees at its base. Ahead was the ruins of the stadium, and beyond that the street. In between was a cluster of buildings. Many of the ruins were less than six feet tall, remnants of walls and columns from the ancient buildings. Some defied time, standing their full two stories with part of the roof structures still intact. It was a random pattern that Saba hoped would provide enough cover to conceal them.

They were halfway down the hill when a clump of dirt flew up two feet to her left. A millisecond later a blast echoed through the ancient buildings, which, even over two thousand years, had never been filled with that sound. Another shot struck closer, forcing Saba to serpentine the rest of the way down the hill.

Saba reached the trees first, and turned with Mako's Glock extended, ready to provide covering fire for him. It wasn't necessary, and he reached the trees a second later. Burga was half-running, half-falling down the hill. She'd had to make a decision to shoot or follow. The terrain made it impossible to run and shoot with any accuracy at the same time. Saba suspected from the placement of the shots that they were more for effect than to cripple or kill them. Without stopping to take aim, a shot from a handgun would be inaccurate.

A left-hand arrow on a sign pointed them in the direction of the Temple of Apollo and then the street. Mako stayed a step behind, allowing him to glance back every few steps to locate Burga. Once they entered the ruins, they scrambled through what remained of the door and window openings and vaulted low walls in what he hoped was a direct path to the street.

They stopped just short, finding themselves standing on top of a stone wall. Below was the field of the stadium, its old structure visible in the columns and foundation walls. A ten-foot drop separated them from the next step in their escape plan. Stairways at each end of the stadium provided access. Unfortunately, they didn't have the time to reach them and still maintain a lead on Burga. Nodding to each other, they crouched and launched themselves off the wall.

The grass below was deceptive. Thinking it would be soft, Saba landed awkwardly, ending up on her side. She looked across at Mako, who had landed on his feet. Embarrassed at her attempt, she snuck a glance over at Mako to see if he had noticed. Some other time she would have to figure out why his opinion mattered—not now. As they ran toward the short side of the field where another drop waited, Saba glanced back and saw Burga aiming her gun at them from the top of the wall.

The only cover was the row of old columns, about four feet tall and nearly as wide at their bases. She followed Mako as he wove his way between them, alternating sides with each column. It looked like one of her old soccer drills, where the coach had placed cones that the players had to dribble the ball in and out of. It was effective, though, allowing only a brief section between columns where they were visible to Burga.

Saba didn't need to look back. Bullets ricocheted off the old stone around them. Burga had remained above. Just ahead was another drop that would bring them to the Temple of Apollo and the street. Without hesitating, Saba ran for it. One last look in the fading sunlight showed Burga struggling to climb down the wall.

"Here we go," she called to Mako, bracing herself. Together they dropped down to the Temple, ran through the ruins and found themselves on a road. It was not a public thoroughfare, just the perimeter loop around the site, but just beyond it, down a grassy embankment lay a wrought-iron fence and freedom.

Scrambling down the slope of the last hill, Saba noticed that the streetlights had turned on. In a few minutes it would be dark and they could make an attempt at the fence without attracting attention. Looking back, she saw Burga. They didn't have that long.

"She'll expect us to scale the fence. Why not follow this service road to an exit?" Mako gasped. He stopped for a second, pulling the paper that the Uber driver had given him from his pocket. Reaching for his phone, he called Lucia, and arranged a pickup.

"What are you doing?"

"I got a driver."

Once again Mako had simplified things.

"Plan." Saba started into an easy jog around the road. By the time they reached the gate, they saw it was closed.

"Park closes at sunset," the attendant said.

"We got a little lost, sorry," Saba replied, as he opened the gate.

"Happens more than you'd think. That's why I'm here."

They were on the sidewalk now, right by the gate where they had entered. To the right was the Arch of Constantine. Through the opening, Saba could see taxis passing by on the road. A second later, with a smile on his face, Lucia pulled up in his Uber.

27

STORM
SURGE

Rome

JOHN EXITED THE POLICE STATION. IT WAS AFTER DARK, AND HE scanned the sidewalk, knowing someone was waiting there. Someone he'd have to explain himself to. By using the State Department get-out-of-jail-free card, he would be required to give a statement. It was not a step he could afford. After calling Alicia, she had backdoored him into the State Department's system, then called them to make sure they knew where he was held. Once past retirement age, every government official knew if you achieved that status you were somebody—not just a name in a computer. Someone would be here to meet him, someone he would prefer to avoid.

A woman caught his eye, and he delayed for a second too long. Had it been a man, John would have looked right past him. Her short skirt was like a magnet that stopped his eyes.

"John Storm?" she asked, walking quickly toward him.

Evading her and getting caught would lead to worse circumstances than the jail he had just exited. "Yes. Thanks for taking care of all this."

"Faith Roberts. I have some questions." She held out her hand.

He bet she did. Instinctively, he guided her down the street and away from the security lights illuminating the police station. While they walked he was able to study her, and saw a resemblance.

"Roberts?"

"That's right, Faith Roberts."

"Your dad work for the agency?"

She turned to look at him, and John knew he was right.

"Why, yes."

Maybe things weren't so bad after all.

"Where's he at these days? We worked together, but I was bad at staying in touch." It was the best way he could think of to ask if his old friend was still alive.

"Not keeping in touch is one of his specialties." She paused.

John suspected she was trying to decide whether to cross the line that separates business from an agent's personal life. It was a decision that would affect how this conversation ended.

"They've got a place outside Scottsdale. You know Dad, loves his golf. Now he's out there every day."

John breathed a sigh of relief, both in how she answered the question and that his friend was still alive. At his age, attrition was starting to take a toll on his acquaintances. "How about coffee or a bite to eat? I had to beg for water in there."

"I suppose, but I'll need you to answer some questions."

"Sure thing. It'll be good to hear how your mom and dad are doing, as well." John calculated that Rome was eight hours ahead of Arizona. In order to extricate himself from this mess, he would need his friend to vouch for him. John hoped he had an early tee time, because interrupting his golf game would be a bad way to accomplish that.

28

STEVEN BECKER

STORM SURGE

Trastevere District, Rome

THEY HOPPED INTO LUCIA'S CAR AND HE TOOK OFF IMMEDIATELY. A glance back confirmed that Burga had reached the road. Mako had pulled Saba in beside him, not failing to notice the electricity that shot through him. There was some kind of connection there. If he could only sort out her allegiances maybe it could go somewhere. Mako felt that she knew it too; the question was, who would acknowledge it first?

He had little to lose. She'd already drugged him and stolen the journal. Now allied because of a common enemy, staying close to her was the best way to retrieve the journal, and what better way to do that than have her share his bed?

While he was still debating whether he should make the first move, he had pushed Saba down to avoid Burga seeing them. His hand slid under the short sleeve of her blouse. The placement of his hand on her arm was an intimate gesture—and she knew it too.

Saba's head turned towards him and their eyes met. There

was something about sharing a life or death experience that brought people together. Their faces inched closer, but just as their lips were about to touch the car smashed into one of Rome's famous potholes. Jostled to the side, Mako collected himself. The moment was over, but would not be forgotten.

A question from Lucia brought Mako back to the present.

"*Destinazioni?*" Lucia asked.

Mako gave him a questioning look, deciding that, as a stereotypical Italian man, Lucia was trying despite their circumstance to flirt with Saba by excluding him from the conversation.

"*Aeroporto,*" Saba responded.

"Sicily, then?" Mako asked.

"That's where this is headed."

The island might have been where this was going, but it was not where everything started, at least for him. "Forgive me if I'm wrong, but you have the journal."

She leaned her face against the window. "About that."

Mako looked at her. Though her body had shifted away, her hand lay on the seat next to him. Usually working alone, covert operators had to depend on their own perceptions of reality. There was often no other way to assess a situation than by talking it through—to yourself. In these one-sided conversations, it was easy to twist that truth. Mako had had more than a few of these talks with himself, the latest being when he came to lying on hard concrete under a ratty blanket by the Tiber. At the time Saba had seemed an enemy after depriving him of the means to complete a valuable contract. But there were two sides to every operation. He'd been around long enough to understand the shifting alliances of the covert world. Now, he just had to convince her it was all right to to shift their alliances to include each other.

Reaching for her hand, he hesitated. The almost-kiss had

come about naturally. Taking her hand would be a premeditated act, and though it was almost trivial, as a step toward gaining her trust it was a major decision. Whether he was thinking clearly or not, Mako wanted her. He'd seen enough to know she was capable, intelligent, fun—if you could call a chase through Rome fun—and beautiful. She was also on the right side of the law.

Just before he touched her, she turned and their eyes met again. It looked like she had made a decision. Moments like this are fleeting, and if he wanted her and the journal, he needed to make his move—now. Sliding his hand across the plastic-covered seat, his outstretched fingers reached towards hers, and he was relieved when they naturally interlaced with his. Their eyes remained locked on each other. She was speaking to him with her eyes, and he hoped they were speaking the same language. Leaning in, he needn't have worried. She moved towards him, closing the space faster than he expected.

No errant potholes interrupted this kiss.

The kiss lingered as they melted into each other's arms, oblivious to the outside world. Lucia was the one to break them up.

"*Excusé, qualcuno ti sta seguendo.*"

While Mako had understood the anglicized words for destination and airport, this phrase he didn't understand. Before he asked, he saw Lucia's eyes in the rearview mirror move to scan the road behind them. Saba had understood and was already looking through the back window, checking the cars behind them. No translation was necessary when Mako saw the barrel of a gun extend from a side window of a car several lengths back. Ready to return fire if necessary, he reached for his pistol and opened his window.

"Don't. Let's try and lose her first" Saba said.

"Persistent, though, isn't she?" Mako had thought they were in the clear.

"Her reputation is like a dog with a bone."

Mako had seen the woman exit Palatine Hill. He had hoped they'd had enough of a lead that they could escape unnoticed. A sudden gunshot told him otherwise."

"Now?"

Saba was speaking urgently to the driver. She reached out and pulled Mako's arm back in the car. "Too much chance for collateral damage. We can't be like them."

Mako understood. He had been trained to evaluate life-threatening situations as well, and she was right. Pulling the gun back in, he woke up his ear fob and got Alicia's attention, asking for help. She quickly understood their situation, and started rattling off street names that Mako could barely comprehend, forget about repeating out loud. Handing the earbud to Saba, he turned to check on their pursuer. Just as he faced the rear window it shattered, blowing glass all over the backseat. Lucia's natural reaction was flight and he accelerated. Saba had been facing away from the window and took it in stride, rattling off directions in Italian. Mako brushed the broken glass off his face, feeling the stickiness of blood along with the tiny pieces.

Moving the threat status to DEFCON 1, Mako pulled the pistol out, and using the headrest for support, aimed out the broken window. Cars were swerving to get out of the way, allowing the pursuer to close the gap, and Mako saw the woman just two cars behind. Her gun was not visible, giving Mako a brief reprieve to evaluate the situation.

Killing Mako and Saba was still not a viable option for Burga. As much as she might want to, sealing their lips would also lose the journal forever. The shots had been fired to let her car get closer to theirs, and maybe even incapacitate it. She'd accomplished the first part.

Burga's driver, one of the men who had chased them earlier, was clearly visible, his face unflinching, intent on following them. As Mako heard Saba talking to Alicia he realized he had underestimated his opponent, who had called ahead to have her man and car waiting for her when she exited Palatine Hill.

The darkened windows of the cars between Mako and Burga obscured her from his sight. Knowing the driver was in league with the woman and not an innocent civilian, Mako fixed his aim again. Alicia had chosen to try to evade their pursuit, sending them down surface streets instead of the highway. Without being in Rome, what looked clear on Alicia's monitor didn't indicate the frantic nature of transportation in the city. The driver directly behind their Uber saw Mako's pistol and immediately swerved to his right, grazing the car in the adjacent lane.

There was a dull thump as the lightweight metals collided. Fortunately for the drivers of the affected cars, there was a wide sidewalk, allowing them to pull off the street. If not for the sidewalk, the chase would be over. Instead, pedestrians scurried into storefronts to evade the oncoming vehicles, allowing Burga's car to pull right behind their car.

Saba ordered a sharp left into a narrow side street. With a squeal of tires, Lucia accelerated into the turn, knocking over a stack of trash cans in the process. Several were tossed to the side, and the rest were crushed as Burga's driver slammed through the debris.

Unable to lose the other car, Mako started to make a contingency plan. Glancing at Lucia's eyes in the rearview mirror, he noticed the man was looking back more than ahead. That could only lead to disaster. With the gunshots, their adventure was over for their Uber driver.

Mako needed to be ready. Older, low-rise buildings lined the crowded streets. Restaurants and cafes were the predominant feature of the neighborhood, which appeared more residential than the other parts of Rome they had been through. There were no ruins or tourist trappings here. It seemed like many neighborhoods Mako had been through in New York, Washington, D.C., and London. It had an old-world feeling, with telephone and cable wires slung between the buildings. It was a place where people lived their entire lives. Where you could be born several blocks from where you died.

Small cafes with outside tables and markets with bins and crates encroaching on the sidewalks attracted Mako's attention. They were the perfect obstacles to help lose a pursuer. In theory, Alicia's tactic of using the tight maze of urban streets to lose Burga was correct. Now, with their pursuers directly behind their car, it played against them. One collision would have them in each other's laps.

Just as he thought it, brake lights flashed ahead, then the squeal of cars stopping suddenly, and finally a rider-less bicycle skidded across the street. Traffic stopped. When Mako looked back, he was staring directly into the barrel of Burga's pistol. Pulling Saba toward him, he opened his car door and pulled her to the sidewalk. Leaving the door open as a shield, he reached into his pocket and threw a wad of bills on the seat. Lucia understood Mako's intent and slowly drove away, allowing Mako and Saba cover as they made for the busy sidewalk.

The vendors and waiters yelled what even Mako could interpret as flavorful curses as he and Saba crashed through the displays and tables. Saba wore the earbud—with Alicia talking —allowing Mako no choice but to follow her. Taking the first three turns available, they found themselves on an avenue with two lanes of traffic in each direction. The markets and restaurants were still present, but the wider sidewalks allowed Mako and Saba to break into a run.

They stayed on the street, dodging cars as they crossed

against the light at each intersection. Drivers slammed on their brakes to avoid them, leaning out their windows making stereotypical Italian hand gestures. Mako had heard somewhere that being flipped off with just one hand was a more casual gesture than being flipped off with two hands—which they saw what was flung at them as they danced through the cars. When Saba crossed the main street, again against traffic, they saw more hands.

Another glance behind him revealed no pursuit. Mako had seen this show before, and kept pressing Saba from behind.

"We need transportation," he gasped. One of the drawbacks of the residential area was a noticeable lack of cabs. "The bus."

Just ahead a bus had pulled to the side of the street. The doors hissed open and a stream of workers exited. "The back doors. Right before they close," Mako called ahead to Saba. She slowed just enough to time their move, and as the last work-weary commuter exited, they slid aboard. Expecting some kind of reprisal, Mako dug into his pockets to pay the fare. Saba pulled his hand back. No one had noticed their entrance, and if they had, they didn't seem to care. Glancing at the driver, Mako saw his focus was on the large side mirror, as he tried to find an opening in the traffic. Rumor had it that a good deal of public transportation in Italy was on the honor system of payment.

Mako and Saba found a pair of seats at the back of the bus. After an interminable wait, the driver found his opening and pulled into traffic. Their heavy breathing was audible to anyone listening, but again, no one paid them any attention, as they waited for their heart rates too slow.

This time their escape looked to be successful and, without a word spoken to Mako, Saba started talking to Alicia, squinting at the route map strategically placed between fragrance ads on the wall of the bus. Mako sat back and opened Google Maps. Punching in "airport," he pressed the bus icon, and the screen populated with their route. He offered the phone to Saba, who at first, intent on studying the map on the bus, pushed it away. After a second, she must have realized what it was and accepted it, giving Mako a smile that reminded him of their kiss.

"We need to make a stop first," Saba said.

29

STEVEN BECKER

STORM SURGE

Rome

"THIS HAS BEEN VERY INTERESTING, HEARING ABOUT MY DAD AND the good old days," Faith said, her smile softening the barb. "But you've carefully avoided telling me why you were arrested and how your name mysteriously appeared on the State Department's watch list."

John used the noisy restaurant as an excuse, feigning he didn't hear, and sat back, sipping his wine. Faith was definitely the daughter of an agent. Trying to find a way to tell her that the information was probably above her pay grade, he asked instead what she did.

"Art."

That wasn't what he expected. "I didn't know the State Department was into art?"

"Not per se. But with the amount of money being paid out for it, its become a currency of sorts. Art has become a primary source of funding for ISIS. The market is flooded with artifacts from Syria and other countries they've invaded. We are working to cut off the money, and with it, the head of the snake."

"Money was how Reagan took down the Soviets." He stopped short, realizing he was dating himself. The chapter in history that he'd been personally involved in had probably been a question on exams now.

"So. Mr. Storm. I do need some answers."

John took another sip. "Hungry?" He asked Faith at the same time as he signaled a server.

"I guess you're starved from prison and all. I'll make a deal with you. Tell me why you were there and I'll keep you company."

Smart, too. John estimated her age to be a few years younger than Mako. He looked at her as if daughter-in-law was written on her forehead. John knew better, though. Mako leaned toward women who lived more on the edge. An art investigator would be of little interest to his son.

He had to remember this was work for her, and her superiors would be expecting answers. The first question was harmless enough and might actually interest her. The second question of how Alicia had inserted his name on the watch list needed to be avoided.

"Deal." The server was already at the table. John ordered a plate of linguini and a pork chop. It took all his willpower to avoid ordering an appetizer as well. The Italians liked their courses. Faith ordered a salad and gnocchi.

"Okay. Let's have it and I'll give you some more dirt on Dad." She leaned back, knowing she had set the hook.

"You're familiar with Caravaggio?" John asked. Her look told him to continue. "You know then that there are rumors the *Nativity* has been recovered."

"Of course, and there is questioning of the authenticity of his other works. The masters were far from saints, and Caravaggio was a down-and-out sinner. Are you familiar with the *Fortune Teller*, Mr. Storm?"

"John, please." He had heard something about it, and even if he knew the story, he was enjoying the lesson. It was as if while she spoke, the daughter-in-law sign on her forehead became neon red.

"Most of the masters had sponsors, and Caravaggio was no different, except he couldn't stay out of trouble. It appears he had few scruples as well, because when a new sponsor showed interest in his original *Fortune Teller*, which he had already sold, he painted another. Back in the day there were no cameras, and comparing a painting in Italy against another in France was somewhat of a challenge. Caravaggio hedged his bets, though, and made some minor adjustments to the new painting. These were well-known at the time, but there were others, which he recorded in a journal."

John laid some of his cards on the table. "It was that same journal that got me arrested. My son and I were chased by men I suspect were with the Mafia, who thought we had it. I disarmed one. The police saw me and thought I was the aggressor." He decided to leave Carlotta Burga's name out of it.

"What happened to the other man?"

"He escaped."

She frowned, the look of distaste on her face telling John that she was not comfortable with arms or aggression. Fortunately, their first courses appeared, pausing the conversation and giving John time to think.

Faith finished first and changed the subject back to more familiar ground. "You know, stealing art to finance nefarious activity has been going on since there have been collectors willing to pay for it without questioning the source. Art is a unique commodity, especially the old masters' works. Each piece is unique, making them worth fortunes. The Nazis probably financed half of their war efforts from selling 'confiscated' art. And a good deal of that was purchased by the Vatican."

"If it is authentic."

"Yes."

John observed a trace of bitterness in her voice. He had studied the relationship between the Nazis and the Vatican prior to and during World War II. Most of their dealings have been whitewashed by history, but Nazi Germany and the Church had had a friendly relationship. With Hitler agreeing to collect the ten-percent tithe on Catholics living in Germany and its occupied countries, and the Vatican being in Italy, an Axis ally, the Holy See, sat on the fence, working the war to their own advantage. Pope Pius's defense of his actions was that the Communists were the larger threat.

"So, Mr. —" she paused, "John. Do you know who has the journal now?" She tried an alluring look that would have most men his age fighting for her, but John knew it was a ploy to get information out of him.

The CIA was willing to pay big money for the journal; now it appeared the State Department was interested as well. His dealings with government bureaucracies told him it would be far from the first time American agencies were bidding against each other, often having no idea they were competing.

"No idea." He finished his pasta and took a sip of wine.

"You seem to know a good deal about this stuff."

The wine glass was empty, and he signaled the server. Without the prop, he was forced to answer. "I've spent a bit of time here." He was at a crossroads with her. She might have knowledge and resources unavailable to him. There was also a fatherly urge to take her under his wing—and to introduce her to his son.

Thinking about Mako, he realized between his release from jail and dinner with Faith, he hadn't checked in.

"Excuse me for a minute." She nodded her assent. He rose,

placing his napkin on his chair. He got up and searched for the restrooms.

Stepping into one of the palatial stalls in the men's room, John took out his phone and dialed Alicia.

"We were wondering if it worked."

"Like a charm. I owe you for that one." It was not a phrase John Storm used often. Get-out-of-jail-free cards were an exception. He quickly filled her in on his current situation and waited for an update.

Alicia told him about Mako and Saba's escape.

John digested the information. "Mako and the woman who stole the journal?" That was an interesting twist. "Sicily?"

"I think your assistance there might be needed. Facial recognition shows the woman who chased you and Mako to be Carlotta Burga. You know who she is?"

"Pretty high skill-set on the thug side of things." John had thought about asking Faith to accompany him. With the confirmation that it was the Mafia after them, he decided against it. If he needed Faith, he knew where to find her. "Okay. Book it."

Before he reached the table, John's phone vibrated in his pocket. He stopped and ducked behind a cabinet stacked high with glasses and bread-baskets. A text from Alicia flashed across the screen. She had booked the flight, and it left in two hours.

Back at the table, John's main course had arrived, and his wine glass had been filled. With the clock in his head telling him he needed to eat and run, he dug in. After finishing most of the plate, he noticed Faith pushing her gnocchi around her plate. He knew what she wanted.

"I've got a flight to Syracuse in just less than two hours. I'm happy to keep you up to date on what happens there."

She popped one of the dumplings in her mouth and smiled. "If I let you off the hook on my other question will you take me with you?"

John pushed his plate forward, knowing he'd been played. Sipping his wine he did a quick cost/benefit analysis, finally deciding that the risk of her tagging along was better than telling her how his name had appeared on the State Department list, and that she might be helpful.

"Agreed. But that card's been played now."

She nodded and popped another gnocchi in her mouth, her smile genuine.

Rome

After they stepped off the bus at the next stop, Saba hailed a cab and gave the driver an address. It meant nothing to Mako, who looked aimlessly out the window. She wondered about that. He seemed so engaged sometimes, then, like a switch was flipped, he turned off. Although many deep thinkers had that trait, but Mako didn't seem like one of them. Still—there was something about him.

As the streets passed by she saw a look of recognition on his face. Saba had spent several days following Mako before the night she had taken the journal, and knew they were heading back towards his old safe house in the Monti district. The cab stopped several blocks from the bullet-ridden apartment, and Saba asked the driver to wait.

The street was packed with cars, with no spaces to even temporarily pull over. There weren't even loading zones. Deliveries in this neighborhood were done in the early hours of the morning. The cabbie said he would have to circle the block.

Mako started to open his door.

"I'll just be a minute." She didn't want to sound rude. She might be ready to let Mako into her private life, but not as far as her apartment. He nodded his acceptance and sat back. She waited just long enough for the driver to turn the corner, then ran across the street, past several buildings, and scurried by two cars and a scooter to reach her building on the other side of the intersection. Sprinting up the four flights of stairs to her apartment, she reached the door and punched the code into the digital lock.

The minute the door opened she knew something was wrong. She'd been in such a rush to conceal her building from Mako that she had failed to check her telltales. Stepping into the apartment, she was glad she had Mako's pistol concealed in the small of her back.

The apartment had been ransacked. Moving quickly, she cleared the space, though that did nothing to cure her anxiety. Ignoring her personal effects scattered over the floor, she went directly to the kitchen. Pulling open the freezer, she saw that, though whoever tossed the place had emptied the cabinets, they had ignored the freezer. Unless they were in the mood for an ice cream sandwich, there was no reason to check the box of treat, from which she pulled out a large Ziploc bag that held the journal.

Breathing a sigh of relief, she quickly grabbed a backpack, tossed in the journal and enough clothes for a few days, and ran down the stairs. At the entrance, she checked the street and, not seeing the cab, ran back to the building where the driver had left her out. Seconds later, before she could catch her breath, the cab rounded the corner and pulled to a stop.

"All good?" Mako asked.

She nodded, afraid her quick breathing would alert him that something was wrong. Swallowing several times, she breathed in and out. Four counts on the inhale to eight counts on the exhale. After several repetitions, she asked the driver to head for the airport.

She knew what question was on Mako's mind, and had already decided on a tactic if he asked. Brushing off a bead of sweat from her forehead, she saw him turn to her. Before the question was out of his mouth, she planted her lips on his.

30

STEVEN BECKER

STORM SURGE

Syracuse, Sicily

THE OUTLINE OF THE MOTOR YACHT GLOWED. ILLUMINATED BY scores of high-power LED lights, it appeared to Burga that the sleek shape floated above the water. In a world where appearances were critical, the yacht was Leonardo Longino's calling card.

Carlota Burga wondered what her reception would be like; she was about to face the head of the crime family. She could see from the look on the face of the man at the helm of the small craft that he was aware of her discomfort. Clenching her fists, a sudden rage came over. It was generally beneficial that her looks disguised a ruthless killer, though in some cases like this, she would like to put the pilot in his place.

Putting things in perspective did little good as she scanned the ink-black water for the telling dorsal fins that she expected. It was more than a rumor that Longino dealt with the failure of his subordinates by chumming the waters and tossing them to the sharks. There was no way to hide her apprehension for the coming meeting—she had failed.

In fact, the yacht *Squalo*, meaning shark, resembled one of the beasts. In contrast to most hull designs, the profile of the bow sloped toward the water, instead of away from it. The foredeck tapered uninterrupted to a five-deck-high structure that seemed as large as a stadium. Painted the same light gray as a Stealth Bomber, and without any adornment, the sleek lines defined the ship. As the *Squalo* lay at anchor, her bow was pointed toward the open waters of the Mediterranean should a fast exit be required.

As the tender approached its destination, Burga saw none of the telling fins in the water, and took it as a good omen. A hatch soundlessly lifted near the ship's stern, swinging open on a previously invisible hinge at the top. The interior of the ship was revealed, and a platform extended outboard of the ship. A subtle course correction by the pilot had the tender alongside the dock, where two men stood ready to receive her.

Burga knew many of Longino's guards, and nodded to the men as they reached over to grab hold of the tender's gunwales. A half-round rub-rail protected the hull and platform from damage as they held the boat and nodded to Burga to disembark. One of the men handed the pilot a small roll of euro notes. With a relieved look on his face, the man departed, quickly accelerating toward the lights of Syracuse.

Burga was dying, literally, to know what kind of mood her benefactor was in. She knew better than to ask the guards. She was scared, but knew any crack in the veneer of her stone-face facade would signal weakness.

"He's in the salon on the bridge level," one of the men said. He approached Burga who, knowing the drill, handed her weapon to him and spread her legs and arms to facilitate the body search, which was standard procedure. Still, she felt naked and alone without the gun.

Turning toward the interior of the ship, she found herself on an open deck containing a variety of vessels. On one side was a pair of jet skis, and a twenty-plus-foot center console. They took half of the space. The other half was devoted to a cradle holding a small submarine. She felt, rather than heard, the door close, sealing her in the ship. With no choice, she followed the guards past a steel door that opened to an elevator. From the bowels of the ship they ascended four levels before reaching daylight, then another four to reach the bridge deck. The elevator continued one more level to a sundeck. Holding a glass door open for her, the guards left without a word of encouragement or even a goodbye.

Burga considered herself an irreplaceable asset to the family. Her contrasting skillsets of art and death was probably why she was still alive. As she approached her boss, she hoped she hadn't overestimated her worth.

"Carlota." Longino waved toward her. "Come have some refreshment."

If she could judge the tenor of their meeting by the greeting, she was on solid footing. Burga knew better, though. She approached Longino, holding her breath that she had read the mood correctly. The brief hug and kiss on each cheek were also standard procedure and no indication of what lay in store.

"I understand we've had setbacks."

It was a statement. Burga had briefed Longino regularly. She couldn't help but notice that he had used "we" instead of "you." For a man who chose his words carefully, it was a good sign.

"I believe the journal is here, in Syracuse. The unveiling of the *Nativity* is in two days."

Longino waved Burga to an adjacent chair.

Burga sat. The silver bucket holding an open bottle of Cristal caught her eye, and she looked at Longino, who nodded. Before speaking, she poured them each a glass and sat back, trying to remember the words she had been rehearsing since stepping onto the plane in Rome.

"Unfortunately, we only have one day. I plan to reveal the painting at a private affair, and will need the journal to authenticate it."

Carlota sat back, using the champagne flute to disguise the look of surprise on her face. The painting had been stolen well before her time in the organization, and she had no knowledge whether the rumors that the Longino family was behind the theft were true or not. But, based on the recent sale of another Caravaggio, the *Nativity* was now worth close to two hundred million dollars. Trying to hide her displeasure at her position in the family's intel loop, she sat back and folded her arms across her chest.

It was out of character for her to ask for help, but the woman and her boyfriend in Key Largo needed to be removed. At this point, her closest resources were in Miami. Though only a few hours away, it was a different world there than the Florida Keys; a place where discretion was less important than making a statement. If asked to handle the couple, she knew her assets would likely make a high-profile mess of it. Biting the bullet, she turned toward Longino, "Mako Storm's associates in Key Largo ..."

With a smirk, he looked at her. "I've got people already on that. Those two will never know what hit them."

Exhaling quietly, Carlota regained her composure. She was safe, for now.

31

STEVEN BECKER

STORM SURGE

Piazza Duomo, Syracuse

SITTING IN THE BACK BEHIND ROWS OF TOURISTS, ONE OF THE inescapable daily trials of life in Italy, Mako and Saba looked up at the *Burial of Santa Lucia*. Ensconced on the white stone walls behind the altar, concealed lighting illuminated the Caravaggio.

"Two hundred million? Not seeing anything special about it," Mako whispered. He could feel eyes shifting from the altarpiece to him as if he were a magnet.

"Shhhh."

Mako looked around the church. He was already impatient. Saba, sitting next to him with her legs crossed and arms folded across her body, looked like she was settled in. Recalling a bar he'd seen kitty-cornered to the church in the Piazza Duomo, he started to get up.

"You should appreciate it," Saba whispered.

"It's old. What'd she do?"

Saba's eyes rolled. "Stood her ground. And was murdered for it. Right here."

"And that'll get you a church named after you. I suppose her relics are here, too."

"Actually, they were stolen during the Middle Ages."

"Damn." Mako stood up. "I'll be at the bar across the street." He had seen enough. Saba didn't move. As he slipped out of the pew and into the aisle, Mako took one last look at the painting. He just didn't get it.

The minute he stepped outside of the old church and breathed in the fresh air of the Plaza, he felt better. He understood the one-of-a-kind thing, though he had no idea how you ranked art, or why anyone would spend hundreds of millions on a painting.

He strolled across the plaza and took a seat at an unoccupied table outside the cafe. A waiter came over a moment later and handed him a menu, which he brushed away. Saba had fed him before she dragged him through the Old City, doing what she called "surveillance," or, since the shops were closed, what he called "pre-shopping." They had already eaten, but his throat was parched. Mako would have liked an Aperol spritz, an acceptable early afternoon drink. Since it was still morning, he ordered espresso. Even for him, before noon was too early to drink.

Doing his own reconnaissance, Mako studied the people walking through the awkwardly shaped plaza. It was possible that the church had been a design afterthought, as the building was crammed in a corner, its entrance only partially visible from the plaza. He had picked his table to observe the comings and goings.

As he sat and people-watched, Mako also studied the architecture, or at least what he could see, of the old church. Saba had rattled off a bunch of dates and styles, none of which he retained. He was half-tempted to Google it just to prove that he had been listening.

He needed to do something to fix whatever he had done wrong with Saba. After sharing that kiss in the cab, she had withdrawn into herself.

To his surprise, this morning over breakfast she had pulled out the tattered journal. Grabbing it and running had occurred to him. Its authenticity had pretty much been established yesterday with the *Fortune Teller*. But their relationship was even more complicated than logistics and emotions. Her Interpol credentials had allowed her to take his gun through security at the airport, and she still had the weapon. For his own peace of mind and sanity, he had to know if they were really allied.

Glancing into his cup, he saw only grounds, and signaled the waiter for a refill. Mako checked his watch while he waited. The church was closed from 11 a.m. to noon, and Saba wanted to use that opportunity to check the Caravaggio against the journal. They had thankfully arrived just as Mass was ending and he knew she was waiting for the priest to reappear. Her Interpol credentials were gold, and there was no reason to suspect her request would be denied.

It was a pleasant morning, but Mako was starting to get jittery from the double dose of caffeine. He decided he would give it another fifteen minutes then head back in. Catching the waiter's attention, he asked for the check, and left a sizable tip, though he knew one wasn't generally required in Europe, learning long ago that generosity often paid off. Besides, Alicia would pick up the tab. He spent the time memorizing the exterior facade of the church, coming to the conclusion that they should charge admission to raise some funds to repair the iron balcony that looked like it was about to fall off its meager supports. The façade reminded him of the buildings in the Old West, where each structure had a fancy storefront, which hid a simple gable roof behind it.

It was time, and he rose, placing the five-euro note under his cup. Before crossing the plaza, he noticed a couple strolling casually toward the church. It appeared to be a father and daughter, but the man looked very familiar. Mako quickened his pace, catching them just as they reached the double green doors leading to the church.

"Dad? What are you doing here?"

Church of Santa Lucia, Syracuse

As they entered the church, John started to make a beeline for Saba.

"That's her," he whispered to Mako.

Mako grabbed his shoulder. "It's cool. We're together." Mako didn't even need to look; he knew it was coming: the shared glance between parents and children that most people outside of the family didn't understand. This was the "What the hell, Mako" look he'd been getting as long as he could remember.

"We've got a limited time window here, and it's right now," Mako said, as he stood aside to allow the tourists, ushered outside by the priest, to exit. The pastor recognized Mako from the earlier conversation and allowed him to pass by.

"We'll catch up later."

"You have the journal?"

"Not exactly." Mako and Saba had decided at breakfast that the pictures of the journal on his phone would be enough to verify if the *Burial* was legit. Their discussion had been intense. Saba wanted to lock the journal in the small safe in the hotel room. Mako's plan had prevailed, and earlier they had hidden it behind a stone in one of the niches in the church.

"What the hell does that mean?" John's voice was louder than he intended. He lowered it and continued. "You're off the rails again, Mako."

"What about your associate there?" Mako glanced at the woman beside John. He wasn't sure what to call her. Clearly close to his age, he looked back at his father, wondering if she favored older men. Deciding the inquisition on both ends could wait, Mako caught Saba's eye. She joined them, nodding curtly to John as they walked toward the sanctuary.

The church dimmed as the priest closed the double doors. "You have a half an hour. The ladder is in the janitor's closet." He pointed to a hallway, walked past them, and disappeared through a small door beside the altar. Mako had no doubt that somehow he would be observing them.

"We need it?" he asked Saba.

"I think so."

"Come on, Pops, give me a hand." Mako didn't want to leave him alone with Saba.

John followed Mako down the hallway. It had been forty years since he had last been here, but he still remembered the layout, and stopped himself from correcting Mako when he opened the door to a storeroom. Mako then moved to the correct one, and removed the ladder.

"Who's your friend, Dad?" Mako tried to phrase the question to be more businesslike.

"State Department."

The Storm family had always operated on a need-to-know basis—no one needed to know anything. Mako probed further. "You think this is a good idea?"

"And you, with the woman who drugged you and stole the journal? I guess that's a good idea?"

"Touché." They both knew they were at an impasse that couldn't be solved in the limited time they had. With an unspoken "Later," Mako carried the ladder to the apse.

Wanting to avoid any further interactions with John, he set

up the ladder and climbed. Hung well above the altar, the four-teen-foot-tall painting reached toward the ceiling, its top well out of Mako's reach. His current line of sight was at eye level with the group gathered around a woman's body.

"You'll have to find something around this level to verify," he called to Saba.

Mako looked down at the trio. John leaned over Saba's shoulder, with Faith at her side. Each person's goals and alliances had been temporarily put on hold as they focused on the phone.

Pinching the screen to zoom in, Saba called up, "I think I've got something. He placed the initials MM somewhere."

"Michelangelo Morisi," Faith said, startling them. They were the first words she'd spoken. "His initials."

"Right, that'll be a piece of cake. A little more direction, maybe?"

"The half-naked man, digging what I guess is her grave. In his beard, Caravaggio says he placed his initials."

Mako stood on the top step, one level higher than the ladder's warning placard allowed. Knowing he was inches away from a multi-million-dollar painting was not reassuring, as he precariously leaned in for a closer look. At this distance the detail was much greater than he expected. He could see the relief effect created by the individual brush strokes.

"Nothing."

"Be patient. He planted it there so a forger would miss it," Saba said.

Mako leaned even closer. Looking for anything unusual, he squinted to try to change his focus. Still nothing. He knew they were running out of time.

"I don't see anything." Having an overview of the group, he could see his father squirm. John Storm might have been many things, but a squirmer wasn't one of them. Something was up. "I'm coming down."

It was easier said than done. Maintaining his balance with only his shins resting against the top of the ladder, Mako needed some support to lower himself farther, something for his hands to grasp. The painting was off-limits, so he extended himself to reach for the half-round molding set just inside of the Corinthian columns located on each side of the painting.

His body turned as he grasped the old plaster. Not wanting to look down, he glanced to the side and saw the door that the priest had exited crack open. He had assured them a half-hour's privacy; Mako expected only fifteen minutes had passed.

The door eased open a little more. Mako had no doubt the priest was watching and listening from somewhere, but it wouldn't be through a cracked door. Old churches had all kinds of nooks and crannies, sometimes placed intentionally, sometimes a relic from a past remodel. The priest would know every inch of the church.

Calling out to the group at the altar would alarm whoever was there, but Mako wanted down. If it was a real threat, standing where he was made him an easy target. The hold on the molding gave him enough security to bend his knees and drop one foot to the rung just below the top. Now that his feet were apart, his balance improved enough that he could release the molding, and he scurried down to ground level.

A sideways glance at the door told him nothing had changed, and he leaned in to look at the journal on his phone. "Someone's behind the door," he whispered, nodding his head to show the direction.

Saba and John betrayed no sign that anything was amiss. Faith, lacking their training, immediately looked toward the door.

Saba and John, both seeing her mistake, reached slowly for

their concealed weapons. To a trained agent, their movements telegraphed their intention. Just as the lights illuminating Caravaggio's painting caught the polished slide of John's 1911, a shot ricocheted off the altar. The door opened and standing there with her weapon trained at Faith was Carlota Burga.

32

STORM SURGE

Syracuse, Sicily

BURGA HAD THE DROP ON JOHN AND SABA, WHOSE WEAPONS WERE still at waist level.

With her pistol trained on Faith, Burga stepped out of the doorway. Either John or Saba could have taken the Mafia boss out, but not before she shot Faith.

"Drop your weapons and step away from the woman," Burga motioned to the first row of seats.

Two grating sounds of steel on stone echoed through the old church as Saba and John dropped their guns.

"None for you, lover boy?" Burga asked Mako.

He was unarmed and raised his hands. "Check if you want."

Burga again gestured for the group to move to the first row. The looks on their faces showed there was no option—at least for now, and they complied, leaving Faith standing alone by the altar.

Without moving his head, Mako scanned the church hoping to find the priest's hiding place. Surely, he would help if he was witnessing this. There was no sign of him. If he was watching from a hidden place, it was well concealed, and Mako shifted his gaze to Faith.

Mascara ran down her tear-streaked face. Behind the smudge marks, he noticed that she was remarkably pretty in a down-home kind of way. Under different circumstances he had no doubt his father would try to get them together.

"The journal, please."

"We don't have it. Only a copy on my phone," Saba explained. "Let her go. She's not part of this."

"Exactly why she is so valuable. Come here." She motioned for Faith to move toward her with the barrel. Meeting her halfway, Burga picked up Mako's Glock, which Saba had dropped, and John's 1911 from the floor and stuffed them into her waistband. "I expect the original is not far. Whatever the case, you have twenty-four hours to bring it to me and I will release the girl unharmed."

"Take me instead. I'm more valuable to you," Saba said.

Mako felt badly he hadn't offered first. He was sure to get a lesson in chivalry from his father later.

"I think not. An innocent American is gold." Burga reached for Faith's arm.

Instead of pulling away, Faith rolled into Burga, taking her by surprise. An elbow to her solar plexus, followed by a backhand slap to her face, threw the Mafia boss off-guard. Before she could recover, Faith grabbed both of her wrists, swung underneath her arms to face her, and smashed her knee into her stomach.

Mako was the first to move. Crossing the stone floor, he grabbed Burga from behind. Before he could restrain her, a gunshot fired. The bullet ricocheted off the stone floor, doing no damage, but it was enough of a distraction for Burga to make her move.

Bringing her knee to her chest, she landed a front kick into

Faith that threw her halfway across the room. In one blow Burga had shown the violent streak she was known for. Mako still had his arms around Burga when another shot fired. Again. using the distraction, Burga elbowed Mako in the stomach.

It was a basic martial arts move, and Mako was ready for it. Opening his stance to avoid the heel ready to slam onto one of his feet, Mako sucked in his gut, avoiding the major force of the blow from Burga's elbow, and crumpled to the floor, hoping she would fall for the feint. Bent over on his knees, Mako waited for Burga to make the next move. Peering out of the corner of his eyes, he watched the woman approach, her pistol rising.

With his head down, he couldn't see the others, and wondered why they hadn't intervened. There was no time to look for them. In slow motion, Mako watched the weapon move to his head. Just as it reached chest level, he swung his leg out, executing a low sweep kick. Burga, unprepared for the move, lost her footing. Mako sprang up and grabbed her, smashing her head back into the stone floor, causing her to release her grip on the 1911, which slid across the floor.

Just as Mako was about to reach for it, he heard an unfamiliar voice. "Leave it and step back with your friends."

Mako hesitated. This was his chance to take control of the situation.

"Do what he says," John said.

Mako backed away from the weapon, and looked toward the side door, which led to the storerooms and janitor's closet. Standing there was a man wearing a black suit, shirt, and priest's collar. He was older, but tall and athletic looking, certainly not a stereotypical priest. The pistol he held extended toward Mako didn't hurt his image, either.

"Put it down, Bishop," John said. He stood and walked toward the weapon on the floor. The priest remained silent. John picked up the gun and pointed it at Burga. "She's the one you want."

"What I want is the journal," the bishop said.

John stepped toward Burga, but the bishop's voice stopped him. "Maybe our Interpol agent can take her into custody."

Saba took the cue. She stood up and walked over to Burga. Turning to Mako, she asked him to find something to restrain the Mafia boss.

"And once she is in custody, you will get me the original copy of the journal."

Mako brushed past the bishop as he entered the hallway. Opening the first door, he scanned the shelves, finding a small roll of twine. Back by the altar, he leaned behind Burga, and was about to squat down to tie the woman's hands behind her back when Burga rose, slamming the back of her head into Mako's chin.

Stunned, Mako lost his balance and landed on his butt. John had the gun, but with Saba and Mako standing right by Burga it was useless. Saba, sensing his problem, started to back away, but before she took two steps, Burga reached behind her back and pulled out Mako's Glock.

She wasted no time. Grabbing Saba around the neck, she placed the tip of the barrel against Saba's temple and started walking backwards toward the door leading to the priest's office. Disappearing through the portal, Mako gasped as a single shot rang out.

John went for the bishop, but before he reached him to strip the gun from his hand, another shot fired, this one much closer. John doubled over in pain, clutching his thigh, where a small circle of blood appeared. Mako, not seeing that his father had been shot, ran to the door. A flash of light disrupted his vision, which was acclimated to the dim church. Instinctively he ducked, but it was the exit door opening. A second later, it slammed shut.

Mako sprinted toward the steel door, passing a body on the floor with blood pooled around the chest. His first thought was Saba. He stopped to verify his fear only to find it the priest. There was nothing they could do for him now. Burga had taken Saba. Mako stormed down the hallway and slammed into the exit door's crash bar. The bar didn't budge. He tried again, taking his frustration out on the door. A second later, he felt John at his shoulder.

"She pinned it, and I can't see where the mechanism is," Mako said.

"I'll take Faith and go out the main entrance. Keep at it."

John left him struggling to free the bar. Several long seconds later, he found the button and, pressing it, opened the door. Squinting in the bright light, Mako found himself staring into a crowd of people. It was lunchtime and the plaza was crowded. Even with his height enabling him to see over the crowd, there was no sign of Burga or Saba.

Faith and Maldonado came running around the corner with John limping behind them. Mako saw his father was hurt.

"What the hell happened?" he asked.

John shot a look toward the bishop. At first Mako thought it might have been because of his language. "It was an accident."

Mako moved toward his father, who held up a hand, indicating he was okay. Faith bent over and bound her scarf around his leg. He winced in pain as she cinched it tightly.

"Where's the journal, Mako?" John asked, as he picked up his gun, which had slid underneath the pew.

Mako had a decision to make. He knew where the journal was, and how to access it. The simple solution would be to call Interpol and alert them to the danger Saba was in, and let them clean up their own mess which would leave them free to recover the journal and complete their contract.

First, he needed a quiet moment to consult with Alicia. At this point, calm heads needed to prevail. Burga had enough of a head start that running aimlessly through the crowded streets of Syracuse was not going to find Saba. Mako had told Alicia of their plan to use the journal to authenticate the painting. At the time there had been no need for the constant communication. He dug in his pocket for the device and, placing it in his ear, tried to connect to her.

There was no answer. He tried again.

"What are you doing?" John asked.

Standing by the side door of the church, they were out of the flow of traffic in the plaza. Faith was trying to clean up her face, while John stared at Mako with a pained look.

"I need to reach Alicia. Burga and Saba are gone. She's our best chance of locating them. Then we need to get you to a doctor."

"What we need to do is find the journal before that bitch makes her talk. You know her reputation. Once she gets what she wants, Saba's dead."

Mako started in the direction of the hotel, leaving his companions behind. Deciding to leave the journal safely ensconced in the stone wall in the nave was the logical decision, though he wasn't sure what he was going to find on reaching it. Despite its maze of side streets, Syracuse, because of its small size, seemed easy to navigate. The old city center was essentially an island, cut off from the mainland by a V-shaped canal. Access to the city was by a single one-way bridge or by boat. Strategic geographically, and with protected anchorages on all sides, the island had been the key portal to Sicily, and then the mainland via the Straits of Messina, for millennium. The list of invaders who had tried to take the city was long, covering the entire history of the Mediterranean.

Syracuse was a city better navigated by bicycle or on foot than with a car. Mako was more concerned with direction than using a particular street. He took off toward the north and the hotel. Initially he made good time, but the maze of dead-end side streets soon had him confused.

Standing with his hands on his knees, trying to catch his breath, he heard his phone ring.

"Stay there. We're just down the block," Faith said.

Disgruntled that he had apparently gone in a big circle, Mako circled back to Faith and John.

"You're lost." She studied her phone.

"Shit," John said, finding yet another deficiency in his son.

"What's the name of the hotel?"

Mako struggled to remember. He knew what it looked like, but the Italian names were so confusing, and having relied on Saba earlier, he had forgotten. He shrugged, resulting in a deeper scowl on John's face.

"Do you have a key card?" Faith asked.

"Fucking brilliant," John muttered.

Mako pulled the plastic card from his pocket and handed it to her. She quickly punched the name of the hotel into the app. "Come on. We're actually close."

That soothed Mako's ego slightly and the Storm men set out after Faith.

Syracuse, Sicily

John Storm might have been his contemporary, but Bishop Maldonado was not about to run through the streets of Syracuse chasing him. His status provided its own set of unique tools, as well as a different set of priorities. He had the Vatican's interests to protect. Turning back to the church, he noticed a score of tourists who had gathered around the front doors, waiting for the church to reopen.

Involving the police would make the church a crime scene, and he couldn't open the doors to the public, either, so he ignored them as he entered the side door. Stopping briefly to say a prayer over the dead priest's body, he carefully stepped over it, and moved to the priest's office. Just then, he heard the front doors open and the buzz of the tourists as they entered the church.

Trying to recall the details of the scene by the altar, he didn't think there was anything amiss there. He hadn't thought about a secretary or other member of the church staff having a key, and he scrambled to the door leading to the altar, fabricating excuses as he went to keep whoever had opened the front doors from seeing the body.

He ran into a middle-aged woman in the doorway.

"I'm in the middle of a meeting in the office. I would appreciate some privacy." He stepped back to allow her to see who he was. Even if she didn't recognize his face, she would respect his authority.

"Bishop? Oh, of course. Can I get you anything?" she asked.

He almost asked for tea, though it was more of a whiskey kind of afternoon. Realizing that would give her an invitation to enter the office, he declined her offer. "This might take quite a while. If you wanted to take the day off, I'm sure Father would understand." He cursed himself for not knowing the priest's name.

"Well, if you say it's all right, who's to judge?" She looked up at the ceiling.

"Thank you. I'll explain to Father."

Maldonado watched her as she walked out. A few of the tourists noticed him, and nodded their respects. He smiled back, and returned to the hallway, making sure the door was locked behind him.

The first matter was to take care of the body. The Church had people for everything—including cleaners for crime scenes. Constantly riddled with scandal, the Vatican employed a network of the faithful to clean up its messes. Once the body was handled, he would call the Curia and request a temporary replacement for the priest who had suddenly taken ill.

He sat at the deceased priest's desk, moving papers around aimlessly. He'd called his secretary in Vatican City. Killing time while he waited for her to complete the list of tasks he had rattled off, he shuffled through the papers, thinking of it as putting the deceased's work in order, rather than snooping.

An invitation caught his eye. One just like it lay in a stack of similar requests in his own office. Having Bishop Maldonado present at an affair was a status symbol. Though this one had interested him, he ordinarily didn't travel for parties—or unveilings, or whatever this was, preferring to remain in the background. Considering the circumstances, he thought it might be wise to attend.

33

STEVEN BECKER

STORM
SURGE

Syracuse, Sicily

MAKO INSERTED THE KEY CARD IN THE READER AND STEPPED BACK, not sure what to expect when he opened the door. A small green light flashed, followed by the release of the electromagnetic lock. Slowly, he turned the knob and pushed the door open. Relief swept over him when he saw there were no bodies on the floor. Wading his way across the ransacked room, he checked the bathroom and closet just to be sure.

Behind him, John and Faith stood in the doorway. A knowing look crossed his father's face. Faith seemed startled. Mako had revised his opinion of her after her attack on Burga. Now, though, he dialed back his expectations for her usefulness. She might have been skilled in the martial arts, but she stood in the doorway with her jaw dropped, looking like she was ready to throw up. John quickly pulled her into the room and shut the door. He silenced her questions with a bottle of water taken from the mini-bar.

Taking the water, Faith escorted John to the bathroom for some first aid.

"He's going to need a new pair of pants," she called back. "I'll have a look to see if he needs a doctor as well."

Mako looked at his clothes strewn across the floor, picked up a pair of the least skinny jeans he had, and tossed them into the bathroom. The condition of the room was no surprise. It was the most obvious place for Burga to look, and she had probably searched it before she went to the church—or had her thug helpers do it. That thought put Mako on the alert.

As Burga had checked the room off her list of possible hiding places, Mako realized they might be two steps behind instead of one. Burga could easily have reentered the church and forced Saba to reveal the location of the journal.

"That priest guy. You knew him, right?" Mako asked John. He moved to the bathroom door and leaned against the jamb. John's bloody pants were in a pile on the floor. Faith leaned over his leg, cleaning the wound with a towel. Once more, he revised his opinion of her a little higher.

"Bishop Maldonado and I have some history." John paused. "Why do you ask?" He winced as she prodded deeper, searching for an exit wound.

Mako wasn't sure if he should tell his father where the journal was. Right now, there was no way, with Faith hovering near, to speak privately. Mako turned to her.

"What's your stake in this?"

"I work for the State Department. They have an interest in art as well."

"What's your capacity?" It was an obtuse way for Mako to discover if she had a security clearance.

John cleared his throat. "I can speak for her. Don't know if you remember Frank Robertson? Faith is his daughter."

"I'd prefer to sink or swim on my own," Faith said.

Mako liked her response. He had noticed how attractive she was earlier—it was hard not to—and after watching her fight, he had felt a stirring of interest. Now add a little sass, and he had to stop himself from looking at her as a potential bedmate—that activity had already gotten him in trouble on this case.

"I'm going to try Alicia again." Mako turned and walked to the windows overlooking the harbor. While he waited for the call to connect he studied the marina. Docks lined a nearby seawall, where brightly colored boats awaited the next round of tourists. Several small fishing boats motored in and out of the marina entrance. In order to do so, they had to pass a behemoth of a ship, one of the sleekest motor yachts Mako had seen.

The call again went to voicemail. His message asking her to call back might have sounded generic, but his phrasing would let Alicia know that he was sitting in a dumpster fire. He disconnected and returned to John and Faith.

Mako knew Saba would not be harmed until the journal was recovered. It was also concealed in a place where either one of them would have to go personally to retrieve it and, considering the priest's dead body was laying in the church, it would have to be after dark when the church was closed. The circumstances may have bought them some time.

"Maldonado. How much does he know?" he asked his dad.

A look only a son would know crossed John's face. Mako saw it. "How much, Dad?"

John looked at Faith, trying to use her for an excuse to leave his cards face-down.

Before he could say anything, Mako shut him down. "Not so fast. You said she could be trusted."

Defeated, John pulled on the loaner pants, looking disgusted with the cut of the jeans as opposed to his dad pants. He looked at the carpet for help. Seeing that the berber was not coming to his aid, he told the story of how he had seen Maldonado swap the paintings.

"It was fifty years ago. There's no telling if anything's changed since then," John ended.

"Except it hasn't. We just verified it as a forgery. Do you think the bishop still has the original?" Mako asked.

"There's only one way to find out. I'd expect he could use our help with the priest, as well."

"Make the call, Dad."

John pulled his phone out of his pocket, found the number he wanted, and waited for the call to connect. "Bishop, John Storm here."

Mako gestured for him to put the call on speaker. The phone lay face up on the bed between Faith and John. Mako stepped closer when the bishop answered.

"Hope your group is all right. Any word from Saba?"

Mako had forgotten that the bishop and the green-eyed woman knew each other.

"Not yet. Her room was tossed, but that was probably before the incident," John told him.

"What can I do for you, John? Seems we've inherited quite the mess here."

"That's why I was calling. Thought you might need some help cleaning up the site. I was thinking you wouldn't want the police involved."

"Right. Church business, not theirs. I'm a little out of sorts here and would gratefully accept your help," Maldonado replied.

"We'll be there in twenty minutes," John said, disconnecting the call.

"Perfect," Mako said. "I saw plenty of bleach and trash bags in the janitor's closet."

"Better get to it, then," his dad replied.

Syracuse, Sicily

Burga hadn't said a word since they'd left the church. She walked half-a-step behind and just to the left of Saba. Assuming Burga was right-handed, that made sense, as the pistol in her pocket would be in her shooting hand, pointed directly at Saba's left kidney.

Breaking the silence with a whisper, Burga directed Saba down several side streets, and through another odd-shaped plaza. Ahead was the water. Arriving at a small marina, Burga directed Saba to board a tender that was waiting for them. Without a word to the pilot, Burga untied the bow line from the cleat, tossed it to the deck, and climbed aboard.

The stunning view of the historic city was lost on Saba as she contemplated her fate. Passing a dozen or so sailboats either anchored or attached to mooring balls, they headed toward the mouth of the harbor. Nearing open water, there was only one ship left, an impossibly large motor cruiser. The gun-metal gray yacht loomed above the small tender as the pilot pulled along-side a platform that had extended from the hull. Two men waited to escort the women off the boat and through a large bay holding several kinds of craft—and a submarine.

An elevator was centered in an open area amidship, with a solid door to one side that Saba guessed were stairs. The four of them entered the cab. One guard pushed a button, and the doors closed with a swoosh. As it climbed through the multi-story structure of the ship, Saba started to grasp a thread of hope. Going up was a good thing. If they'd wanted her dead, the anchorage, or lower levels, of the ship would have been her more likely destination.

She tried to formulate an escape plan, but every idea had weaknesses and had to be discarded. When the elevator doors opened, she still had nothing. One of the men prodded her out of the cab with what felt like the barrel of a gun. She might not be dead, but it was a reminder that she was in grave danger. Only the knowledge of where the journal was hidden and how she played it could save her.

All she could hope for was that Mako and John Storm would make an attempt to save her, or at least call Interpol. Hoping for the former, she needed to clean up this mess before she informed her superiors what had happened. Saba had started to like the father and son team, especially Mako. He had shown backbone in the church, a trait she was surprised to see. The problem was that time was against them.

Seated at a table was a man wearing an off-white linen suit. A straw hat similar to a classic fedora sat on a full head of almost-black hair, with just a hint of gray mixed in. Sitting there, reading a newspaper and sipping what looked like a cocktail, she knew his disinterest was feigned. But he held all the cards.

"Saba Dragovich. A pleasure, my dear."

The accent and endearment were fake as well.

"Please, sit down and join me. We have much to discuss."

He didn't introduce himself, nor did she need him to. The object of the past several years of her professional life, Leonardo Longino, sat in front of her.

Before the gun could find her, Saba moved to the chair directly across the table from him. It was a small strategic move to at least allow her to observe him. Burga sat between them.

"Food, drink?" he asked.

Saba realized she hadn't had anything to eat or drink since breakfast. There was no point in being stubborn. Whatever lay in store for her, sustenance would be required. "Yes, please."

The man snapped his fingers, and three uniformed servers appeared. Plates of smoked fish, cheese, fruit, and bread were placed on the table. Another man poured what she guessed was white wine in her glass.

"Water, too, please, if you don't mind,"she asked.

With a flourish of his hands, Leonardo dismissed the staff, and started loading his plate. Saba followed suit, noticing that Burga ate only sparingly, and drank no wine. The food was excellent and she ate her fill. Finally, Longino snapped his fingers again. The staff came forward and the plates disappeared.

"You are wondering why the first-class treatment." He paused, making sure she took in her surroundings. "In truth, I need you as an ally."

She couldn't hide the surprised look on her face.

"You see, I want to expose the forgery as much as you do. I think, though you might not want to admit it, that we have a common enemy. You know the old saying," he laughed at his joke. "It seems the party that wants the journal to go away is the same one that has the original painting."

Before any words came out of her mouth, she knew. Her brain buzzed, trying to process the information he had just revealed. She knew all about Maldonado and the Church's scam to replace the art in their control with forgeries. They'd been doing it for years. Maldonado thought he was impressing her, but she had just seen the originals in the vault in the basement of the Sistine Chapel—or at least the tubes and crates containing them.

"I want the journal to prove the painting is a forgery. The bishop wants to destroy it and perpetuate their fraud."

In one sentence her world turned upside down.

She swallowed. "How can I trust you?"

Burga snickered.

"It seems my associate doesn't seem to care how the journal is obtained. But you have a choice. There is a party tonight. An unveiling, if you will. You can be my guest, or ... " He glanced at Burga, who was still smiling.

34

STORM
SURGE

Noto, Sicily

SEVERAL G-FORCES PINNED MAKO AGAINST THE PASSENGER DOOR as Maldonado sped around another turn. Gravity released him as the car straightened, but he remained vigilant. Looking ahead, he saw the road continuing to wind around the hills of the Sicilian countryside. With a firm grip on the door handle, he watched the olive groves and pastures fly by.

"Think the crates'll hold up?" Mako asked the bishop. Maldonado had produced the old wooden boxes that Saint Lucia's stolen relics had been previously been stored in. The bishop had vetoed the garbage bags Mako had produced for the task. It had been a gruesome task to dismember and pack the priest's remains, certainly not the respectful burial the priest probably deserved, but the only way to remove the body from the church in daylight without attracting unwanted attention.

Maldonado eased his foot off the accelerator—slightly.

As the religious authority, Maldonado had ultimately ended the discussion of how to deal with the priest's remains. It was left to John and Mako to do the dirty work while Faith cleaned the blood from the old stone floors. When they were done, the church reeked of the bleach that erased all signs of the struggle.

Thankfully, Maldonado kept the speed down, which helped keep Mako's still queasy stomach in place.

They had showered and changed, then met back up, first to dispose of the body, and next to attend the unveiling.

"Exactly where are we going first?" Mako asked. He had been following their route on his phone. Their ultimate destination was a castle on the outskirts of Noto. The E45 highway that followed the coast had been an easy ride, allowing them time to decompress after the gruesome work of cleaning up the church. Now, climbing into the foothills, the road and scenery had changed.

Before they entered the city, Maldonado turned to Mako. "Can you get me directions to the Noto Cathedral?"

Mako did as he was asked, anxious to be rid of the body in the trunk. As the virtual woman's voice rattled off the turns, he wondered what had happened to Saba. He had expected some word, either from Burga, if she was still captive, or from Saba directly, if she had managed to escape. There had been no sign of them at the church or in the plaza.

Maldonado made a last turn and stopped near the cathedral. Its architectural styling was Baroque, with the same features evidenced everywhere they turned. Maldonado had mentioned the conformity had something to do with most of the country being rebuilt after an earthquake—or eruption of Mount Etna. Mako couldn't remember.

The bishop passed the entrance, made a quick call, and turned right onto a side street. A priest met them at a gate, which he opened to let them in.

"Let me do the talking. The priest is trustworthy."

"Like he won't ask questions when we bring in the crates and deposit them with him?" Mako asked.

"There are many ways to ascend in the church. Being a good priest is only one of them," the bishop replied.

Faith exited the backseat and walked around to the other door to help John. With her assistance, he climbed out using the cane he had taken from the church in Syracuse. He seemed to enjoy the attention Faith was giving him. Mako got the distinct impression that his father thought she was a better daughter than he was a son.

The priest waited for them by a side door. Faith helped John while Maldonado talked to the clergyman. That left Mako alone by the trunk to deal with the two boxes. A small wheelbarrow helped, but it still took two loads. Maldonado and the priest were on bent knees praying while Mako set the remains in an underground crypt. The crates were placed with as much decorum as possible and, the clergy appeased, Mako slid the stone back in place, making sure it sat properly.

"I could use a drink after that," John said.

Mako glared at him, but kept his tongue. Having a gunshot wound to his leg begged a little sympathy. The inevitable fight could wait until they were alone.

"On to the party, then?" Mako checked over the area, using a broom the priest offered to clean the floor. Having done as much janitorial work as he cared to do in several years, Mako walked outside and waited by the car.

Faith emerged first. "He was shot, you know."

"Dear old Dad. Yes, I know."

"Well?"

"You expect me to fawn over him. You're doing a good enough job for the both of us."

She inched closer, hands on her hips. "What's your problem?"

Thankfully, just then John, Maldonado, and the priest appeared. The priest walked past them and opened the gate. A few minutes later they left the city and headed back into the foothills.

35

STEVEN BECKER

STORM SURGE

Mediterranean Sea

THE SOUND OF METAL AGAINST METAL STARTLED SABA. AFTER concluding their meal and conversation earlier, she had been "assigned" a cabin one deck lower than the deck where they had eaten. A rumble accompanied the sound, which she identified as the anchor being raised. Longino had said something about a special gathering later, but she hadn't expected a boat ride to get there.

From the bed she could see the old fortifications of the city that had repelled many invaders. Saba moved closer to the window for a better look, being careful not to disturb the dress that had been left for this evening. She was still undecided on whether to wear it or not. Doing so would surely please Longino, and maybe that was what she needed to do. He had not answered her last question about the importance of the gathering. Maybe complying would be one more step in a relationship they both knew was based on deceit.

It was a way of life Europeans had become accustomed to since Caesar had conquered Gaul: the strategic partnership of enemies toward a common goal. Saba could easily dress up for him—for a purpose.

The old stone walls built on the rocky shoreline to protect the city passed from view. Her cabin was starboard side, so with land visible, they had to be moving south. Not surprisingly, she had been searched and the burner phone Mako had given her taken.

As they moved away from Syracuse into the open Mediterranean, Saba started to worry. No one knew where she was and the next landfall—if the party was a ruse—was Africa, a place where little good happened to Interpol agents. Malta was also a possibility. Recalling her art history, the island had been another stop on Caravaggio's trail of paintings—and bodies.

Studying the coast as they motored south, she tried to memorize any distinctive landmarks, thinking they might be important. Towns passed by, some merely fishing villages, others, with long beaches, were tourist destinations. After a while it all started to look the same and she gave up. Soon after that, a knock on the door informed her that she should be ready to disembark in an hour.

Possibly the highlight of a very bad day was the luxurious tub in the bathroom. Working the timeline backwards, she decided a twenty-minute soak would fit and started to run the water. A few minutes later, settled into the foamy bubbles, she closed her eyes and tried to relax. Whatever was on the agenda for the evening, she needed her wits about her.

It was an odd feeling, sitting in a tub of water inside a ship floating on the sea. Whenever the bow of the ship plowed through a wave, the water in the tub reacted accordingly. She started to wonder about the physics of the reaction and if it was something she could use to escape. The clock was ticking and if the movement of the water in the tub was the best she could come up with, Saba decided she had better check the fit of the dress.

After a quick cold shower to rinse off, she was dressed, and ready with ten minutes to spare. Exiting the bathroom, she was startled to find an ice bucket with a bottle of Cristal and a single flute sitting on the nightstand.

Checking outside through the window, all she could see was water and Saba started to wonder again where they were. Before she could assess the situation further, right on time there was a knock on the door. With nothing to be gained by delaying and her curiosity piqued, she downed the last sip in the flute, the single glass she had allowed herself. The door was locked from the outside, a not-so-subtle reminder of her status, and she had to wait for the guard to open it.

Dressed in a chauffeur's uniform, he nodded to her, and led her down the passageway to the elevator. They exited on the same level she had come in on. Expecting the tender to be waiting to take them to the mainland, she was surprised to see a black SUV. It was pulled toward the retractable ramp where the tender had dropped her off from earlier. A peek at the opening showed the ramp was resting on a large dock.

Longino entered, distracting her from looking further. He nodded in the direction of the passenger seat. The chauffeur moved to the door, opened it, and she slid in. The door was closed and, once Longino was seated next to her, the driver started over the ramp. Saba checked the interior of the spacious SUV, wondering where Burga was. Longino with his chauffeur was far from benign, but without his lead henchwoman, maybe she had a chance.

"Where is this castle?" Saba asked. She was dying to know where they were. *Not far*, was all she received by way of an answer. With each intersection the SUV continued to climb the hill leading out of the harbor. Glancing back, Saba could see the reflection of the sun setting on the water. It was a beautiful view, but that didn't help with the location.

The SUV left the city behind, and started along a winding road. It was a narrow, two-lane street with no shoulder. Along either side, the locals were using the early evening reprieve from the heat to harvest the olive trees. With nothing else to do except observe, she watched as they used an ingenious method to collect the ripe fruit. Instead of picking them, they spread large blankets and tarps on the ground and beat the branches with long rakes. Scores of ripe olives fell onto the blankets, which were then gathered up and dumped into bins.

Saba had started counting turns and trying to judge time. She had a good idea how fast they were going, but soon lost count as the SUV rounded a final turn and stopped in front of a tall, wrought-iron gate.

The driver pressed a button and spoke into the intercom. With a loud buzz the gate opened and they entered the grounds of a large estate. She'd thought Longino had been exaggerating, but there was still enough daylight for Saba to see the well-groomed lawns leading up to a substantial building that could only be described as a castle.

The driver dropped them at the entrance, and swung the SUV into a larger cobblestoned parking area. At least a dozen other vehicles were already there, their drivers standing to the side smoking cigarettes and talking. If there was a way out, it might be here, she thought.

Before she could plan any further, Longino led her through a high, rectangular entrance. Looking up, she noticed a gate hung above them, originally installed to drop down, entrapping the barbarian hordes and allowing the archers stationed on the battlements to decimate their ranks.

They entered a courtyard, which was actually a classic killing zone with high towers on all three sides, with crenellations left and right. She couldn't stop herself from looking up to see if there were archers waiting.

Finally, they reached a pair of doors. The right was ajar, and Longino led her into what looked like a great hall. Instead of armored warriors ready to protect the keep, small groups of well-dressed people sipped from crystal flutes and picked at the trays offered by uniformed waiters.

Some of the faces looked familiar and she started putting names to the wealthy and powerful art collectors, at the same time wondering why so many were assembled here. A waitress, seeing them without drinks, scurried over with a tray of flutes, offering one to each. Saba took it, more out of courtesy and for something to do with her hands. She was intent on escape, not drinking.

Feeling like a puppy on an invisible leash, she followed Longino around the room as he shook hands with the men and pecked the women on the cheek. Saba continued to match names with faces, noting that if the paparazzi had been present they would have had a field day with the diverse attendees, most of whom would never be seen in each other's company. She had met several of the collectors before. Some cast furtive glances at her, while others looked away. Saba knew it was her companion who stopped them from approaching. These were the rich and powerful, and she knew she was a beautiful woman. There could be no other reason why none had approached her.

Working their way through the room, she noticed another group enter. A buzz started, as if the guest were someone even more powerful than they.

To her surprise it was Bishop Maldonado, followed by the Storms and Faith.

Castel Noto, Sicily

Their eyes locked together. Mako couldn't keep his gaze from drifting down to her dress, and for a long second, he almost forgot the circumstances that had brought them here. When he was finally able to break the magnetic force that held them together, Mako stood back, observing the scene. She was with another man. A quick scan of the room showed no sign of Burga, which he took as a good sign. That bit of luck gave him the courage to approach.

Reviewing his inventory of opening lines, he had just selected one when the ringing sound of an object striking a crystal glass silenced the room. Mako had been so focused on Saba that he didn't realize it had come from the man at her side until he was just feet away. He clinked the glass again. The guests formed into an uneven semicircle around him. This gave Mako the chance to slink away and blend into the crowd. Once he had situated himself, he glanced over at Saba, who was waiting to catch his eye.

From her expression, he garnered that she was all right—at least for the moment. Relaxing slightly, he scanned the room for John and Faith. They were across from him. Rather than join them, he decided it would be better to remain apart.

An expectant silence hung over the room. It was broken by several people shifting toward the middle of the group. A solemn-looking Bishop Maldonado crossed the polished stone. He approached the man with Saba. A speculative murmur started through the room as they spoke in hushed tones for a minute. Even before the bishop made his entrance there had been a palpable tension running through the crowd; now, as their conversation ended, it had built to a crescendo. Maldonado stepped away. There was no handshake, only what looked like an uneasy truce.

"Thank you for coming. It is my honor to welcome Bishop Maldonado," the man said.

There was a light spattering of applause. The glass clinked again, and Mako noticed movement in a hallway adjacent to the reception. Four men pushed a large cart with a drop cloth covering it. The shape soon registered in Mako's mind, and he realized it was an easel with a painting underneath the tarp. The men wheeled it next to the man, then moved into a formation where each took a quarter of the room. They stood at-ease, with their hands crossed in front of them. The "relaxed" pose fooled no one. The weapons secreted under their jackets were clearly apparent.

"It is my pleasure to bring back to the world a long-lost painting." He waited for the murmurs to die out. "Some had speculated it no longer existed. I am here to tell you otherwise." He paused, letting the room speculate as to what was under the tarp.

He waited until the crowd quieted then, with a flourish, pulled back the tarp. The fabric fell to the ground and a prearranged spotlight illuminated the painting. Mako recognized that the style was very similar to the painting on display in the church in Syracuse. He guessed it was a Caravaggio, and from the reaction of those gathered, he knew it was an important one.

The crowd inched closer in shocked silence.

"Caravaggio's *Nativity with Saint Francis and Saint Lawrence*."

The man allowed the crowd to speculate quietly for a few minutes. Mako eavesdropped on several conversations, picking up the man's name: Longino. Instinctively he tapped his ear, but there was no earbud in place, reminding him that Alicia was AWOL. Some of the others were staring at their phones, wanting to communicate the revelation to their bankers or patrons. There was little doubt this was a prelude to a sale. Mako pulled his phone out, immediately noticing the "no service" icon at the top of the screen. Longino had chosen the location for more than the dramatic effect.

Longino called for silence. "A little history lesson for those unaware of the circumstances of the *Nativity*.

"Nothing about Caravaggio's life was pedestrian. It is most fitting that the painting we see before us was stolen exactly fifty years ago from a church in Palermo."

Mako connected the dots: Stolen art. Sicily. Burga. Longino. And Maldonado. Clearly, Maldonado was trying to hide the connection between the Church and the Mafia. The journal added another level to the intrigue and the first question that popped into Mako's mind was if the painting was a forgery. Only the journal could authenticate it.

Mako half-listened as Longino filled the vacuum caused by the unveiling by sharing a snapshot of the artist's life.

"Had Caravaggio been born today in L.A., instead of Milan in the sixteenth century, he'd be king of the rappers."

The group spoke in hushed tones after that statement. Mako's attention moved to Maldonado. He wanted to gauge the bishop's reaction.

Longino continued, "You think I jest, but not really. Every move Caravaggio made in his life was because of his tendencies toward violence. From Rome to Naples to Malta to Sicily, Caravaggio left a trail of paintings, and blood in his wake.

"He rarely had any money, having to barter paintings in exchange for protection. This extended as far as the Knights of Malta, where the Grand Master allowed him to provide an altar-piece in exchange for his knighthood."

Mako knew a sales pitch when he heard one, confirming his theory that the painting was for sale.

"Caravaggio never worked from sketches, he just painted—a part of his brilliance."

"Can you authenticate it? Do you have his journal?" a voice asked from the crowd, interrupting him.

"I have a letter of authentication."

Mako wondered how Longino had authenticated the painting without the journal—unless ... He looked over at Saba, but there were no clues in her expression.

Movement across the room caught his attention. Bishop Maldonado was moving through the crowd. Mako had noticed his look of surprise after the painting was revealed. That look was gone, replaced by what could only be called fury.

As the bishop approached Longino and the painting, the group collectively took a step back. The room fell silent.

Mako scanned the nearby faces and saw his father growing restless. He suspected the old man knew more than he was letting on. Every eye in the room was on Maldonado as he moved towards the canvas. Most of the people gathered thought it was nothing when he stuck his hand in his pocket, but Saba, John, and Mako knew otherwise.

John reacted first. Pushing past Faith, he started toward Maldonado, who was only a few steps away from the painting, but was hindered by his wounded leg. Mako watched as he stumbled. He knew John was the only one in position to reach the bishop in time. He had to trust his father.

Longino's men inched closer, but seeing no immediate threat, they remained several paces away.

In two steps and a hobble, John reached the canvas at the same time that Maldonado's hand pulled free of his pocket. It wasn't a gun, or even much of a weapon—just a pocket knife, which he flicked open. If not for the journal and their own attempt at authenticating the *Burial* earlier today, Mako would have had no idea what the bishop was up to.

Deciding to save a painting was different than saving a life. To save a person, just redirecting the thrust could result in less damage being done. With the painting, a slash anywhere on it would cause it to be ruined.

Mako didn't know why the bishop was determined to ruin the Caravaggio, but as the knife flashed, he had no doubt about the bishop's intention.

Maldonado raised the knife. His hand started its downward motion.

"Stop him!" Mako heard John call out.

His father, limping badly on his wounded leg, was not going to reach the bishop in time. Longino's men were to the side and slightly behind the painting. The bishop had been careful to use the large canvas to screen his movements.

Hearing John's warning, the guards instinctively drew their guns. There was a slight pause as they looked to Longino. The mob boss nodded, but it was too late. Mako had to do it himself. He had inched close enough to reach Maldonado and, leaping toward the bishop, he reached for the hand that held the knife and slammed it down, taking himself and the bishop to the floor.

The knife clattered across the stone floor, and was quickly picked up by one of the security men. Mako rolled off the bishop, leaving the security guards to haul him to his feet. Mako was only feet from Saba. A smile crossed her lips, and he felt the heat rise in his face. Before he could respond in kind, the bishop's voice chilled the room.

"This is clearly a forgery." Maldonado played the priest card. He shrugged off the grip of the guards, who were loath to manhandle him. "It is my duty to see that this painting is destroyed." He looked at Mako and John for support.

Mako knew the odds were against them. Two more security guards arrived and moved into position in front of the painting. The bystanders had drifted back into the shadows of the great hall. They were watching, riveted to the drama, but out of harm's way.

"Step back, Bishop. As far as I know, you are not a qualified appraiser. Let's leave it to the experts, shall we?" Longino tried to defuse the situation and salvage what he could of the unveiling.

"The Church commissioned the original. It belongs to God," Maldonado countered. The bishop stepped forward, but the security guards closed the gap between him and the canvas.

Longino spread his hands out. "Then why would you want to destroy it before it can be authenticated?"

Mako thought that was a good question. He scanned the faces again, noticing something was still off with his father's. The rest of the crowd had stepped back, leaving the six of them, Longino, Saba, Maldonado, John, Faith, and Mako, around the painting. Mako needed answers. He slid across the room to stand by John.

"What do you know about this?" Mako whispered.

"Not now. We just have to make sure the painting is not harmed."

"Does that mean out of the hands of a mobster?"

"You're damned right it does," John responded.

Mako could see his father was agitated. Gripping his hands into fists, John had a scowl on his face. Before they could decide on a plan, Longino whispered an order to the guards, who started pushing the easel holding the canvas away from the fracas and toward the back of the room.

"Nothing we can do now, except get out alive." John muttered something about losing the battle, but not the war.

Mako realized this might be their chance to grab Saba. She was still by Longino's side, glued there by the occasional glance from one of the guards. As sideways as the reception had gone, Mako wouldn't be surprised if bullets would be served up next.

He felt naked, having been stripped of his weapon by Burga earlier.

He, John and Faith moved slowly out of earshot.

"Let's get out of here so we can put ourselves in a position to follow," John said, starting to limp toward the door.

"What about Maldonado and Saba?" Mako asked.

"Leave the bishop, get the girl." John hooked his arm in Faith's, using her as a crutch to accelerate his exit.

Longino frantically waved his hands, directing the staff to pour drinks. They reacted quickly and flutes of champagne were trayed and disbursed. Music started to play in the background. Thinking the drama was over, groups stepped out of the recesses.

Longino started to mingle. His focus now on salvaging the evening, he left Saba standing with the guards.

Mako stepped out of the shadows and approached them.

Longino was deep in the crowd now. Two of the guards were wheeling the easel away, while the other two restrained the bishop. There would not be a better time. Mako had to assume, if given the choice, the guards would watch Maldonado and protect the painting, leaving Saba their third priority.

Mako moved closer, carefully gauging the guards for any reaction. There was no need to attack; he only needed to get close enough to Saba to get her attention. Fifteen feet separated him from the group around the easel. It had been only two or three minutes since John and Faith had left. Unless they'd run into trouble, they should have the car around front any second.

Saba was watching him. He nodded, hoping to communicate to her it was time. Mako watched her gaze swing around to the guards. A questioning look crossed her face, asking him how he was going to do this.

It had to be now. The guards shifted suddenly. Mako turned his head to follow their gaze and saw Burga step out of the shadows. Reaching for Maldonado's arm, the bishop started to object. Mako didn't know or care what was happening between them. If anything, it was a welcome diversion. As the guards stepped closer to break up the pair, he held out his hand. Saba moved toward him. With a quick look over her shoulder, she took his hand, and followed him through the room.

36

STORM SURGE

Key Largo, Florida

ALICIA HAD TO DECIDE BETWEEN HER PASSION AND HER CAREER. The morning charter had gone well and, with only four divers, TJ and one of their part-time divemasters had handled it easily. Looking down at the dock from their kitchen, she watched the afternoon group assemble.

TJ and Alicia each supported their individual causes. His was veterans' groups and the reputed benefits diving had on treating PTSD; Alicia's was working with the disabled to allow them to dive. They also shared a common goal of preserving the reef, and worked with several coral reef restoration programs when they needed volunteer boats. Today allowed them to combine all of these interests, but it would require that she leave the war room and be out on the water.

With the reef less than five miles from the mainland, they were within range of the cell towers. That was the deciding factor. It was evening in Italy now, and she expected a quiet night. The gunshot wound to John's leg was troubling; however, Mako and John assured her that it was more of a nuisance than a problem. She was well aware of the Storm gene that enabled them to effortlessly lie about themselves. All she could do was hope John had enough sense to stay off the leg and take it easy, at least overnight.

She decided to go on the dive trip.

One of the first lessons Alicia had learned at the Agency was that making decisions by committee rarely led to the right choice. However, with John and Saba in the mix now, it was required. Not directly part of their operation, she knew John had no problem acting as a lone wolf and Saba had already shown she had her own agenda. Either could endanger their contract if they weren't dealt with properly. In order to sort this out, a decision had been made by consensus adding John and Saba to their partnership with Mako.

There were two people who knew where the journal was. With Saba being held by Carlota Burga, the plan they had decided on was to clean up the mess in the church and observe it tonight. If there was a chance to get Saba back alive and retrieve the journal, all the better.

Opening the refrigerator, she relished in the cold air for a few minutes while she pulled out several drinks. There were times, mostly in August, when she felt like pulling up a chair and sitting there. Technically the worst heat was past, as they had slid into fall, which for the Keys meant round three of summer. The skies were clear and blue with only a few puffy cumulus clouds decorating it. Reaching for the sunscreen on the counter, she liberally applied it to her face, grabbed a hat, sunglasses, and the cooler, then headed downstairs.

TJ was onboard talking to the two adaptive divers, who remained in their wheelchairs on the dock. She nodded to the men, and looked down the dock for Jen from the Coral Restoration Foundation, who would handle the coral installation. After their checkout dive had gone okay, the adaptive divers were scheduled to harvest and plant coral this afternoon. Veterans, especially those with PTSD, benefited from the gravity-free world underwater, without the rules and threats that caused their anxiety. That same environment allowed disabled divers the ability to dive.

In addition to the checkout dive, they'd already done a tour of the foundation's facilities, where they had crafted the "trees" that held the small pieces of coral as they grew. Their first dive this afternoon was scheduled to be a tour of the coral nursery, a sandy area in twenty feet of water off Hawk Channel, where the PVC trees were placed. The second dive was planned for the reef, where the divers would "plant" the small coral pieces using epoxy to secure them in place.

"You okay with this?" TJ asked as Alicia hopped onto the gunwale to help the first disabled vet into the boat.

"As long as one of us is by the cell phone, we're probably good. How much trouble could those two get into in four hours?"

TJ knew it was a rhetorical question and laughed. Neither wanted to think about the truth. The two Storms together were volatile enough that they could light a fire without a match.

Alicia worked with the two men, transferring them from their wheelchairs to the gunwale, where they spun around and dropped to the bench. The two leaned over and started to sort out their gear. Jen appeared around the side of the house, struggling with a bin and a large coil of rope. Alicia went to help her, taking the rope from her hands.

"What's with that?" Alicia asked, as they walked to the boat. She had done several of these trips and never needed rope.

"Hemp rope. We've been trying to wind it through the larger pieces of coral and see if it attracts growth. It's organic, so it'll decompose without harming the reef or marine life."

Back by the boat, Alicia hopped aboard, dropped the coil on

deck, and reached for the bin holding the supplies they needed. Jen stayed on the dock ready to help with the lines.

TJ fired up the engines, and Alicia climbed up the ladder to the flybridge. She handed him her phone and descended to the deck to brief the divers.

"You all know Jen," she started. "She's already given you an overview of what we're going to do, right? Once we get underway, I'll do the dive briefing. The weather's looking pretty good, so I expect we'll get in at least two dives."

TJ called down for Jen to release the lines. Tossing the bow first, Jen moved to the stern, untied the line from the cleat, leaving a half-turn still around the base and, with the bitter end in her hand, stepped onto the gunwale and down to the deck. Using the twin engines, TJ pivoted the bow out and called for her to release the line.

A half-mile of canals separated them from open water. Figuring they had about five minutes before the engines would make it impossible to hear, she moved between the men and explained the first dive.

It was a pretty straightforward twenty-foot dive. Being shallower than the thirty-three-foot limit, there were no decompression-related issues to worry about. Jen would show the vets how to harvest the coral that they would take to the reef and plant during the second dive. Alicia would be alongside, making sure the divers were weighted properly and comfortable in the water. The nursery was in a protected area inside the reef where there was generally little current; once they were on the outside that could change dramatically. The key to the adaptive divers' success was proper weighting. That would be her main focus on the first dive.

Just as she finished the engines surged. After having been re-powered with twin diesel Cummins engines, the converted thirty-eight-foot sportfisher ran faster than many similar boats.

Time was a key factor in the success of a charter operation. The additional horsepower cut close to an hour off each trip, allowing them to run three charters a day during the long summer light.

When they were past the last marker delineating the navigable channel from the shallow flats on each side, TJ nudged the throttles forward again. Ten minutes later they were circling the coral nursery. TJ stopped, allowing the boat to drift in the current. Once satisfied, he steered the reciprocal course of the drift, and anchored a hundred feet up-current of the waypoint.

The divers had inflated their buoyancy control vests and were waiting when Alicia splashed into the powder-blue water. She surfaced, gave TJ the okay signal, and released the air in her BC. Alicia stayed behind with the two divers and worked with them until she was certain that they were weighted properly, while Jen led the way toward the PVC towers. Once the two men looked comfortable, they exchanged okay signs and headed toward the nursery.

The coral "trees," ten-foot-tall pieces of PVC pipe with thinner, shorter PVC "branches" attached with T-connectors, were planted in the sand. Dangling pieces of coral were suspended from them with monofilament fishing line, which made the trees look like Charlie Brown Christmas trees.

Alicia checked the men again then started the collection process. At ten-minute intervals she caught her divers' attention. Pointing to her pressure gauge, she signaled for them to indicate how much air they had left. With a full tank being about three-thousand PSI, and the safe limit to surface five hundred, after a half hour she expected each diver to have about a half-tank remaining.

The first diver laid two fingers on his forearm, indicating he had two-thousand PSI left. The second diver set only one finger down. Divers ran the gamut in air consumption and there was little you could predict ahead of time. She would have to watch the second diver, and made a mental note to check again every few minutes.

With mesh bags full of coral to plant, they surfaced twenty minutes later, and with TJ's help climbed aboard. Alicia helped TJ with the anchor while snacks and drinks were offered around. With the second site a little more than a mile further out, TJ motored at a relaxed rate while they changed their tanks over for the second dive. With the shallow depth of the first dive, there was no need for a surface interval, but with the seas running two feet from the southeast it would have been a bumpy ride at a higher speed.

By the time they had reached the second dive site, the equipment and divers were ready to get back in the water. Alicia moved toward the men, squatting between them for the dive briefing. This dive was more complicated: deeper and with more current than the nursery site. Jen had already shown them how to epoxy the coral to the reef during the dry-land training this morning. She would do a quick review and turn it over to Alicia. The powder blue water color told Alicia that they hadn't crossed over the reef yet. She told the divers they had about ten minutes before the next dive. Wanting to check her phone before they splashed, she started for the stainless-steel ladder that led to the flybridge.

A wave caught Alicia off-guard as she set her foot on the first rung, dropping her down to the deck. She looked back, only to find a gun pointed at her. Both of the divers had pistols out. One was aimed at her, the other at Jen.

"Come down to the deck," one man yelled, motioning the barrel up at TJ.

"You two in the cabin," the other man ordered the women.

"Bring the phones down, too," the first man said as TJ descended the ladder. He and Alicia exchanged worried looks.

There was no choice but to comply. As Alicia moved back into the cabin she tried to think of anything in it that could be used as a weapon. There were no guns aboard, not even a bang stick. Dive knives were fairly useless as weapons. With their thick, short blades forged for prying as much as cutting, they were more of a tool. The mandatory flare gun came to mind. There were two onboard; one below decks and one on the bridge. Even if she could get to one, firing it on their own craft was a recipe for disaster. The cartridges could easily start a fire and kill everyone aboard.

She and Jen huddled together. One of the men kept his pistol trained on them, while the other tossed their phones overboard, and grabbed the hemp rope that Jen had brought. Moving to TJ first, the man bound TJ's hands behind his back, then tied his ankles together, leaving him squirming on the deck. Then he turned to Jen and Alicia.

37

STORM
SURGE

Castel Noto, Sicily

ONCE PAST THE ONLOOKERS, MAKO QUICKENED HIS STEP JUST AS Saba pulled her hand from his. The regular tapping of her heels on the stone floor suddenly ceased, and he glanced back to see she had stopped. Before he could question her, she removed the stiletto shoes that Longino had provided for her.

A few seconds later, now unencumbered, she caught up to him. They were out of sight of the guards and Mako maintained a fast walk, expecting a guard to be at the entrance. Once the doorway was in sight, he slowed. Though he would have rather run to the doors and smashed through them, acting normal was their best chance to escape. Through the open door of a room that looked like a converted coat closet—or in the case of a castle, an armory—Mako could see a single guard was focused on several small screens, probably monitoring what was happening in the reception room. Slowing further to appear as if they were just leaving, they walked by. The man merely nodded to them. Once past him, Mako fought the urge to look back, breathed out, and pushed the door open.

The SUV sat only feet away. Mako ran to the car, opened the back door, and waited while Saba, treading gingerly over the crushed limestone paving, climbed in. Before the door closed behind him, the car spun out, surely leaving ruts from the tires. John was at the wheel, his wounded left leg not a problem driving the automatic vehicle. They sped down the driveway, only to see a set of headlights flash behind them as they turned onto the road.

Mako could only hope another guest had seen them leave and decided it was in their best interest to exit as well. After making a left turn, John accelerated. Mako, straining to see behind them, saw the headlights again. They appeared sooner than he expected, and unless the guest was a Formula One driver, they had company.

"Car on our tail," Mako called out to John.

"Got him." The SUV shuddered as John accelerated. "The lights are low to the ground. Looks like a sports car. I saw an Alfa Romeo in the parking area."

"Shit." Mako grabbed the handle above the door as John took a hard turn. To reach Syracuse and the journal, they would have to negotiate the same steep, winding road they had come up. With the high center of gravity of the SUV, these conditions would heavily favor the sports car.

"Open the glove box," John ordered Faith. She had been so quiet that Mako had forgotten she was there until she handed John his 1911.

When a bullet ricocheted off the rear bumper, Mako, once again, regretted being unarmed.

38

STORM
SURGE

En route to Syracuse

MAKO FELT THE OUTSIDE WHEELS LIFT AS JOHN TOOK ANOTHER tight turn. The winding roads of the foothills favored the sports car behind them. Mako looked back, noticing its headlights were brighter now. Able to speed around the turns faster, the Alfa Romeo was steadily gaining. The best Mako could hope for was a mechanical failure. It was an Italian sports car—the inevitable breakdown would happen—but when?

The shots had stopped, either from not wanting to send the SUV and its occupants over the guardrail to their certain deaths or because the road was winding enough not to allow their pursuers to aim.

Mako suspected it was the former. "Whoever it is, they want us alive."

"Everyone who knows where the journal is hidden, is in this car. They can't afford to lose us," Saba said.

"Maldonado knows if he's checked the security cameras," John muttered.

Mako looked back at the car, now only a few hundred yards

behind them. The sports car gained on them on the turns and fell back on the straightaways. Mako wondered about that, thinking its occupants might be worried that the SUV would return fire.

"Maldonado has access to the church, and if he knows the journal's there ... " John said, loud enough for them all to hear this time.

"Now that we're all together, it's our top priority, anyway," Faith said.

Mako slid over, trying to catch a look at her in the rearview mirror. These were the first words she'd spoken since they'd left the castle. Faith had proven to be quiet and pragmatic, the kind of person that when she spoke, people listened.

"She's right," Mako agreed.

"So, to the church?" John asked, leaning his body into the door as he took another hard turn. "Once we're out of the foothills, we'll have a better chance of losing him."

Mako saw the lights of a town below them. Pulling out his phone, he opened the maps app to see where they were. From this distance all he could see were two church spires with lights spread out in between. The classic Sicilian town: church on the bottom of the hill; church on the top. The rest of the town falling in between.

"Why not lead them right to the church? Let them expose themselves, and see who it is," Saba said.

The road straightened out as it descended to the town. Mako could see John's eyes flit to the rearview mirror, both to check on the car, but also to catch Mako and Saba's eyes.

"It appears we have two enemies, but that's not what's important. The journal means nothing if we can't figure out who benefits from possessing it." John laid out the problem.

Faith turned sideways in her seat. "Follow the money."

Before he could respond, Mako grabbed the headrest of the

seat in front of him as the car barreled around another turn. John had already voiced his displeasure with Italian drivers several times. With the thickening traffic, his complaints became more frequent. He'd quickly adopted the gestures of the locals. Releasing the wheel, he flipped off each car that offended him, almost as if he was enjoying himself. The lights of the town were approaching, forcing John to resume his concentration on the road ahead, and allowing them time to think.

"This is the time to speak up if you want to ditch whoever's back there," John said, as they passed a sign for the highway two kilometers away.

"I'd like to know who it is," Saba said.

"Me, too. If we're going to figure out who the enemy really is, we need to know who's back there," Faith said.

"One thing is guaranteed," John said, as he cut the wheel to the right and accelerated onto the ramp. "There's never one enemy."

Mako knew that was the truth. "Okay, so we take a speed limit ride back to Syracuse and see what they do?"

"Fine by me," John said. Reaching under his thigh he pulled the .45 he had placed there, and handed it back to Mako. "Just in case."

Mako took the 1911. After ejecting the magazine and checking how many rounds it contained, he did a chamber check, then reinserted the magazine. The full magazine settled him, though he still didn't know who pursued them, or if they were outgunned.

Once John had settled into the left-hand lane, they all glanced behind, trying to locate the sports car's headlights. A steady stream of traffic was pouring in from the entry ramp and merging across the lanes of traffic, making it difficult to distinguish the Alfa Romeo. Several vehicles had the low profile of the sports car, making it impossible to tell if they were still being followed, and which car it might be. Mako chambered a round, and set the pistol on his lap—just in case.

As the miles ticked by, theories were discussed and discarded. Faith was extremely helpful in analyzing the ins and outs of the art world. Saba seemed closed-minded—in her opinion, everything went back to the Church. Mako couldn't help but think she had some kind of axe to grind. He filed that away for future thought. John was quiet. He had determined, after several unannounced lane changes, including one where he drove on the exit lane until the last second to flush out their pursuers, that the Alfa Romeo was indeed behind them. It had remained a consistent three or four cars back, only making one mistake when he feigned the exit.

Mako let most of the talk between Faith and Saba go in one ear and out the other. His job was to recover the journal and turn it over to Alicia's contact. He fully understood it was not that simple, but chose, as he tended to, to look at what was in front of his face, rather than chase ghosts.

John appeared to have heard enough.

"They're both forgeries."

"How can you be so sure?" Faith asked.

"We proved it this morning with the journal," he answered.

"I don't think it's quite that easy," Faith said, turning in her seat to see if Saba would back her up.

Mako noticed Faith's eyes as they lingered on him before shifting to Saba. He'd seen that look before. She wanted his approval as well, and sensed a cat fight.

"She's right. You've got to step back in time into both the political state of Italy in the early 1600s and Caravaggio's personal state of affairs." John provided the history.

"The last part's easy. He was a twisted mofo," Mako said. "I'd like to have a beer with him if he were around today."

"He's not far off." Faith brushed a strand of hair away from her face and smiled at Mako. "Italy wasn't really Italy then. It was broken into several areas controlled by the Papal States, Spain, and countless bandits-turned-mercenaries, several of which grew to what were essentially small armies with hundreds of cavalry and infantrymen."

"What's that got to do with our boy?" Mako asked.

"They all wanted a piece of him, either literally or figuratively, and sometimes both. Caravaggio was licensed to carry a sword in Rome, probably not a good idea, as the outcome was a murder that saw him exile himself rather than face the authorities. He continued his exploits, leaving a string of artwork, and blood, behind him."

"Okay, the dude was stone cold. Bring it back to the Church and the paintings."

John stopped the conversation as they approached the bridge leading into Syracuse's old town. "We need a plan."

As if they all expected the elder Storm to have one, there was a long pause as the SUV crossed the V-shaped channel. Mako turned back to look, and with the thinning late-evening traffic, was able to see the sports car.

"We either set a trap, or draw them out," Saba said.

"Maldonado is in the wind," John said. "It makes sense to check the church first. If he finds the journal while we're dicking around with whoever is back there, this is all for naught."

They were just a few blocks from the Piazza Duomo. "Sounds good," Mako said, lifting the pistol from his lap. "How about you drop me around the corner over there? I'll take a position where I can see the entrance."

"Not without me, you're not." Saba had her hand on the door handle.

Mako knew he had no choice. Any delay and he would be caught in the headlights coming toward them. The SUV slowed. Mako glanced at Saba, who nodded that she was ready. Simultaneously, without waiting for the vehicle to stop, they opened the doors and bailed out on each side. Separating, they sprinted for the cover of the shops lining the road.

Without slowing, the Alfa Romeo sped by a few seconds later. Mako caught Saba's eye across the narrow street. He gave her the all-clear sign, and she sprinted across. They found themselves a block away from the small café where Mako had spent an hour this morning. His larger tip might pay off now, as It appeared the same waiter was still working.

Taking Saba's hand, to appear more as lovers rather than spies, he felt the familiar tingling when she returned the pressure. "The café." Mako led her across the street. They took an empty table, and sat next to each other instead of across. The catty-cornered seating arrangement allowed them a clear view of the church's entrance.

Twice while they waited for their espressos the Alfa Romeo circled the block. Mako took out his phone and texted John an update. He knew from his childhood that communication was the way to settle down his overly anxious father. The last thing he needed was for the old man to go all cowboy. Between Faith's inexperience and John's injury, they were all better off if that pair waited in the car.

Mako had his phone in his hands when the car passed again, and took a chance at taking a picture. The tinted windows prevented him from seeing the occupant, but he was able to get a shot of the license plate.

"Can you run this without getting in trouble?" Mako slid the phone across to her.

"Shouldn't be a problem." She pulled out her own phone and texted someone the tag number.

They sat in silence for a few minutes.

"The Church connection. You think there's something there?" Mako decided to try and draw her out while they waited.

Saba brought the cup to her lips and sipped the dark brew. "It's a long twisted story."

Again she was cut off as the Alfa Romeo came into view. This time it stopped in front of the church. The driver's-side door opened and Maldonado appeared.

"Shit," Saba whispered through gritted teeth.

Mako was thinking the same thing, wondering where you drew the line when a bishop was involved. The question resolved itself when Burga stepped out of the passenger door. The gun that had fired on them earlier was no doubt hers—or the one she had taken from him. In the dim light of the entry Mako could see Maldonado unwind his tall frame from the driver's seat. Together, like old friends, they walked toward the side entrance.

39

STEVEN BECKER

STORM SURGE

Key Largo, Florida

THE TWO "ADAPTIVE" DIVERS SET THEIR TANKS AND GEAR BY THE tuna door, a passage cut through the transom used to haul big fish aboard. Alicia drew her breath in as one of the men fired several shots at the deck. The distinctive smell of fuel wafted through the bullet holes. At least one shot had hit the tank. The man waited an interminable minute, then he and his partner geared up.

Questions were pointless. The only saving grace was the fuel was diesel and would burn, not explode. That might give them enough time to escape—or cook them alive.

TJ was a gamer, boat captain, and dive guru. He'd been caught up in some of Mac Travis's adventures, but only in those capacities. This was not in his wheelhouse—or Alicia's. She was an analyst; her only experience in the field was with Mac's side-kick, Trufante. Learning from the wily Cajun was a different curriculum than the agency taught. Hopefully something had stuck that would get them out of this mess.

One of the men set his mask in place, cleared his regulator, and stepped off the swim platform. Alicia bit her tongue as she watched him stand easily. The wheelchairs had been a ruse. She had suspected something was different about these two during the checkout dives yesterday. Both men had muscular legs—it should have been ample warning. Her passion had over-ridden her gut. Alicia could see the guy's head bobbing in the two-foot waves behind the boat as the other man found and turned on the switch for the manual bilge pump. The diver in the water disappeared a moment later, a swath of bubbles the only sign of where he had been.

The smell of diesel was thick in the air as the second man prepared to dive. Sticking the weapon in the cummerbund of the BC vest, he pulled something out of one of their dive bags before tossing them both overboard. He appeared in no rush, as he donned his mask, swung his right arm around his back to snag the regulator hose, and set the mouthpiece in his mouth. With one last look around, he revealed the object he had taken from the bag.

Leaning over, he raised the hatch that covered the bilge, and flicked the wheel, which sparked when it came in contact with the flint. A second later Alicia watched as the yellow glow of a flame flashed against the dark bilge. The diver dropped the lighter, paused to make sure it had caught, and ran for the bow. Alicia lost sight of him as he vaulted off the front of the boat to avoid the fuel slick floating back in the current.

The terror in the groups' eyes was illuminated as the bilge caught fire. Seconds later, following the trail of fuel pumped overboard, the water surrounding the boat was ablaze. She caught TJ's and Jen's eyes and saw their panic. It was up to her to get them out of this. All she could think was, "What would Trufante do?"

40

STORM
SURGE

Piazza Duomo, Syracuse

"WELL, I GUESS YOU'RE RIGHT. THE CHURCH IS RIGHT IN THE middle of this," Mako said, after they absorbed the implications of Burga and the bishop working together.

"And, if John is right about the cameras, they know where we hid the journal." Saba paused. "I should have thought about it, but we were in a church ...." They might appear to be BFFs right now, but Carlota Burga's notorious for her lack of patience." Saba leaned into Mako for a better view of the church.

Mako accepted his part of the blame as well. Despite the situation, it was hard not to enjoy her touch. It lasted for only a second as the bishop disappeared inside the building. Mako rose, and dropped a ten euro note on the table. The earlier extravagant tip had proven worthwhile; he just had to remember to update his expense account, which usually meant texting Alicia whenever he spent anything. There was no doubt it pissed her off, but he wasn't about to do paperwork. Thinking of Alicia, he checked his phone as he followed Saba around the corner.

There was nothing. No missed calls, voicemails, or texts. Very unusual. Once the bishop and the journal were squared away, he would have to find out what had happened to her.

Saba ducked into the recessed doorway of one of the shops lining the street. Mako followed her, peering over her shoulder. Burga had followed Maldonado into the church. Seconds later the door closed.

"Come on. Maybe he left it unlocked. He knows we're around here." Mako started for the door.

Saba pulled him back. "Don't you people believe in backup?" She gave him a frustrated look. "Call John and tell him what we're doing."

"I've got his gun. He's got nothing besides a greenhorn and a shot-up leg."

"How about we ditch your daddy issues? He's a trained agent."

Mako knew the only course was to comply, and texted John rather than calling. A second later his phone vibrated with a text saying "OK." Mako turned back to Saba. "We're good to go."

"Give me that thing. Do you even know how many rounds are left?" She took the gun, ejected the magazine, and checked the chamber.

"Only need one. Maybe two if he's quick."

"Okay, there are seven and one in the chamber. This thing weighs a ton." She inserted the magazine, and handed it back to Mako.

"Old school likes his .45s." Mako settled his right hand around the grip. "Not so bad if you don't have to conceal it."

Saba gave him a "whatever" look, checked for traffic, and walked off. After crossing the street, they placed their backs against the old stone walls of the church. It was a conspicuous pose, but with the lights on in the window behind them, it was better than being seen.

Mako pointed to the left, past the church. If they wanted to check the door they would need to avoid the windows. Six inches shorter and probably way more limber than he was, Saba lowered herself and duck-walked past the windows. She passed the door and continued another ten feet to the end of the building.

Mako followed, though not as gracefully. When they were both past the building, they turned. "It's too risky to look inside," Mako said.

"You can't see inside the part of the chapel where we stashed the journal, anyway."

"Guess we wait 'em out," Mako said.

"It's the best option we've got. Why don't you have John bring the car around? At least we can be comfortable," Saba said.

The only thing that changed over the next few hours was that John got grumpier. It was his typical old-man state of affairs, only exacerbated by the gunshot wound. Mako had been shot twice before, both to areas thick with muscle. There would be no lasting damage, but he knew his dad would hurt like all hell for the next few days.

"I can't take this anymore. I'm going out to get him some pain meds," Saba said, pointing to the reflection of a green cross in a window down the block.

There was little to debate, and they agreed that she would be okay to go alone. Mako and John were relieved to be free of her for a few minutes. As soon as the door closed, Mako started questioning his dad.

John quickly recounted the story of how he and Faith met outside the police station in Rome, that he knew Faith's father well, and, in his opinion, she could be trusted.

"Don't know if she can shoot, but she handled herself better than most when bullets were flying," he finished the summary.

"You know I'm sitting right here, right?" she said.

The two Storms gave each other a look that was almost a grin.

Saba returned carrying a larger bag than a bottle of pills required.

John popped the lock just as Saba was about to knock on the glass. Saba opened the door, slid into the seat and passed drinks and snacks around. Lastly, she handed John a bottle of pills.

He held the bottle close to his face. "This is the real McCoy here." He struggled with the childproof lid for a long second before opening the bottle. He dispensed two, then paused and waited for a third to slide onto his hand before popping them into his mouth and chasing them down with the bottle of water Saba had brought.

"He said to take only two, and that's if the pain is really bad."

"I can read," John snapped.

Mako supported his decision to overmedicate if it would take the edge off his mood.

"Sorry. I appreciate you getting them for me." John paused. "I've kind of built up a tolerance over the years. I'll be fine."

Mako wondered how Saba had walked into a *farmacia* without a prescription and emerged with narcotics, then realized her Interpol credentials had probably done the trick. Studying her face, he wondered if she also might have used the interlude to call for backup.

They sat silently for the next hour. It was getting close to midnight, and they watched as one at a time, like dominos falling in slow motion, the lights in the stores and cafes went out. By one a.m., the street was deserted. The only illumination came from several streetlights and the light bleeding through the windows of the church.

"Was there another exit? I just remember the front and side doors," Mako asked.

There was a long pause.

"Dad?" Mako leaned forward, expecting an answer. John Storm was meticulous about noting those kinds of things. John's head bobbed and Mako realized he was asleep.

"I'm going to take a walk." Mako had been cooped up long enough.

"I'm going with you. If anyone's looking, a couple walking will seem more normal than a single man," Saba said.

"You okay with dear old dad?" Mako asked Faith.

She nodded, and leaned over and tilted John's head back against the seat. "Yeah, we're good."

Mako and Saba crossed the street. He looked back at Faith, and could see her face illuminated by her cell phone. Both he and Saba knew better than to allow it, and he regretted not being thorough with stake-out procedures. The light from the phone would act like a beacon to anyone looking.

He was about to go back and tell her when something creaked, breaking the silence. Their heads turned toward the door. It was the unmistakable sound of a rusty hinge. The small island that held the church was not a good climate for metal. They were only feet away from the door when it cracked open, spilling a narrow stream of light onto the street. It was quickly extinguished. Mako and Saba hugged the wall, using whatever skills they had acquired over the years to stay invisible.

Mako could tell from the bishop's height that he came out first. Burga, following close behind, closed the door, and scanned the street. She looked to each side, and then forward, but not behind her. Mako glanced across to the SUV, which would have looked vacant if not for the light from Faith's phone. It was out of place enough to attract Burga's interest. Whispering something to Maldonado, she pulled out her pistol, and crossed the street.

Burga was on her before Faith realized anything was amiss.

Her inexperience had shown with the use of her phone, also making Mako wonder if the car doors were locked. He didn't recall hearing them click when he and Saba had left, but Faith could have done it any time after.

The answer was evident when Burga opened the driver's-side back door and slid in. Faith had lifted her head. The phone illuminated the interior of the SUV enough for Mako to see the gun trained on her. Burga called for Maldonado. In several long strides he crossed the street and entered the car through the passenger rear door. A minute later John's head jerked up and the car was rolling.

STORM SURGE

Key Largo, Florida

ALICIA COULD FEEL THE HEAT OF THE FLAMES ON HER FACE AND knew they only had another few minutes before the fire compromised the hull and the boat sank. She looked at TJ, who was also desperately looking for a path through the flames, and Jen, who remained stoic. Alicia could tell from the reflection of the flames in their eyes that they were as scared as she was.

"What would Trufante do?" she said out loud, looking around for a knife or anything else that might cut their restraints. Her eyes found the dive tanks. The gear had been switched over to fresh tanks, but it sat across the deck with a line of flames blocking the way. She didn't know how to reach it without injuring themselves. Feeling the roughness of the rope around her wrists, she couldn't figure a way, even if they could cross the deck without being burned, to get into the water.

One way or another, the ocean was going to save them or kill them.

"We have to get in the water," she called over the crackling flames.

"Goddamn, I liked this boat," TJ howled. It had been totally refitted after his adventure with Mac Travis.

"We have to get in the water," Alicia repeated. It was her mantra, and she repeated it over and over to herself. Her intermittent yoga practice had given her enough flexibility and balance to allow her to get to her feet. Standing right next to the gunwale, she could easily roll over into the water, but what then?

A loud crack from inside the hull told her that time was running out. She felt the flames on her face, the fire hot enough to singe her hair.

"Let's just get to the tanks. We'll figure out part two from there," Jen said.

Her and Jen's tanks were side-by-side, strapped to the portside gunwale with bungee cords. Hoping her dive booties would protect her feet, Alicia started hopping across the deck. Flames danced around her and she gagged on the smell of burning hair as she braved the flames. Alicia made it first, with Jen right behind, looking like Medusa with tiny specks of flame burning the tips of her long hair. TJ was last. Just as he reached the area engulfed in flames came another crack and he dropped, looking as if he had been cut off at the knees. The extra hundred pounds he carried had caved in a compromised section of the deck.

Alicia was by his side in seconds as he struggled to extricate himself. It was no use. It was as if he were stuck in quicksand; his movements weakened the deck further and, instead of releasing him, it started to engulf him more. Alicia's efforts seemed futile.

If they escaped this, she needed to pump some iron and he needed to lose some weight. First, they had to get past the "if."

A figure broke the wall of flames, and Alicia saw Jen approaching with the end of the coil of hemp rope dangling behind her. Alicia knew what they had to do, but with their hands restrained she had no idea how. Something Trufante had said about her tendency to make things harder than they were came to mind, and the answer came to her.

"Put that end through the rope around his hands." She moved to Jen and awkwardly took the end of the line. Backing up to TJ, she dropped the line between TJ's body and his restraints, then squatted down and picked up the end. Grasping both sections in her bound hands, Alicia reluctantly backed away, knowing that if she dropped one, TJ was lost.

Alicia knew that the ocean was their only chance. Flames had spread across the deck, inching close enough that they started to lick the base of the cabin and flybridge structure. The stink of burnt fiberglass permeated the air, making Alicia's eyes water. The ball cap she had been wearing protected some of her hair, the rest had been singed. She heard a splash and realized Jen was gone. Turning back to TJ, their eyes met, the panic clear. He yelled something across to her, but his words were sucked into the flames.

"Go!" TJ's plea finally reached her.

Alicia was glued to the deck, paralyzed by indecision. "What would Trufante do?" she asked herself again.

A woman's voice called out from the water. Turning toward it, she saw Jen's dripping-wet head bobbing in the waves.

"Help!" Jen called out, handing a metal cylinder to Alicia. She fumbled with the pin, finally realizing she didn't have the dexterity with her hands bound to operate the fire extinguisher.

"I need you. It's going to take both of us to set this baby off." Alicia set the cylinder on the deck and reached backwards over the gunwale, hoping the unbalanced position didn't send her into the water, and helped Jen back aboard.

Alicia realized that Jen had braved the flames, and grabbed the fire extinguisher from the side of the flybridge. Unable to recross the deck, she had dived overboard, and swam around to Alicia, all the while holding the heavy cylinder behind her back.

They would need a little luck, Alicia thought, but it was the best, and only, idea they had going. Standing back-to-back, Alicia pulled the pin and together they depressed the lever, while Jen tried to aim the nozzle. The first blast soared over the gunwale. On the next several attempts the two women danced around the deck, trying to focus the spray on the area around TJ.

Slowly the flames surrounding him were extinguished, and the empty canister dropped to the deck. The fire in the cockpit had been partially extinguished, buying back a few precious moments, but flames continued to creep up the cabin.

The two women scanned the deck and surrounding water.

"We'll never get him over the side," Jen said.

A third loud crack startled her, and Alicia watched as flames reappeared in the extinguished areas. Alicia looked around for something to cut their bonds. Every edge she saw was rounded to prevent injury in rolling seas. The cabin had some old kitchen knives, but it was impassable now.

She felt the heat of the flames intensify. Fire shot up the sides of the boat, engulfing the cabin and flybridge. Like the finale of a fireworks show, the Bimini shade cover flared like a torch.

There was nothing to do but abandon ship, and hope the EPIRB placed in a cradle inside the cabin hadn't been destroyed by the flames. The device would activate if the boat sank, and automatically alert the Coast Guard of their position.

Remembering the life raft strapped to the foredeck, Alicia tried to make her way to the skinny passageway between the cabin and gunwale. She had to turn back. Everything in front of her was engulfed in flames.

The respite the fire extinguisher had bought was gone.

"The tanks!"

Jen understood and moved toward one of the two tanks with their BCs and regulators attached. Sitting on the bench in front of it, she struggled to figure out how to get into it. Under normal circumstances the diver slid their arms through the vest and buckled the cummerbund. Jen struggled to stick her bound hands backwards through one arm hole. Giving up her attempt to wear the equipment, she stood, looked over her shoulder, and reached behind her back for the inflator hose.

Alicia immediately saw what she was trying to do. If they could inflate the BCs and toss the gear over the side, they might be able to swim toward them. The inflated vests would be more than adequate flotation devices. It was an awkward maneuver, but they managed to get two tanks over the side.

A third for TJ would have been ideal, but there had been only four divers and the saboteurs had taken two of the rigs. The fire had breached the cabin door, consuming the interior of the cabin, where the rental gear was stored. Alicia turned back to TJ. The fire extinguisher's magic had worn off and flames were closing in on him. It was time to go, but first they had to free him.

She turned toward him, but the deck cracked again, making the decision for them. It would have been difficult to pull him out before. Now, waist deep in fiberglass, there was no way. As she watched him struggle, a solution came to her.

Alicia glanced over at Jen. "Go over and grab the tanks. I've got one more thing to try and I'll be right with you."

Jen gave her a worried look. "What about TJ, we can't leave him!"

"I've got an idea. Now go." Alicia watched Jen move onto the dive platform and jump in feet first. She didn't have time to wait for her to surface. If she didn't, there was little Alicia could do about it.

With her hands still bound behind her back, Alicia's feet were her only tool. Fortunately, she had on her dive booties. The five-mil neoprene was still damp from the first dive and offered surprising protection as she crossed the flaming deck to where TJ was stuck.

Though she didn't have much field experience, as a teen Alicia had trained in the martial arts. Along with the mandatory piano lessons, her dragon mom had thought it best that her diminutive daughter be able to protect herself. At the time, Alicia had doubted that either type of training had much real-world value. She had been wrong about music, as it clearly had aided her in math and logic. The usefulness of martial arts was about to get tested as she bent her knees, breathed in, and jumped straight into the air.

The guttural sound she instinctively made when she landed, as well as the cracks that appeared in the deck, were proof that martial arts had been good for something. She might not have been able to take out multiple attackers—or even one—but she knew how to channel her energy into a strong blow. The deck paid the price of her education several more times as she moved around TJ, jumping every few inches to weaken the deck around his girth.

The damage she caused would make pulling him free more difficult. But that was not the direction she intended to save him. With a glance she grabbed the ends of the rope. "Hold onto the line and I'll see ya on the other side."

The look on his face told her he had no idea what she was up to. With no time to explain, she leaned over and kissed him hard, told him she loved him, and bailed over the side of the boat.

42

Syracuse, Sicily

MAKO'S EYES FOLLOWED THE SUV AS IT TURNED RIGHT ONTO A side street just past the square. As much as he liked to think himself self-sufficient, instinctively, when he was in trouble, his go-to was Alicia, and he pulled out his phone. The call again went to voicemail. Starting to worry about her silence, he tried TJ's number with the same result. He thought about calling Mac Travis down in Marathon. Living on an island twenty miles from the mainland, he wasn't sure there was cell service that far out, or if Travis would take his call. Mac might not care much for Mako, but he knew he would help Alicia. Deciding to give it a little more time, he put the phone back in his pocket, deciding that if Alicia was still missing in the morning, he would try to reach Mac.

When Mako looked back up, he found his eyes locked on Saba's. They each had different motives regarding the journal, but he judged the distress on her face to be authentic.

"We need to see if Maldonado found the journal," he told her.

"Agreed," Saba said, taking a step across the street.

Mako reached the side door right behind her and stood watch while she tried to open it.

"Locked."

Mako reached into his pocket and retrieved his billfold. "I got this. Keep an eye out."

Saba complied. Mako found the black graphite card that contained the embossed tools of his lock-pick set. The thin pieces dropped into his hand when he pushed them out of the card, and he went to work. The age of the lock should have made it an easy operation, but the saltwater and humidity in the city had found their way into the mechanism, making it difficult to feel for and then turn the pins.

The position of Saba's body blocked a good deal of the light. It didn't matter, though, picking a lock was done more by feel than sight. Mako could see the plug and that was what mattered. Finding the bottom of the keyhole with the small end of the tension wrench, he gently applied upward pressure to the tumbler. Then, he inserted the rake, a two-inch-long tool with peaks and valleys. With a back and forth sawing motion, he pushed the pins above the shear line. The rust made it harder than usual, but within a minute the handle turned and they were inside.

A flashing red light caught their eyes. "Alarm."

Saba pushed him aside. "I got this one."

Mako held his phone up, letting the screen illuminate the keypad. Saba worked her fingers around the device, found the release and opened the cover. With only seconds before the alarm activated, she unceremoniously pulled out the circuit board.

They stood frozen, waiting for the blare of sirens, until the device went dark.

Relieved, Mako again held his phone in front of them as they navigated the hallway where the body of the priest had lain only hours earlier. Entering the chapel through the side door by the altar, he glanced up at the forgery of the *Burial of Santa Lucia*. The recessed light fixtures surrounding the painting were the only illumination in the chapel, making it hard to see in the nooks and crannies of the old church. Inside the enclosed area, Mako turned on his phone's flashlight, and moved toward the small niche where they had hidden the journal. The space appeared to be undisturbed.

He could feel Saba exhale on his neck as she came up behind him.

"They could have put it back," Saba said, moving around Mako and kneeling in front of the stone they had hidden the journal behind.

43

STEVEN BECKER

STORM SURGE

Key Largo, Florida

THE FLAME-KISSED WATER FELT WARMER THAN SHE REMEMBERED from her dive. It might have been the fire's effect on the surface, or her internal temperature, which was probably through the roof from standing on the burning deck. Either way, it didn't matter.

Before Alicia had fallen over the side with the ends of the rope in her hands, she'd seen Jen floating on the surface grasping both BCs. Her plunge wasn't graceful, but all she could manage considering her bound hands and feet. Kicking like a mermaid, she reached Jen and waited. The burning fuel slick was still growing, and would until the bilge pump burnt up, or the tank emptied. This forced them to continuously kick away from the boat—and TJ—hoping the water would protect the inch-thick rope from the flames.

"Do you think anyone's seen us?" Jen asked, scanning the skies.

Twilight was closing in, probably obfuscating the smoke plume and any chance it could be seen from land. The fire itself would be visible to any boats in the area, but burned too low to the water to be seen from the mainland. There was a formula for determining how far away something was visible along the horizon, but it escaped her now. Their chance for rescue decreased with every minute that passed, as the light diminished with the sunset.

Alicia's expectations were low, as the fire had totally consumed the foredeck and flybridge, and she expected the boat to be underwater in minutes. Rotating her body in a circle, the water around them appeared empty. In this case, the same formula worked backwards; anyone within range with a higher perspective might be able to see her. While it seemed like hours since the "adaptive" divers had set the boat on fire and taken off, it had likely been less than five minutes. Help could be minutes away—or not.

Their attention was drawn to the boat, which belched out a large black cloud laced with sparks. At the same time the rope in her hand, the lifeline to TJ, went limp.

It meant one of two things: either the fire had severed their connection and TJ was engulfed in the conflagration on the rear deck, or he had fallen through into the water when the deck disintegrated.

Alicia started to swim closer, entering the field of flames to find out TJ's fate. A hand grabbed her shoulder and pulled her back.

"There's nothing you can do without killing yourself in the process."

Alicia still held the ends of the rope in her bound hands. One thing she could do was pull, and hope she was still connected to TJ. To help, Jen kicked backwards to counteract the effect of the retrieval of the line.

Their bound hands restricted their movements, making the attempt futile. When Alicia stopped to regain her bearings, something jabbed her stomach. Realizing what it was, she called Jen over.

"Can you grab this?" Alicia swept the BC to the side, revealing the hilt of a sheathed dive knife clipped to the vest. Jen worked her way toward it, trying to decide whether to use her teeth or hands—there was only going to be one chance.

"Use your hands." Alicia made the decision for her.

Alicia, having already released her BC to expose the knife, was frantically treading water. Jen rotated enough to grab the hilt and, with a grunt, pulled the knife free of the sheath, but in the process fell off the BC. They were both drifting freely now, with their equipment barely in reach.

The women struggled into a back-to-back position. Gritting her teeth, Alicia felt the cold steel against her wrist, then her arms were pulled down. The sawing motion continued. As badly as she wanted to try and pull free, she restrained herself, knowing that any unexpected movement might knock the knife from Jen's hands, and drop it into the depths.

"It's through!" Jen swam back around to face Alicia.

Alicia, feeling her restraints fall free pulled her hands apart. Relief was short-lived, as their equipment and the two ends of the rope connected to TJ floated just out of reach.

Alicia grabbed the knife from Jen's iron grasp, cut the rope around her ankles, then quickly freed Jen. Seconds later they retrieved their equipment. With one arm through the shoulder strap of her BC, Alicia grabbed the two ends of the rope.

Slowly she started to haul the slack line in. With each pull her heart dropped, knowing the odds of TJ being on the other end were slight.

Ten pulls in, tears streaking her cheeks, she continued. At fifteen pulls, she imagined she felt something. Fighting off hopelessness, she yanked with all her pent-up frustration. At first she thought the line was just snagged—until she felt it pull back.

44

STORM SURGE

Church of Saint Lucia, Syracuse

"WE NEED TO SEE IF IT'S STILL HERE." SABA REACHED FOR THE stone they had dislodged earlier.

Mako knew she was correct. With his father's and Faith's lives in jeopardy, the disposition of the journal would be key in getting them back.

"Okay, we look, take it, and get out of here." With Burga holding the hostages, Mako badly needed some leverage over her. He looked at Saba, who was trying to extricate the large stone, and wondered what would happen if the journal was there. After taking advantage of him at the original exchange, Saba somehow still managed to hold all the cards.

Pulling the gun from his waistband, she saw it and he caught a flicker in her eye that told him she hadn't made up her mind about what to do. He hadn't intended on scaring her, and swung the pistol grip in his hand. Removing the magazine, Mako drew back the slide and caught the round as it fell from the chamber. Without any live rounds to accidentally discharge, he took a firm grasp on the barrel, and used the butt to hammer away the loose material.

Small pieces of dirt fell onto the church floor as Saba pulled at the corners of the stone. It yielded easily, much more so than when they had first extracted it. That meant little. With a final pull, Mako removed the stone. Before he could set it down, Saba reached into the void between the interior and exterior walls.

Her hand came back empty.

"Shit," faintly echoed off the stone walls, as they both said it at the same time.

Mako picked up the gun. Saba had fooled him once, and he was not going to let it happen again. With the barrel pointed down, he motioned her to the side and reached his free hand inside the niche. There were no tricks this time, for he felt only loose pieces of rubble and chunks of old mortar.

"Shit," Saba said again.

"They found it," Mako said.

"It appeared that they were fast friends," Mako said. He set the gun down and replaced the stone. Rising, he scuffed his foot along the floor to scatter the sand and dirt. Stepping back, he couldn't tell that anyone had been here.

"We've got to follow them," Saba said.

"We have a slight transportation problem. It's almost four a.m." Mako pulled out his phone and checked his Uber app. "If they even have Uber here, there's no one working."

Saba pulled out her own phone. Mako peered over her shoulder and saw that she had opened the maps app. "They've got to be heading for the yacht. The harbor's less than a half mile." She started for the side door.

Leaving the church, Mako and Saba took off through the sleeping city. They ran past the silent two- and three-story masonry buildings, the apartments above the stores and restaurants on the main floors dark. Crossing a wide avenue running parallel to the water, they stood at the old stone balustrade and scanned the harbor. The ship was nowhere in sight.

"What now?" Mako asked. He pulled out his phone and tried Alicia.

"It's three-thirty in the morning. Who are you calling?"

"Alicia. It's only nine-thirty there." The shrill ring of the phone echoed in his ear. Finally, the call went to voicemail. Mako left a message, probably the tenth since the last time they had spoken. "I'm worried something's happened to her. I haven't been able to reach her or TJ since yesterday."

"I've got some connections in Miami. I can make a few calls and have someone check on them."

"Cool." Mako shared Alicia's contact info, realizing after he sent the message that Saba probably already had it. She knew way too much about him and their operation.

Saba texted someone and looked up at Mako. "What would she do if you find her?"

Mako thought for a second. They had been in a similar circumstance on another job. "There's some kind of program that shows the location of all the commercial and many recreational vessels. Takes their location from their radar transponders or something. Maybe we can find Longino that way?"

"It's AIS. Stands for Automatic Identification System. There's an app for that." Saba started working her phone.

Another Alicia, was all Mako could think while he watched Saba peck at her screen. Again, he wondered what had happened to her and TJ, thinking it might be time to call Mac. A glance at Saba confirmed she was still concentrating on her phone. Mako turned away, found Mac's number in his contacts and hit connect.

It was a surprise when he heard the gruff voice mutter *hello*.

"Mac, it's Mako Storm." He let that sit for a minute. They'd met previously and there weren't many Mako's out there. A second later it registered.

"Hey. What's up?"

That was Mac. No small talk—ever. Mako explained his concerns.

"You think tomorrow's soon enough to run up there?" Mac asked.

Mako would have liked to think so, but decided to take a stand. "It's been too long since either of them has answered." With three pages of confidentiality clauses embedded in their contract with the CIA, Mako tried to keep the details sketchy.

Mac sensed his artifice. "Look, Mako, I'm happy to check on them. They're friends of mine, but I need to know what I'm walking into."

Mako thought about it for a second and told him everything.

"On it. I'll run under the Seven Mile Bridge and follow the coast up to Key Largo. Not the fastest way, but there's a good chance they're on the water. I'll be in touch."

Mako heard the call disconnect. He'd spent enough time in the Keys to know that traveling by boat between the hundred-plus islands was often the best route. It was definitely the one that Travis was most comfortable with. Feeling better about the situation now that Mac was involved, he turned back to Saba.

"Anything?"

She was pinching, panning, and zooming her phone. "If I knew the name of the ship it would be a lot easier."

"Describe it to me," Mako said.

After a thorough description, Mako started entering search terms into his phone's browser. After entering "largest private yachts" and hitting images, he handed the phone to Saba.

"That's it." She clicked the picture, which took her to the designer's website. "Largest private yacht in the world—*Squalo*." Handing Mako back his phone, she entered the name into the search bar of the AIS app. "Here. It's heading this way." She handed the phone to Mako.

The enlarged icon showed the name, registration information, course, and speed of the vessel. She was right. Doing the math based on their current location and speed, he figured they'd be here at dawn.

"There's not much we can do until it gets here. Burga and Maldonado have gone to ground, but they'll waiting for the yacht to arrive. Maybe we should get a few hours sleep?" Saba asked.

"Or talk."

STORM SURGE

Key Largo, Florida

ALICIA TUGGED THE LINE HARDER THIS TIME. SHE FELT THE resistance as well as the counter force of Jen trying to hold her out of the flames.

"Kick hard and we'll pull him out," Alicia called over her shoulder. She had never realized how loud a fire was and waited for some kind of confirmation that Jen understood. When the younger woman called back and Alicia felt the turbulence from her kicking feet, she followed suit.

Doing the best they could to avoid being dragged back into the flames, they pulled together. Thankfully the resistance didn't waiver, nor did their sense of urgency. Alicia felt like her face was sunburnt and realized they were pulling themselves into the fire, not pulling TJ away. They were only feet outside the ring of flaming debris burning on the water. Panic came over Alicia and she stopped pulling.

Devastated, Jen swam around to face her.

"We can't give up. There's something on the line."

"Feels like it's just dead weight. He's gone," Alicia wailed, the ends of the rope hanging loosely in her hands.

Their circumstances didn't allow her to wallow in pity for more than a few seconds. Finally, she regained her composure and noticed the current had pulled them away from the flames. With little wind, the incoming tide would eventually take them toward shore—if it didn't turn first. Alicia was too low in the water to see the twinkling lights yet, but she had been out here many times for night charters and knew safety was just over the horizon.

Alicia continued to grasp the ends of the rope. There was little resistance, and all she could hope for was that whatever— or whoever—it was attached to was drifting with them. Finally, they reached an area far enough away from the burning boat that even if it exploded they would be safe. Handing one end of the rope to Jen, they started to retrieve the line again. It was time to find out what was on the other end.

As they pulled the resistance increased, taking them back toward the flames. They were twenty feet away from the outer edge when a bulge appeared on the surface. It looked like one of the manatees that frequented their canal in the winter months. The bright yellow T-shirt that TJ had been wearing identified the bulge as human. Now they had to see if he was alive.

Alicia dropped the line and swam, using her BC as a kick-board, toward the inert body. Reaching it, she found Jen by her side. TJ lay face down on the surface. It took both women to roll him over.

"We've got to get him in a BC," Jen said.

The inflated vest would act like a flotation device and allow them to evaluate TJ's condition without him sinking. "I'm a medium, you're a small. Not much help with Mr. Extra-large here."

"It's the best we've got," Jen said,

Alicia released the tank and BC she had been using. Jen grabbed them, raised the inflator hose out of the water, and released enough air to allow them to wiggle the vest under TJ's body. There was no point in trying to squeeze him into the too-small shoulder straps, so Alicia pushed his arms backwards through the shoulder strap and fastened it like a bandolier. The buckle clicked and Jen inflated the BC, leaving TJ bobbing on the surface. The tank acted as a counterweight, rolling TJ onto his back.

While Jen freed TJ's hands and feet, Alicia wasted no time. Positioning herself directly above his face, she followed the blow, tap, talk, or BTT protocol, that she and TJ taught in their freediving classes. Blowing lightly on his eyes, she tapped his cheeks, and spoke his name, all with the hope that he had not inhaled any water during the rescue. If he had, it would be for naught. The protocol called for three taps, but she continued on, slapping him harder out of frustration.

A harder breath caused some movement behind his eyelids. Reinvigorated, she continued the procedure until TJ opened his eyes. They were not out of the woods yet, but it was a start.

"Talk to me, TJ, talk to me," Alicia pleaded.

Saltwater spewed from his mouth. "I'm good."

"Thank God. Take it easy now. We're a safe distance from the boat, floating toward shore." She didn't want him to look back at his beloved vessel, which was now only a low line of flames on the water. The boat had probably sunk and within a few minutes, when the diesel burned off, there would be no sign of it at all.

"The boat?" he asked.

"Gone. We need to focus on getting to shore. Are you hurt?"

"Shit, everything hurts." He paused and wiggled his extremities one at a time. "I seem to be in one piece."

Alicia couldn't hold back. She put her arms around him and

planted a big kiss on his mouth. As she began to move away, she noticed that the combined buoyancy of TJ's body and the inflated BC held her out of the water. That gave her a few seconds to relax and think.

They were safe, and afloat. The calm seas and warm water were no immediate threat, either. Alicia knew the key word was immediate. Despite the temperature being in the mid-eighties, over time the ten- or twelve-degree difference between their bodies and the ocean would put them in danger of hypothermia. Added to that, they were five miles from shore. There was a very real chance the tide would turn and, instead of gently taking them toward land, pull them back out to sea.

Marathon, Florida Keys

Mac Travis set the phone down and hopped out of bed faster than his knees would have preferred. Mel, his long-time girl-friend, rolled over, pulling the sheet over her head, and ignoring him. As Mac was a part-time salvor, part-time commercial fisherman, and part-time boat bum, she was used to his early rising and erratic hours. Mac slid his feet across the Southern yellow pine floor to find his flip-flops and avoid any lurking scorpions, thinking that Mel might actually prefer it when he was gone.

With his primary—and only—footwear on, Mac grabbed a pair of cargo shorts and a T-shirt from the dresser, and went to the bathroom, where he dressed. Using the light from his phone to navigate the bedroom, he found the door without incident and closed it behind him.

It was too late for alcohol and too early for beer, so Mac filled his water bottle and headed down the stairs of the stilt house. One of two structures on the island, the other being a small storage shed. The house had originally been built by

Wood, Mel's father and Mac's mentor. Destroyed by a fire bomb shot by a rogue CIA agent a few years ago, Mac had rebuilt the structure. It was strong enough that, though the storm surge from Irma had reached the top step, it had weathered the hurricane with only the loss of a few solar panels.

Using the flashlight on his phone, he followed the narrow mangrove-lined path, swatting mosquitoes as they tried to zero in on an unexpected midnight snack. A hundred steps later he stopped to open the gate, screened with mangrove branches to blend into the backdrop of the island, and stepped onto the beach. The dock was new, built only last year. Back in the day, Wood had enjoyed his privacy, having simply a lone piling to tie off a boat.

Since Mel had moved back to the Keys it had been one improvement project after another, starting with satellite internet and most recently the improved dock. Three boats bobbed gently there on their lines. *Ghost Runner*, his custom forty-two-foot steel-hulled trawler; *Reef Runner*, a twenty-four-foot center console; and a new addition from his last adventure, a Surfari motor sailer. Not knowing what he was going to run into, he'd already decided to take the trawler. It was the best combination of speed, efficiency, and size. The trawler looked like a commercial fishing boat, which it was in part, but had been re-powered several years ago allowing for a comfortable cruising speed of thirty knots.

Mac turned the battery switch on, and started the engine. While the 800-horsepower Cat C-18 warmed up, he turned on the electronics package, a dual touch-screen setup. Once the unit powered up, he set the left-hand screen to radar and the right to the chartplotter function. Things hadn't always been so high-tech aboard *Ghost Runner*. What he had once resisted, he now relied upon. Mac touched various waypoints already entered into the unit, and connecting the dots, the plotter created a route through the Seven Mile Bridge and up the coast.

The Gulf, or backcountry, side of the Keys was not somewhere you could run a straight course. The flats, shoals, sandbars, and small islands made navigation difficult during the day, and without electronics a risky venture at night. Once he was satisfied with the route, he pressed GO and cast off the lines.

Before he allowed the autopilot to take over, he cut a hard turn around a submerged rock standing sentinel just outside the small channel leading to the dock. Once clear of the hazard he engaged the autopilot. He'd always been a John Henry kind of guy and it had taken mounds of evidence to convince him that the electronics could steer a straighter course than he could. Now that he was convinced, he checked the gauges and course, then went forward into the small cabin and made a cup of coffee.

When he returned to the wheel, Mac could see the lights from the old Seven Mile Bridge just ahead. Taking control back from the autopilot to navigate through the narrow channel between the large concrete pilings, Mac steered toward the red lights marking the opening of the demolished swing bridge. Once clear, he continued past the new, higher span, and steered through the channel marked by the one square and three triangular placards mounted to pilings. They were colored red and green, as well as numbered, but in the dark of night he had to rely on their shape. Keeping the triangular shapes to port, he followed the channel leading through the shallows to Hawk Channel. When the depth finder read thirty feet of water, he turned the controls back to the autopilot. Hawk Channel, running parallel to land on his port side and to the infamous reef on his starboard, was a safe deep-water passage through the Keys.

Despite the channel's consistent course, Mac continued to

monitor the chartplotter, and keep a watch for other boats. The reef, on his starboard side, had claimed hundreds of boats that had failed to respect the deadly coral. With an estimated time of two hours to reach Key Largo, Mac sat down to think.

First, he did something he should have done originally, and called Alicia's and TJ's separate cell phones. Mako had never appeared to be the brightest bulb in the chandelier. It was worth the few minutes it took to confirm that neither was answering. Both calls went to voicemail without ringing, a sign they were turned off, which added a bit of urgency to Mac's concerns.

As he transited Hawk Channel, new landmarks he could rely on fell in his wake. Sombrero Key Light and the high-rise condo at Key Colony Beach were in his rearview mirror, and the flashing white lights marking the Tennessee Reef Light and Alligator Reef were tiny white dots on the horizon. Other than the Long Key Bridge and the Channel #5 and Channel #2 bridges outside Islamorada, there was little else out here except for a few anchor lights from boats fishing on the reef, and the few houses whose occupants were still awake on the islands.

Another cup of coffee and and two hours later found *Ghost Runner* off Key Largo. Mac again reclaimed control of the boat and, respecting the flats adjacent to the channel, turned to port and set course for the red piling, now just a flashing light, marking the entrance to the channel and TJ's dive shop. The unanswered cell phones had been his first clue that something was amiss. When he turned to enter the side canal where TJ docked his boat behind the shop and found it empty, he knew they were in trouble.

The one shot that they were safe was the chance they were on a night charter. That thought did little to lower his ever-increasing apprehension. There was good cell service several miles past the reef, and still neither had taken his calls.

He pulled up to the vacant dock. Leaving the engine

running, Mac used one line to secure the boat, and hopped onto the dock. The few minutes it took to check the house and dive shop yielded no clues. Mac returned to the boat, hopped back over the gunwale, released the single line he had used amidship, and swung the bow around. As he traveled through the canal, and then the channel, he hailed TJ's boat. He didn't expect an answer, nor did he receive one, on channel 16. Switching to channels 68, 69, and 72, he repeated the call on the off-chance that they weren't monitoring the main hailing frequency. No replies came back.

The Keys' ecosystem begins just offshore of Miami and runs seventy miles past Key West, ending in the Dry Tortugas. It encompasses a vast amount of water, but the area where dive charters operated was relatively skinny. Looking seaward, Mac saw several white lights, the anchor lights from boats probably snapper fishing. Concentrating on the slice of water between thirty-five and one-hundred feet in depth, he turned his attention to the left-hand display. Mac set the zoom to ten miles, and scanned the area.

From two miles away he was able to identify the lights ahead with the blips on the radar screen. With a pretty good idea of the area where TJ and Alicia operated their night charters, he turned to the east. There was no other way than to check each boat and see if it was theirs.

Mac cruised over the reef. What would have been a dynamic color change, a palette of shades from white to indigo during the day, was just ink-black water now. Cruising south, Mac reached the sixty-foot line and turned to port. Heading east, he ran down the reef, slowing for the handful of boats, checking them as he passed.

None was TJ's.

With Carysfort and Alligator Reefs showing on the opposing

outer rings of his radar, Mac halted the search. He cut the engines to an idle, set the bow into the waves, and sat back to think. The obvious place to start was with Mako. In order to find Alicia and TJ, he needed more information. Reluctantly, he picked up his phone and called Mako.

46

STEVEN BECKER

STORM
SURGE

Syracuse, Sicily

MAKO WAS HAVING A HARD TIME DECIDING IF THE HURT LOOK ON Saba's face was real or contrived, though it didn't matter.

"Start at the beginning. We've got time," he said.

Silence settled around them, broken only by the gentle lapping of the waves against the seawall.

"My father's life is at stake here. And Faith."

Mako glanced over at Saba, who looked more vulnerable than he had seen her. Under other circumstances it would have been a romantic setting, watching the harbor of an ancient city under a star-flecked sky. That wasn't the case now. As much as he was attracted to her, he needed to know. He sensed a battle within her. There was no point in rushing her—they had all night.

Finally, a few long and uncomfortable minutes later, she turned to him.

"I can't reveal sources, but I can give you the facts."

"All ears," Mako said. He thought about taking her hand in

his, but felt the gesture out of place, and if he thought that, it surely was. *Be patient*, he told himself.

"The forgery took me by surprise, too, as did the unveiling."

Having expected that, Mako nodded, but it was not the information he wanted. If she wanted to go backwards in time, that was fine, as long as she ended with stealing the journal from him.

"It starts and ends with the Vatican, and their representative for all things art is Bishop Maldonado. He was the one who reported the journal as being missing."

"And that I had it."

She paused for a second and looked out at the water. Mako followed her gaze, but there was nothing to see. Before returning his eyes to her, he noticed some activity around the docks. Mako suspected it was fishermen, who often left before sunrise to get the morning bite then be back in time to sell their catch at the market and avoid the afternoon winds.

"You were hired by the CIA. Do you know who their client was?" she asked.

Mako thought about that for a second. It was a question well worth asking—as soon as he could find Alicia. He looked at his phone, seeing that it was after four a.m.. He thought about calling her again and decided it was pointless. Mac was on his way, and there was nothing he could do from here.

"I don't know." It was not an answer he liked giving. Turning the tables, he asked, "Doesn't the pope have people for that?"

"The Swiss Guard, I guess." She paused. "But, when you have that much power there's no harm in reaching out. They are also trying like hell to look innocent in all this."

The murky waters were starting to clear. "Reaching out, like to Interpol, and the CIA, through Maldonado?"

"Yes. Corruption seems to be embedded in the Vatican like the plague," she said.

"So, Maldonado asks the CIA and Interpol to find Caravaggio's journal, but why? And why did you steal it from me, if they were going to get it anyway?"

"Money. We work for free," Saba said. "Your contract was probably well into six figures."

Mako knew the answer, but chose not to disclose it. There was often enmity between contractors and government workers. "I'll go along with that for now, but not buying all the way in." Mako started feeling better about the theft. At least it wasn't personal.

"How do Burga and Longino fit into this?" Mako asked.

"Now we get to the meat of it, and why Maldonado is so freaked out. It's no secret that under the Sistine Chapel is a huge cache of art—much of it likely stolen. Caravaggio is only one of the artists. His commissions, especially in his later years, all hang in churches. And, for all his reputation, there are damned few of them. He worked by himself, rather than set up a shop with apprentices who facilitated the process, like the other masters did. There was more than one brush in the paint pot on many masterpieces. Caravaggio painted on the run."

"Good history lesson, but it doesn't answer my question." Caravaggio was starting to fascinate him; the seedier side of the art world had his attention.

"Collateral."

"They borrow against stolen paintings?"

"Yup."

47

STEVEN BECKER

STORM
SURGE

Key Largo, Florida

"Mac?"

It was Mako's voice. Then another, an unknown woman in the background. He assumed he was on speaker.

"Try the Coast Guard?" she asked.

Mac paused, not recognizing the voice. Mako caught his hesitancy and did a quick introduction. Not caring about the prickly tone he was conveying, Mac ignored the question. "Might be a good idea if y'all filled me in."

The tension on the other end of the phone was palpable.

Finally, Mako was back on the line. "Just a contract that's gone bad. The details don't really matter."

"The details always matter," Mac responded, thinking it was typical Mako. He would much rather deal with his father. "Where's John?"

Another pause. Mac was about to express his frustration when Mako broke in.

"That's another problem."

"Mako, and whoever the hell you're with. You've got two missing persons here, both friends of mine. I know your shit is top secret, but I'm going to need something to go on."

Mac could hear Mako and the woman talking in the background. While he waited for them to decide what to tell him, he started to consider his options. Like the woman had suggested, there was the Coast Guard. They kind of did this for a living. Breaking into the dive shop and seeing who had chartered the boat was also an option. This was not his first rodeo and Mac figured by the time the Coasties got their skivvies on and met him, hours would have elapsed—and he wasn't certain, though the boat wasn't at the dock, that they were on it—or were even really missing.

Mako came back. "Honestly, I don't know how any of this is going to help." He paused and briefed Mac on the journal as well as the Church's, and the Mafia's, involvement.

Mac knew he was leaving out details, but this was something to go on. "I'll get back to you," he said, and disconnected the call, staring at the dark water, looking for answers.

The ocean is hard enough to read during the day. At night its many times more difficult. Even with the moonlight highlighting the dappled crest of the waves, he couldn't see in the troughs. Man-overboard drills emphasized that one person physically point at the victim. It was that easy to lose sight of someone—in daylight. He had checked all the boats that fell inside the radar screen with no luck. He didn't want to think it, but if they were in the water, there was little he could do until morning.

The best option was checking the dive shop. At least he could see if they had a charter and who had booked it. With that as a logical place to start, he spun the wheel toward shore and pressed down on the throttle.

Twenty minutes later, Mac steered *Ghost Runner* into the small canal behind the shop. He slid into the now vacant space

TJ docked their charter boat and, using the lines waiting for its return, tied off his boat. Leaving the engine running, he navigated the narrow dock without the flashlight on his phone. The small beacon would attract attention he didn't want. Once on dry land, the security lights high up in the second-story eaves illuminated the area around the house.

Just before he reached the stairway to the living quarters, he saw two wheelchairs sitting underneath the concrete stairs. Curious, he gave them a cursory glance, until he saw the Marine Corp logo on the back of each one. That meant nothing in itself. A few months ago, he and Mel had driven up here to get some help decoding an encrypted hard drive. Alicia and TJ had made short work of the problem, and the four had gone to dinner. He remembered Alicia talking excitedly about working with adaptive and PTSD divers. As much as he didn't want to consider the possibility that the veterans were involved, under the circumstances, he was forced to consider it.

The rub was the business they were in. In a perfect world, veterans would be without reproach, but reality was far from that. Many, after resigning their rank, hired on with the independent contractors the government now relied on so heavily. The pay and benefits far exceeded what they were used to, but not all the contractors were good—or ethical. Unfortunately, the wheelchairs were no coincidence.

Mac continued toward the storefront. He had spent some time in the war room upstairs, and recalled not seeing a scrap of paper anywhere. Out of curiosity he had looked. As he moved around to the front, where the dive shop was located, he could only hope they used paper calendars for their bookings—otherwise he would be out of luck. It didn't matter. When Mac saw the metal grill pulled across the glass storefront he had no choice but to try upstairs.

With multiple deadbolts, the entry door to the apartment

looked like it was in Chicago or New York, not Key Largo. There was no way to gain access, aside from kicking it in, and that was if it wasn't steel reinforced. To reach the windows he would need a ladder.

Back at the boat, Mac looked at the VHF, trying to think of a way to access the network of fishermen and boaters without alerting the Coast Guard. Channel 16 was the main hailing frequency, which the authorities routinely monitored. Instead, he dialed up Channel 79. Channels 68 to 72 were often used by recreational boaters, but he chose the one the commercial guys preferred.

At first, no one answered when he hailed as *Ghost Runner*. Realizing his boat had only recently been named by Trufante's girlfriend, Pamela, and most boaters wouldn't recognize him, he called out using his own name. Several seconds later a voice came over the speaker, acknowledging him. The name of the other boat was not familiar. As with his own vessel, that meant little. He would likely know the captain. After thirty years in the Keys he had many contacts and was well known through the string of islands.

"Looking for a pair, maybe more, of divers. Anything out there?" Mac knew from the clarity of the connection that the responding boat was within his search zone. VHF ran on line of sight, which usually meant a maximum of ten miles.

"Nah, ain't nothing out here. Even the snapper bites off."

"Keep an eye out, if you don't mind. *Ghost Runner*, out." Mac was about to set the microphone into its holder when another vessel hailed him.

"Yo, Travis, that you?"

"It is, what'cha got?"

"Seen a few of these yellow chemical lights floating out there a few minutes ago. Thought it was just trash."

Mac knew exactly what he was talking about. There was a good chance the lights were attached to BCs. "Can you shoot me your coordinates?"

STORM
SURGE

Syracuse, Sicily

AFTER TALKING TO MAC, MAKO AND SABA REMAINED QUIET, UNTIL a sudden sound made both turn toward the entrance of the harbor. The engine of a ship coming their way was clearly audible over the sounds of the early morning fishermen preparing for their day. The pre-dawn light showed the silhouette of a massive motor yacht.

"Longino?" Mako asked.

"That's his." Saba scanned the harbor. "We've only got a limited view here. We need higher ground with quick access. I'm sure they'll stash John and Faith on the ship. We need to stop them before they reach it."

"You're right about that," Mako said, glad that her first priority was his father and Faith, not the journal. Looking back at the outline of the buildings behind them, he found what he was looking for. "That hotel there." The only other buildings taller were churches.

"That'll work." Saba got up and started walking.

By the time they covered the dozen or so blocks to the Grand

Hotel Ortigia, the sun was casting its first rays on the building. "Rooftop restaurant," Mako said, seeing the sign beside the entry doors.

"You know as soon as we order, Burga will show up."

"Portability, dear. We Americans have some things perfected. I think I've eaten more meals in a car than at a table."

The only way to describe her derisive laugh was European. Regardless, she followed him into the hotel. The elevator took them to the top floor, where they entered the restaurant.

"We'd like a table overlooking the harbor," Mako asked one of the waiters.

They were led to a small table and ordered espresso. Positioning themselves so they could see the harbor through the mass of the lattice-style concrete railing, they scanned the breakfast menu. When the waiter returned they ordered breakfast.

"So." Mako glanced back at the restaurant to see if their conversation could be overheard. This early, only a few tables were occupied and those were scattered around the dining room and balcony. They were safe.

"Back to the Vatican."

Saba sipped from her cup. "Right. The Institute for the Works of Religion."

"Say what?"

"The Vatican Bank." She waited until she had his attention. "The Church would rather talk about sex than money." She had him now. "I'll spare you the history lesson."

Mako nodded, not sure if she was ridiculing him or just wanting to save time. He waited for her to continue.

"Until World War II the Church was constantly teetering on the verge of bankruptcy. During the war, however, they prospered, mainly as money launderers. Cloaked with their religious status, the unique entity was allowed to do business in the United States and other allied nations. Fortunes were amassed.

"No one really knows what assets they have, and though there have been reform efforts, the Church wants to keep them secret. There is a rumor that there's trouble now. Pope Francis wants transparency, and it couldn't come at a worse time. Between the lawsuits against them for child abuse and some bad management decisions, they are having to borrow to pay off the multi-million-dollar settlements. The art is collateral. They did the same thing with securities in the 80s"

Their food arrived. Digging in, Mako summarized. "So, they have a basement loaded with artwork that may or may not be forged, and they use it to pay their bills."

"Basically."

"And now Longino's wanting to go off the reservation and sell the *Nativity*."

"I haven't wrapped my head around that situation yet, but it sounds that way."

With one eye on the water and another on their plates, they ate in silence, quickly devouring their breakfast. Mako sat back first. The food had cleared his mind, and a thought occurred to him. Before he could verbalize it, Saba interrupted him.

"Look, something's going on down there."

49

STEVEN BECKER

STORM
SURGE

Key Largo, Florida

WITH THE COORDINATES ENTERED, MAC RELEASED THE LINES AND spun the bow toward the main channel. Seconds later he was on plane heading toward the location the fisherman had given him. Tempering his expectations, he knew a sighting of two fluorescent glow sticks was far from confirmation that TJ and Alicia were alive. Several other explanations quickly came to mind. Parents gave their kids the sticks to play with all the time. The tide could have taken them out to sea. A more probable explanation was they were discarded by a fisherman who had used them while deep-dropping for swordfish. When fishing deeper than a few hundred feet, the lights helped attract the predators.

Despite having the GPS coordinates, current and drift needed to be factored into his route calculation, making finding the two light sticks akin to finding two needles in a haystack. Searching like this, on a micro level, the vastness of the ocean was revealed.

As he approached the waypoint, Mac kept a vigilant watch, scanning the water with his binoculars while the autopilot steered *Ghost Runner*. Back and forth he swept the glasses, searching for any sign of life on the ink-black water.

An alarm from the chartplotter told him that he was approaching the spot. Mac set the binoculars down and steered toward the icon on the chart, then slowed and waited for the boat to drift. Once a true sailor's art, through the use of electronics judging currents and drift was now more of a science. Zooming in on his location, Mac watched the thin line on the screen that showed his path of travel. He set a mark, then reached for his phone and opened the stopwatch. When a minute elapsed, he made another mark, then measured the distance. The chartplotter showed him the direction, while a quick calculation gave him the speed.

Figuring it had been about thirty minutes since the fisherman had spotted the glowing dots, Mac extrapolated the distance at just short of a half-mile and spun the wheel to maintain his direction. His excitement built as he approached the center of the area he had calculated. Stopping well short of the spot, he set the throttles at idle speed, engaged the autopilot and started scanning the water.

Mac knew his calculations were rough. With the large surface area of his trawler acting as a sail, the boat would be drifting faster than an object low to the water—like a body. Glancing at the chartplotter, he saw it was about a hundred yards to the waypoint, the area he expected to find them. As he approached his anxiety increased.

There was nothing on the water.

50

STEVEN BECKER

STORM
SURGE

Syracuse, Sicily

JUST RISEN ABOVE THE HORIZON, THE SUN GAVE MAKO AND SABA plenty of light to make their way back to the harbor. It also brought out the early morning crowd. They were slowed every block or so by tourists and locals getting a head start on the day, as well as merchants loaded with goods that they were taking to the open-air market. The former moved out of their way; the latter, burdened down like mules, continued to stumble along, forcing Mako and Saba onto the street where they faced another challenge—Italian drivers.

They finally reached the marina in time to see a small skiff already halfway to the yacht. Four people could clearly be seen sitting by the stern. It was too far to see their faces, but Mako knew his father's body language from a distance. He was one of the passengers. That left Burga, Maldonado, and Faith.

Mako didn't wait for Saba. He vaulted the stone rail, landing roughly on a walkway leading to the docks. There was no reason to look back. He felt Saba right behind him. They reached a dock where several tourist boats were tied off and stopped. From the selection of old motors in front of them, there was no way to reach the larger vessel before the skiff did.

"It'll take them a while to get that beast moving," Mako said, hoping they wouldn't be ready to sail upon receiving the passengers.

"We can't take that chance." Saba walked up to one of the captains and offered her hand. A very brief negotiation ensued, and she handed him a few bills, then waved to Mako to join her. Boarding the twenty-odd-foot open-deck boat, the captain cast off the single line, and spun the wheel toward the behemoth.

The man said something in Italian.

"He wants to know if we're sure we want to go to that ship. Says it is dangerous."

"We might not have too," Mako said. "Tell him to hold up."

They were about halfway to Longino's ship when a panel on the ship's hull rose, then disappeared, and a dock extended. The skiff with Burga, John, Faith, and Maldonado approached and was received by two men. Drifting on the blue water of the harbor, Mako and Saba watched as John and Faith were escorted onto the dock and, with one of the men holding their arms, disappeared from view. Burga and Maldonado remained.

"Tell him to head back to the dock," Mako told Saba, who relayed the message to the captain. The relief on his face was evident. The remaining man on the extended dock handed a long cylindrical tube to the skiff's captain. Once the tube was secure, he released the dock line. Mako was about to look away when Maldonado, Burga, and one of the thugs stepped back aboard the skiff. The small craft quickly sped away from the larger vessel. Before it had traveled ten yards, the hull panel was back in place, concealing the access.

"Pretty slick," Mako said, glancing over his shoulder at the approaching skiff. "Might want to ask your boyfriend here to speed it up a bit."

Saba ignored the reproach and said something to the captain. After a furtive glance over his shoulder, he complied, probably breaking the no-wake ordinance. He clearly wanted no part of the mega-yacht or its passengers.

What were they up to? If they had the journal, why not take off? Bringing Maldonado back to the mainland had to be risky. The bishop was a well-known figure—in Italy, almost a celebrity. For the time being they were forced to keep their theories to themselves as the old two-stroke engine made it difficult to talk.

"Over there," Saba said, directing the captain to a different dock than they had disembarked from.

Seconds later they sprung from the skiff and hustled up the ramp, hoping no one had seen them.

"They're going to the church. That tube has to hold the original painting."

"Maldonado's covering his tracks," Saba agreed.

They ran into the city, weaving their way through the growing throng of pedestrian, bicycle, scooter, and vehicular traffic. Knowing their destination, they didn't mind blending in with the crowds. It concealed them, as well as slowed Burga and Maldonado to a point that Saba and Mako actually passed them on the other side of the street. Hoping they hadn't been seen, Mako and Saba took off at a run.

Reaching the church they saw the main door open. A couple exited as another entered.

"This is going to be interesting. I guess the secretary has a key," Mako said.

"Hopefully, the only thing she'll find amiss is the priest absent. C'mon, let's get inside before Burga and Maldonado get here."

They ran for the pair of green doors. Mako yanked one side open, nearly barreling into an older couple. Saba scolded him in Italian. Head down, he backed off, and held the door for them. Saba entered behind him. Together they slid along the back wall, trying to stay out of sight of the handful of early morning tourists wandering through the church.

"There's an upstairs balcony." Mako grabbed Saba's hand and led her to the stairway to their right. Across the opening to the stairs an old chain held a small sign in Italian that Mako deciphered as "no admittance." Slowly, so as not to attract any attention, they ducked under the chain, and climbed the stairs to the balcony. Mako walked down the slight grade of the seating area, stopping at the fourth row. Taking two aisle seats, he and Saba scanned the church below. They could see most of the main floor, but the angle of the balcony helped shield them from view. Just as he settled into his seat, he saw Burga, Maldonado, and the thug enter.

Words were exchanged. Burga and the thug with the tube stepped back into the shadows, while Maldonado walked purposefully toward the altar.

"Tell me if I'm wrong, but it looks like he's in charge," Mako said.

"Or Burga has given him his orders."

Saba didn't elaborate as the secretary walked forward to meet the bishop. It was readily apparent from her body language that she was in awe of the man, who spoke to her. A few minutes later the church was cleared and the doors locked.

"Guess that chain across the stairs is high security here," Mako said.

"Sshhh," Saba whispered. "We don't know where Burga is."

After locking the main doors, the secretary said something to the bishop and entered the doorway near the altar that led to the offices and side entrance. Once the door was closed,

Maldonado gestured toward the shadows and they watched Burga and the other man walk toward the altar. The cylinder was handed to the bishop, who dropped to one knee, set it on the floor, and with a pocket knife pried the end of the tube off. He withdrew a rolled-up canvas.

51

STORM SURGE

Key Largo, Florida

MAC POPPED THE TRANSMISSION OUT OF GEAR, ALLOWING THE boat to drift. He generally took pains to go unnoticed, and using his searchlight went against the grain. Having given up on finding the glow sticks, at this point he felt using the light was a last resort. Reaching toward the ceiling of the cabin, he grabbed the swivel control linked to the light that was mounted above and hit the on switch. The beam shot out in a wide arc, illuminating the water in front of him. He immediately knew why he hadn't seen the glow lights.

A huge mat of sargassum spread out around him; there was no way the small glow lights would be visible through the weeds. That gave him some hope. Using its handle, he swung the light, watching the beam carefully as it moved across the water. Mac knew staring at the light would ruin his night vision, as well as attract attention, but there was little choice.

Glancing down at the chartplotter, he realized he had overshot the mark. He moved the throttle forward to its first stop and spun the boat 180 degrees, running a reciprocal course to the waypoint. The big diesel purred as it moved the boat at four knots. Mac continued to study the weeds ahead. The bow broke through the large clumps and the propeller dispersed them as he passed, making him think a reciprocal heading would provide better visibility.

After running a quarter mile past the waypoint, Mac spun the wheel and reversed course. It was much easier to see now that the light reflected off the water instead of the weeds. As he approached the waypoint again, he continued forward for another two hundred yards to compensate for the additional drift. Mac swung the searchlight back and forth, becoming more anxious with each pass. He knew he was running out of time.

The steady beam of the light was suddenly broken by a flash on the surface. It could have been a fish foraging for small bait-fish in the broken weeds, or a reflector. Hoping it was the latter, Mac dropped his speed to a crawl and inched forward. He saw it again, and this time, heard a voice.

Dropping to neutral, he hopped onto the foredeck and bent over the rail. Three figures were huddled together using two BCs as a makeshift raft. Two pairs of eyes squinted in the light; the eyes of a third, a man, remained closed. Mac knew immediately from the short dreadlocks that it was TJ. Mac reached back and swung the light to the side. Alicia and another woman looked up at him.

"Alicia, it's Mac," he called down to the bodies in the water, knowing he and his boat were just silhouettes to the women.

"Mac Travis?"

"Mako called. But let's get you out of the water. Stay there, I'll swing around and pick you up by the dive platform."

"TJ's hurt. He's going to need medical attention."

"Let's get everyone on board first. Then we'll see to him." Five miles from shore, he could probably reach a waiting ambulance before a helicopter trauma unit would be in the air.

Moving back to the helm, he judged the group's position in the water, deciding to back away from them and make a wide circle to keep them clear of the propeller. He doused the searchlight, taking a few long blinks to help his night vision return, then without taking his eyes off the three pulled back and circled around. Once they were within a few feet of the dive platform, he set the transmission in neutral and ran to the transom, grabbing a long-handled gaff on the way.

From his position up-current of the group, Mac extended the gaff towards Alicia and waited for the boat to bring it within reach. She lunged for it, grabbing the hook. Handing it off to the other woman, she stayed with TJ while Mac pulled the woman to the platform. She released the hook and looked up.

"Jen?" He knew her from the Turtle Hospital in Marathon. Mac could see her face was covered in soot. "What the hell happened?"

"We've got to get TJ up here," Jen interrupted.

Mac again reached the hook out to Alicia. She latched onto it with one hand, with the other firmly around TJ's neck. Mac slowly pulled them toward the boat. When they were close, Jen held onto TJ from the dive platform while Alicia climbed out of the water. Between the three of them, they hauled TJ from the water, onto the platform, and through the transom door. Another time, there might have been a joke about hauling the biggest tuna ever landed onto *Ghost Runner*, but Mac saw the burns on TJ's skin. Realizing how serious the situation was, he ran to the wheelhouse, tossed Alicia his phone to call for help, and pushed the throttle to the limit.

52

STORM SURGE

Syracuse, Sicily

MAKO AND SABA SAT SLOUCHED DOWN IN THEIR SEATS NEAR THE rear of the balcony watching the activity below. It was a little surreal observing the group below clearly committing some kind of crime, from what was essentially a theater seat. All that was missing was popcorn.

Fortunately, the acoustics of the old stone building worked in their favor and they could hear the conversation, at least between Burga and Maldonado. The third man stood menacingly over the other two, clearly there for protection.

"They don't have the expertise to do this themselves," Saba whispered.

Mako flinched, silently watching the group below to see if the sound of her voice had carried. The thug was a bellwether, more concerned with what was going on around them, while Burga and Maldonado stared at the painting. From the man's unchanged demeanor, Mako assumed he hadn't heard.

"We're still not sure what they're doing," Mako whispered.

"Changing the painting out—what else?"

Mako recalled his previous experience while he had inspected the painting from a ladder. Unless they had scaffolding somewhere, or a mechanical lift, there was no way two or even three men could manage the task. Though the painting was only canvas, the physical size of the painting alone would make it difficult.

Mako returned his attention to Burga and Maldonado, and shot forward when Maldonado withdrew the journal from his pocket. His job was to get the journal back, and only one man stood in his way. Once he had the journal, he would have some leverage to free his father and Faith. Slowly his right hand moved behind his back to his father's .45.

Saba must have realized his intentions. Her hand reached across and grabbed his before it reached the pistol. Their fingers seemed to naturally intertwine, but Mako knew this was more of a restraint than a romantic gesture.

"There's a bigger picture here than just the journal," Saba whispered, squeezing his hand to let him know he wasn't alone in this.

Mako wasn't sure what their relationship was. In chapter one he had been a victim; chapter two, they had acted like wannabe lovers, and now, an uneasy partnership had settled over them. He wondered if there would be a chapter three after this was over. His long-standing Storm defect, an inability to express emotion or verbalize things, wasn't going to help.

Just as Mako was about to protest, a loud beeping sound came from outside the main entrance. The thug looked at Burga, who nodded. Mako and Saba instinctively slid down in their chairs as he crossed to the double doors. From the balcony they had no direct view of the entrance, which was underneath them. Mako thought about moving to the railing for a better look, but when a shaft of light penetrated the church and the beeping sound grew louder, he knew what was happening.

The claxon filled the building, echoing off the stone walls as a mechanized lift came into view. Once it cleared the seats, the church fell into shadows again as the doors were closed.

Mako moved his gaze to Maldonado. The bishop was unfazed by the activity. On his hands and knees, he studied the painting, checking the journal that lay beside him every few minutes.

The lift was moved into place and Burga, the security man, and the two mechanics fixed their attention on the bishop.

Maldonado looked up at the altarpiece as if thanking God and rose. "It is the real thing."

Mako gave Saba a questioning look. "What now?"

"If they are planning on taking down the forgery and hanging the original, let them make it right. Then I'll arrange for backup and arrest them for possession of the forgery."

"And the journal?" Mako asked.

"I'm not so sure your contract will be worth anything if the Church is the benefactor."

The incessant beeping had stopped and Mako looked down at the work being done behind the altar while he thought about her answer. The high-lift had been positioned in front of the painting. The basket, holding the two men who had delivered the equipment, started to rise. Powered by batteries, the lift elevated the men to the top of the painting in relative silence. With the men working to remove the forgery the church was far from quiet, and Mako felt at ease to continue the conversation.

"I need to find Alicia," Mako said, pulling out his phone and studying the screen, which showed only his wallpaper. There were no messages or voicemails. He thought for a minute. "If I can deliver the journal to the CIA contact before they find out Maldonado's behind this mess, they'll pay."

"Maybe we can work something out." Saba squeezed Mako's hand, then picked up her phone and started texting.

Mako assumed she was arranging for backup to arrest the bishop and Burga. They sat in silence for what seemed like hours as the two men removed the forgery and started to install the original painting. It took a while, but as Mako watched, he slowly came to the realization that Saba's plan wasn't going to benefit his father and Faith.

"John and Faith are aboard the ship. If you arrest the gang here, there is nothing keeping Longino from killing them."

"You're assuming he has any intention to release them."

"Truth." He needed to do something to change the playing field.

The muffled sound of his phone ringing took him by surprise. Reaching into his pocket, he pulled it out and silenced the ringer. It was too late, the sound had reverberated through the cavernous church. That the name on the screen was Alicia's did little to help when all eyes swung up to the balcony.

Mako and Saba ducked, but Burga and her associate were already running toward the stairs. Maldonado called an order to the men working on the painting. It wasn't audible to Mako, who was crawling along the row of seats behind Saba. He expected it was a command to speed up to their work.

"Is there another exit?" Mako whispered.

Saba didn't answer. With an awkward bear crawl, she was moving toward the other end of the balcony. Once she reached the end of the aisle, they were left staring at a blank stone wall. There was only one egress.

"Follow me, and stay low."

She turned toward the last row of seats and started up the slight incline. When they reached the rearmost row, they crawled back the way they had come. Mako understood the ploy. Their pursuers would likely start at the bottom and work toward the top. They reached the end of the row and waited.

Burga was first to appear. With a pistol held in front of her, she scanned the balcony, then started toward the first row. The other man followed, beginning his search a few rows higher. Mako knew they wouldn't escape undetected, but their goal, at least the immediate one, was to get off the balcony.

Once Burga and the thug were past the halfway mark of their respective rows, Saba dashed from cover to the stairway, Mako right on her heels. He waited until they were on the stairs before risking a look back. Burga had seen them and reversed course, calling to her man. Hopefully he and Saba were far enough ahead.

Taking the stairs three at a time, Mako passed Saba, reaching the ground floor first. Looking around, he locked eyes with Maldonado. When the bishop reached into his coat pocket Mako knew why, before seeing the cold steel of the pistol. A shot fired, ricocheting off the stone. Mako grabbed Saba's hand and ran toward the green doors.

Reaching the doors, he threw the bolt and pushed into daylight. He heard the unmistakable sound of pursuit behind them. Immediately he sought cover and, with the lunch crowd on the streets and in the cafes, he used the bodies of the people to screen him and Saba from Burga and the thug.

Before leaving the plaza, he risked a glance back. Burga and her accomplice looked determined.

Disregarding the bystanders, Mako and Saba pushed and shoved their way through the crowd. They were closing the gap.

"We need to lose these two and get back to Maldonado. He has the journal," Saba said.

"The market." Mako didn't wait for an answer.

"It's by the marina, too. Maldonado is sure to be heading for the boat."

They took off at a dead run, leaving the plaza behind. A quick turn into a side street allowed them to put some space between them and their pursuers. Mako had speed, and Saba wasn't far behind. Burga was lithe, but her man was muscular and heavier. Advantage: Team Storm.

There was no need for a map or directions. Both the market and marina were located in the northern end of the city, which was just over a quarter-mile wide. It would be impossible to get lost if they stuck to the main streets, which would provide better cover.

Mako was hitting his stride as they entered a traffic circle. He headed toward a fountain gracing a small island in the middle. Once they reached it, a large avenue branched off from the northern point of the circle. Sprinting through traffic, they reached the street and ran, dodging between the road and sidewalk to avoid pedestrians and vehicles.

A large excavation labeled *The Temple of Apollo* was directly in front of them, with another plaza laying just beyond. Mako had seen enough Roman ruins for two lifetimes in the last week, and sped past it without a second look. The outskirts of the market were not an organized affair. Carts selling everything from seafood to shawls were parked intermittently along the sidewalk, forcing the pedestrians into the street. Dodging the small groups of tourists milling around the few vendors that had set up their carts, Mako and Saba found themselves in the midst of a throng of people heading toward the main market. There was no choice but to slow their pace.

This worked to Burga's advantage. Screams coming from behind alerted them to the proximity of their pursuers—close—too close.

Reaching the main thoroughfare, Mako and Saba turned right, hoping to lose their pursuers in the crowds of people milling around the stalls. If they were going to make a move, it had to be now. Several shots rang out and the crowds darted for cover. People were yelling, screaming, and crying, but Mako could see no sign of injury. His best guess was that Burga had fired the shots into the air to disperse the crowd.

Whatever her intent, it worked. The street was empty, the crowds of shoppers hunkered down in between and underneath the stalls. Only a lone sandwich-maker wearing headphones continued to work, oblivious to what was happening around him. Several more shots were fired, sounding like different weapons from the previous blasts. This time bullets ricocheted closely around them.

"We've got to find cover," Saba said, breathlessly.

Mako could tell from her voice she was almost spent. He was feeling winded as well. What they needed to do was eliminate their pursuers, not avoid them.

Mako skidded to a stop, swinging behind a cart for cover. He pulled the 1911 from his waistband and, fighting to control his heaving lungs, took aim at Burga and the man coming toward them. Both shots missed.

"Give me that," Saba said, yanking the pistol from his hands.

Somehow, she had caught her breath. Mako watched as she leaned around the corner, using the building for support. She extended both arms, and lined up the sights on the thug. Pausing for a brief second, she slowly squeezed the trigger. Mako was close enough that the spent casing hit him in the head, temporarily distracting him. When he looked up, the man beside Burga was on the ground.

Saba shot again. This time Burga was ready and darted behind a lamppost. As Saba fired once more, Mako clearly saw the intense look on Burga's face.

He dropped to the side just as a shot rang out. It went wide. They were too close to aim now. A gunshot at this range could easily kill the shooter. Mako frantically looked around for another weapon.

"Get down. I got this," he yelled to Saba as he rose and ran to the next stall. Seafood lined its counter, and he spotted the head of a swordfish. In a macabre display, the vendor had cut the head off and set it on the counter with the bill standing vertically. Beneath it was the body of the fish, cut up for sale.

Mako lunged for the bill, slashing his hands on its surprisingly rough surface. Swinging around in one smooth movement, he surprised Burga, who was speeding toward him. She tried to stop. The look of horror on her face when she realized her fate was small consolation to Mako as the bill pierced her chest.

53

STEVEN BECKER

STORM
SURGE

Key Largo, Florida

THE STILL WATER INSIDE THE MARINA REFLECTED THE AMBULANCE lights, doubling their intensity. With everything tinged in red, the scene around them looked ominous. Mac squinted as if it were daylight as he approached the dock. Once they had gotten TJ aboard and were underway, Alicia had called 911 and set up a location to transfer TJ to an ambulance.

To make matters worse, the full marina had little room to negotiate the approach. It was probably a simple matter during daylight hours. In the dark of night everything was harder and the flashing red lights made it even more difficult.

"I can't see a damned thing," Mac called out to Alicia as he dropped down to idle speed. The approach to the dock was hidden in the blinding lights.

"Haven't seen a light show like this since the last time I saw the Dead," TJ said, causing both Mac and Alicia to smile.

She reached across, grabbing the microphone for the VHF radio and hailing anyone monitoring channel 16. The response was immediate. The lights were extinguished. Flashes seemed to continue as Mac's eyes adjusted to the sudden darkness. Blinking rapidly to encourage his night vision to return, he waited until he could see the dock and eased into an empty slip.

EMTs, firemen, and uniformed police officers streamed toward the trawler. Mac deflected all questions until TJ was strapped to a gurney and rolling down the dock toward the ambulance.

"You want me to go with you?" Mac asked Alicia.

"I have to go home and figure this out. We've got assets in the field." She must have realized how cold she sounded. "I want to be with him, but there's little I can do there."

Mac thought the "assets in the field" part sounded funny, especially if she was referring to Mako. He understood her conflict. "I'm not feeling like running back to Marathon in the dark. I'll snag a ride to the hospital and stay with him."

"I'll go with you," Jen said.

Alicia rushed up and threw her arms around him. Mac held on, letting the pent-up emotions of the last few hours pour out. He felt her ease the pressure on him, and released his grip. "You good?"

"Yup. Let me know how he's doing. I've got some payback to arrange." Alicia disappeared into the shadows.

Another smile crossed his face. Mac had been the one to introduce the couple. He remembered when he had first met Alicia. Straight out of the office, she had been as green a field agent as there ever was. She had proven to be willing to learn, and tough as nails. He glanced again at the shadows where he had last seen her, but she was gone.

Mac looked around for someone associated with the marina to ask where he could tie off *Ghost Runner*. Before he located anyone, the officers assigned to the call cornered him. Mac bit his tongue. His relationship with authority had never been good.

Now, they were looking to him for answers he didn't have, and he suspected the worst.

"You're Mac Travis," one of the officers said.

It was a statement, not a question, and there were no hands extended. Mac studied the man's face, looking for a clue as to how he knew him.

"We'll need a statement." The other officer pulled a pad and pen from his shirt pocket.

"That was one of my best friends they just took to the hospital. I'd like to get over there and be with him."

The two men looked at each other.

"Look, I got a call that he was missing." They hadn't seemed to notice Alicia was gone. "Ran up from Marathon to see if I could help. A fisherman said he had seen something on the surface. I found them and brought 'em in. That's it."

"Sounds like your typical Mac Travis story." The officer peered around Mac and looked at the boat. "Trufante's not hiding down there, is he?"

Mac knew he was guilty by association. It was not surprising they recognized him because of his wayward deckhand. "He's got nothing to do with this."

"Hey, I was there, too," Jen said. The officers had been so focused on Mac that they hadn't noticed her.

Without any obvious crime, the officers backed away slightly. "How about we give you a ride to the hospital and once your friends squared away, we'll have a chat?"

Mac knew that was the best deal he was going to get. "That'll work."

54

STORM SURGE

Syracuse, Sicily

IN THE DISTANCE MAKO AND SABA COULD HEAR THE DISTINCTIVE European sirens closing on the scene as they fought their way through the crowd gathering around Burga's body.

"Where'd Maldonado go?" Mako asked once they had extricated themselves from the group.

"I didn't see," Saba said. "We had more pressing matters."

"He's got the journal."

"With the forgery replaced and the journal in hand, there's no doubt he'll run for Vatican City. He's protected there."

Mako continued walking. They were on the fringe of the market, just a block from the water. He crossed the street and stood at the cast-iron railing built to keep people off the rocks below. There was a fair amount of boat traffic now. The size and shape of the various crafts were mostly the same. Studying them for a minute, Mako determined that it was their course that allowed an observer to discern their purpose. Fishermen returning to port with their catch came from the open Mediterranean. Tourist boats ran along the shoreline, showing off the historic city from the water, giving the same view that scores of invaders had had over two millennium.

He recalled seeing the monster yacht from the balcony of the hotel, standing sentinel over the harbor on the other side of the island. He was just about to head down the road adjacent to the V-shaped channel that separated the old and new cities. While Mako's attention was focused ahead, Saba scanned the water.

"There!" She pointed to a man climbing aboard a small skiff. "Maldonado."

Mako changed direction even before she finished the sentence. He ran closer to the water, looking for a boat they could use. Paying for one would be preferable, but he was prepared to steal one if there was no other way. This side of the harbor was mainly privately-owned vessels, most of which were moored Mediterranean style, parallel to each other, and with their sterns to the dock to save space. Even if he could find a captain and vessel willing to take him, it would be too time-consuming to extricate the boat from its mooring.

Just to the side of a long grouping of docked boats, Mako saw a fishing boat tied to the seawall. He ran toward it, finding it unoccupied. From the disorder on the decks it appeared the boat had just returned from a morning trip and the crew was now trying to sell their catch to one of the local vendors.

"Duck!" Saba called to Mako, who was looking around for the captain or crew.

Just as he heard her command a boat passed by. There was no mistaking the passenger—Maldonado. Mako moved behind the wheelhouse to screen himself from the bishop's view. Once the boat passed he moved away from the helm. Before he resumed his search, he noticed the key in the ignition.

With the boat carrying Maldonado headed toward Longino's yacht, he didn't have time to find the captain.

"Come on. We're borrowing this one." Mako cranked the key

hard. The sound of the starter engaging the flywheel was like nails on a blackboard, and for a long second Mako thought the boat might be abandoned because of a breakdown. Just as he was about to release the key, the motor turned over and caught. With a cloud of smoke puffing from the old engine, Mako pulled away from the dock.

Saba stood in the bow, calling in her Interpol voice to any boats in the way to move aside. Mako, focused on pulling away from the dock and accelerating, had a moment's panic when he looked ahead and noticed the low clearance of the first bridge. Only a few feet above the deck, the canvas top would never clear it. Fortunately, one of the boats ahead either hadn't heard or heeded Saba's calls and Mako watched as a crewman, using a pole, dropped the top just as the boat passed underneath the bridge.

"Can you lose this thing like that?" Mako called to Saba.

She had seen it as well and, with only seconds to spare before he would either crash or have to stop, she dropped the Bimini top. Mako ducked as they passed beneath the first bridge. Once the second was in sight, he accelerated, hoping the clearance was the same. He almost had his head shaved, as the second bridge was set a least a foot lower than the first.

Ahead they could see the harbor, the monster yacht standing sentinel over the smaller ships. The whitewater from the wake of Maldonado's boat confirmed his intention. Even over the grumble of the old engine of the fishing boat, Mako could hear the sound of the anchor chain as it reverberated across the water, confirming what he already suspected: The ship would depart as soon as Maldonado reached it. Their destination was likely Rome. Knowing where they were going was little consolation. With every mile they grew closer to the Vatican, the Holy See's protective bubble grew stronger.

Mako goosed the throttle to get as much speed as he could

from the engine. He had already learned the sweet spot where he could push it without flooding the carburetor. It didn't matter, though. It was easy to see they would never catch Maldonado.

They needed a new plan.

55

STEVEN BECKER

STORM SURGE

Key Largo, Florida

Branches whipped against Alicia's legs as she ran through the landscaping that separated the marina from the adjacent properties. She was moving in the direction of a big, bright strip-mall shopping center. It was as good a plan as any.

Her first priority had been to avoid the first responders. She had to have faith that TJ was in good hands and there was nothing she could do to help, though she was grateful that Mac and Jen had offered to be with him. That assuaged a little bit of the guilt encompassing her.

As she ran, the feeling of never being good enough, instilled by her mother, haunted her again, and she cursed herself for not seeing that there had been something funny about the adaptive divers. Growing up, she had learned to use the guilt as fuel for her fire, and now it burned hot within her. She was going to fix this.

Putting TJ from her mind was harder than she thought. Taught at an early age to compartmentalize and control her emotions, TJ had gotten by all her defense systems when they met three years ago. Now, she realized how attached she was to him. It wasn't a bad thing, but Mako and John were out there and they needed her, too.

Breaking free of the shrubs, she stepped onto the pavement. Glancing down at her bare and dirty feet, she realized what the rest of her must look like. At least she had found one of Mel's sweatshirts in the cabin of Mac's boat, though finding a ride home covered in soot and slime might still be tough.

A cab pulled up to a bar near the end of the strip center. The back door opened and a couple stepped out. Alicia sprinted across the lot, sliding into the just-vacated seat before the door closed. The driver turned around, giving her a weary look. There was no judgment in his expression as he asked where she wanted to go. Driving a cab in the Florida Keys, he had seen it all.

Alicia released a pent-up breath as the cab rolled out of the lot. She hadn't realized she'd been holding it, and now tried to alleviate the symptoms she was feeling from lack of oxygen in her bloodstream. She recognized the signs, and began to breathe more evenly. Once her respiration rate was under control, she increased the length of her exhales to engage her parasympathetic nervous system. By the time the driver pulled into the small parking lot in front of the shop she had regained her composure.

The driver waited patiently while she ran upstairs and punched her code into the lock. A moment later she returned downstairs with his fare and a large tip to ensure his silence.

Alicia ran back upstairs. On the way to the war room, she grabbed her insulated mug with the dive shop's name stenciled on it, and filled it with filtered water from the spout on the sink. She chugged the first glass, then refilled it and headed to the war room. They had stopped using bottled water at home and on their charters to help alleviate the plastics crisis; now, each diver was given an insulated mug they could fill from a large water cooler onboard. Passing the pantry, hunger pangs shot through her, and she opened the cabinet and grabbed a bag of chips.

Water and food in hand, she pushed open the door of the war room and went directly to her desk. With her phone either destroyed or floating off Fort Lauderdale in the Gulf Stream current, she opened up a VOIP connection and clicked on Mako's contact information.

The electronic ringer sounded several times before going to voicemail. Alicia moved the angle of her chair to get a better view of the screen on her left, and typed in a string of code. A spinning wheel appeared on the monitor, and a few seconds later an icon appeared on a large map. With the mouse, Alicia zoomed in on the area, noting it was Syracuse. Moving in closer, she saw it wasn't really in Syracuse, but the water off the coast. There was no doubt she had missed something over the last few hours.

She typed a quick text and sent it to Mako, then followed the same procedure with John. The result was the same—voicemail. Tracking John's location found him, or at least his phone, in the same area as Mako, but a half-mile or so further offshore. She left him a message and sat back helpless as she watched the two dots on her screen converge on each other.

That helpless feeling lasted all of ten seconds, just enough to take a sip of water. Alicia's mother had beaten that useless attitude out of her at an early age.

Staring at the dots on her screen, she started to pull up the traffic and security cameras in the area. Though slower at it than TJ, she was still able to populate most of the screens with different angles of the market area and harbor. Though her focus was on the water, she couldn't help but notice the group of people and first responders gathered around what appeared to be a body in the street. An adjacent camera gave a better view. A blond-haired woman she instantly recognized as Carlota Burga lay on her side with what appeared to be ... a swordfish bill through her chest? There was no sign of Mako or John, but there was little doubt this was their handiwork.

Slightly relieved, she worked the cameras near the water, noticing nothing outside of the usual boat traffic. Looking through the database of available cameras, she noticed one that she hadn't accessed, a buoy camera, used for a visual on the state of the seas and waves. It was a long shot.

Clicking on the icon, she waited while the image buffered and loaded. It took her a minute to acclimate to the camera angle, which was aimed from the open Mediterranean toward the shore, instead of the opposing view the other cameras displayed. There, in the middle of the screen, was a huge, gunmetal gray yacht.

Alicia grabbed a screenshot and a few minutes later was scanning a file about the ship—and its owner. After reading it, even if the dot for John's phone wasn't directly on it, she would have suspected the ship had something to do with the journal.

Her eyes panned the screens, stopping on the empty captain's chair in the center of the room. Moisture clouded her eyes for just a second until she wiped it away with the back of her hand. She would not feel sorry for herself, it wasn't in her DNA. Glancing at the screen on her phone, hoping for an update from Mac and Jen, she saw nothing and decided to call.

Mac answered on the third ring. TJ was being treated. The word was that he would be okay. It would take some time for the burns to heal, and they would likely leave scars. Alicia was already imagining some cool tattoos to cover the injuries when, relieved, she thanked Mac for the update and disconnected.

Turning her attention back to the screens, she saw John and Mako's icons merge. Feeling excluded, she sat back, stuffing chips into her mouth, hoping the calories would jump-start her brain. She needed to find a way aboard the yacht—at least virtually.

56

STORM SURGE

Syracuse Harbor, Sicily

SABA POINTED TOWARD THE ACCESS DOOR AS IT LIFTED INTO THE hull, knowing it was the only entry point. A second later, the tender dock appeared, sliding over the water, ready to receive Maldonado.

The best Mako could hope for was to disrupt their plans. He assumed, being armed with only the .45, they would be outgunned and outmanned.

"I'm going to try and get on board," Mako yelled over the engine noise.

"You'll never get in. They're sure to have three or four goons waiting there, and I didn't see any other openings."

As they approached, Mako realized she was correct. There was no time to circumnavigate the ship. He would have to trust her.

Maldonado's boat was only feet away from the dock. Two men emerged from the hull to help him aboard. From a quarter-mile away, Mako could see they were armed. The bishop's boat coasted up to the dock and, without stopping, one of the men helped Maldonado onto the larger ship.

Turning the wheel over to Saba, he moved to the bow. She maintained speed, halving the distance to the tender dock in a matter of seconds. A loud *clank* startled them as they passed the bow. Water streamed down from the anchor and chain as it locked into place. Simultaneously the ship shuddered and started to move. It was scary, even though Mako knew they were not in immediate danger. Ships this size took a long time to gather speed or stop.

Passing amidship, they were within a hundred feet of the tender dock when the platform started to recede into the hull. Just as it disappeared, the door closed, leaving a smooth sheet of metal. There was nothing to be done now—except they were in a different kind of trouble.

The flare of the hull concealed them from anyone wanting to fire on them from above. That was the good news. The bad was that the boat started to move much faster than Mako had expected. The sea churned and the yacht picked up speed as the huge propellers displaced the surrounding water.

"We've got to get away from the stern. This close we could get sucked under." Mako didn't know if Saba understood, but she reacted quickly, swinging the wheel to take them on a course perpendicular to the ship. A space slowly opened between the two craft. They had avoided one hazard. Looking back, Mako saw they were not clear yet.

As the yacht built speed it needed an extra push from the engines to put it on plane. The result was a huge wave, which loomed large over their small boat. The captain would surely be asking for all power. There would be several more waves behind the one currently threatening them.

"You ever surf?" Mako asked, moving towards to the wheel, and glancing back.

Saba followed his gaze and her eyes widened. "That?"

She slid to port, allowing Mako to take the wheel. He'd ridden some waves in his time, but the behemoth behind them was not in his wheelhouse. What he did know was that they had to increase speed—quickly. If they could match the speed of the wave, there was a chance; if not, they would be gobbled up and swallowed.

"Hold on!" Mako yelled. He pushed the throttle to its stop, failing to remember that the old two-stroke engine needed to be coaxed, not whipped. In response it started to stall. Mako released the pressure on the throttle. The engine sputtered back to life. He didn't know it, though, because the ship's engines were so loud it drowned every other sound.

The wave was twenty feet behind them, and looked to be as tall. The best they could hope for was that it wouldn't break. In the event it caved in on itself, they would be lost in the power of the white water.

Mako gunned the engine again. This time he stopped just a little short of full power and, hoping for the best, looked back again. It was ten feet away and closing fast. He felt the wave pull the water from beneath the hull, sucking its energy and slowing the boat even further.

The bow dropped. The angle was almost forty-five degrees, steeper than Mako had expected. In addition to his fear of being swallowed by the wake, they were now in danger of pitchpoling. Breathing in, he let his old surf training kick in. His father had berated him for spending so many hours on the water. Hopefully it would pay off now.

This was the critical time. He needed to at least match the speed of the wave. Fighting his desire to push the throttle to its stops, he slowly accelerated. The engine reacted.

Mako felt the energy of the wave take the boat. It didn't matter what he did now, the ocean was in total control. The bow rose slightly and the boat took off. Mako could have shut the engine down for all the good it was doing. Despite the danger, a smile creased his lips, as the wake carried the boat forward, until a few hundred yards later, when Mako felt their speed drop slightly. It was time to figure out an exit strategy.

Looking behind them, he saw several more rollers. As long as they didn't take them beam on, they would be safe. With a firm grip on the wheel, he accelerated slightly to gain steerage, and turned about thirty degrees to port. The boat escaped one wave, and gently passed another one. It wasn't until he felt Saba beside him that his tunnel vision receded. He had been so focused on the wave, he had forgotten everything else—it might have saved them.

A different urgency overtook them as the seas flattened out beneath the hull of the fishing boat. Passing back under the bridge, they raised the Bimini top and returned the boat back from where they had taken it. Three men stood on the seawall with their arms crossed. Mako felt Saba reach for the pistol. He stopped her when he saw one of the men smile.

"Son of a bitch. How you rode that wave! I didn't think she had it in her."

The men tossed lines across the void and helped tie off the boat.

"Sorry about that. We looked for you, but had no choice," Saba said.

They weren't interested in her flirtatious appeal. It was Mako and the wave they were interested in.

It appeared that a trip to a local tavern was in order, until Mako's phone rang. He glanced down at the screen.

"Alicia," he said to Saba. As they walked away Mako could still hear the men recalling how their boat had surfed the wave.

Syracuse, Sicily

Mako and Saba sat at an outside table in a small cafe. They had wanted to leave immediately and track down the ship, but Alicia had brought them back to earth. There was no boat in the harbor capable of running down the behemoth. They would need to wait until the destination was certain and fly there. She was tracking the vessel's route on one of her screens, giving Mako and Saba real-time updates to its course. The yacht was headed north, leading them to conclude the destination was Rome. There had been a chance they would continue on their tour of Caravaggio's paintings, or rather murder sites, as they were intertwined. That would have led to Malta, where the painter had spent a few years prior to Sicily—until another murder caused him to make a remarkable escape from the dungeons of the Knights.

"We know where they're going. It has to be Rome," Mako said.

"Not so fast," Alicia said. "Sending you a link."

Mako's phone pinged and he opened the web address showing the boat traffic in the area. She had placed a circle around Longino's ship.

"Do you see it?" Alicia asked after a few minutes.

"Yeah, they're heading north, like we thought."

"Again: not so fast. If their destination was Rome, they would be making a beeline for the Straits of Messina. Instead of the direct and deep-water route, they are hugging the coast."

Saba leaned over the phone for a better look. "Catania. They're going to drop Maldonado off."

"The international airport." It was where they had flown into several days ago.

"We need to go after him," Mako said.

Mako knew from the tone of Alicia's voice he was being

impulsive. "Maldonado has the journal, that's ink and paper. It'll survive and now that the painting has been replaced he won't destroy it; he needs it. I'd be a little more concerned about John and Faith."

Mako hadn't forgotten about his father and the girl. Still feeling the endorphin high from his ride on the wave, he was thinking he was Superman.

"I can gather some resources to stop the ship and get John and Faith," Saba said. "Mako might be right. We need to go after the journal."

Mako had noticed a change come over her. His gut told him it concerned the journal escaping her grasp, and not about their adventure. Maldonado winning the game was not going to sit well with her."

"It will certainly be easier to get you two to Rome than to plan a raid on a ship. Maybe we should leave that bit to Interpol," Alicia said.

All three acknowledged that it was the smart move. It would take a military-style action to subdue and board Longino's ship.

An uneasy quiet settled over the table. The waiter brought their food, a veal dish for Saba, and what he was told was freshly caught swordfish for himself—he couldn't resist.

"I'm hoping everything is all right with TJ. I like those two," Mako said. He stuffed a large bite of fish in his mouth and chewed. Looking up from his plate, he saw something different on Saba's face. She reached over and took his hand.

"I'd like to meet them someday." She applied enough pressure to get a reaction. "We should get to Catania tonight. Catch the first flight out."

Mako picked up his phone. "I'll let Alicia know."

"It sounds like she has her own problems. We can take care of it ourselves."

57

STEVEN BECKER

STORM SURGE

Key Largo, Florida

ALICIA FOUGHT OFF THE WEARINESS RUNNING DEEP IN HER BONES. The war room had no windows to distract her; it was her circadian rhythm smacking her in the head. Between being up for more than twenty-four hours and the escape from the burning boat, her body was beginning to shut down, starting with her brain. She knew her mind had started to wander in the last few hours and she was only doing busywork to take her mind off TJ.

The clock on her monitor told her it was past dawn. Fortunately, there were no charters booked for today. She made a note to contact the future bookings. Without a boat, their operation was effectively out of business. None of that mattered now. It was TJ and the journal that she needed to focus on.

Mako and Saba were on their way to Rome. The yacht had passed through the Straits of Messina and was still heading north. She had no luck when she tried to confirm Maldonado's whereabouts. That didn't surprise her. The bishop was crafty and was likely traveling under an assumed name—or in one of the Vatican's private jets.

Stretching, she rose from her chair and left the war room. It was indeed morning, and after a quick shower, she grabbed a cup of coffee and headed out to the hospital.

Sitting in a chair near TJ, Mac's head was resting on his chest when she entered the room. She was thankful that he was still here. Letting him sleep, she ignored him and moved around the other side of the bed. On the trip over she had tried to align her expectations with TJ's condition, hoping that would prepare her. The image in her head fell short of what TJ looked like.

Bandages covered most of him, though there was no seepage, which she took to be a good sign. His head was wrapped as well, leaving holes for his eyes, nose, and mouth. Several plastic bags were hung on the rack beside him, dripping drugs and other fluids intravenously. Looking up to read the labels, she recognized one as an antibiotic. Another was saline.

Following the clear line to his arm, she noticed a blocked-off tube, probably for the pain killers. Her gaze drifted up to his face and she jumped back in shock as his light blue eyes met hers.

"Hey, babe," he said, his voice muffled by the bandages.

"TJ, are you okay?" She felt stupid asking the question. He clearly wasn't. "Pain?" she drilled deeper.

"Some," he said, his eyes moving to the clock on the wall.

Below it, Alicia noticed a whiteboard with his pertinent information. On top was the nurse's name and extension. She scanned the rest of the board, noticing that he was due for his next round of pain meds anytime. Picking up the phone, she dialed the extension and asked the nurse to come by.

The opioid epidemic governed pain management. Pain meds were no longer issued automatically. You had to ask, after telling the nurse how much pain you were in. The scale was near worthless. Alicia had read somewhere that most people replied their pain level was a ten. The problem was that once the meds wore off, the on-ramp to the next dose was steep.

Alicia could see the lines around TJ's eyes soften as soon as the nurse injected a dose of morphine through his IV. A few minutes later, they closed and he was asleep. Alicia motioned to the nurse that she would like to talk outside, and the two left Mac and TJ.

The nurse looked familiar, but Alicia couldn't recall her name. She leaned over, trying to read the hospital ID. "Nancy, is the doctor around?" Though spread out, the Keys were pretty much like every other small town, except for the influx of tourists. People knew each other. If you didn't know someone personally, you at least recognized them.

"I know what you're thinking. It's not anywhere as bad as it looks."

"That's a relief."

"Doctor rounded earlier, and wants to keep him overnight for observation. The bandages and antibiotics are more precautionary." She put a hand on Alicia's arm. "He's going to be all right."

Alicia started to thank her, but Nurse Nancy cut her off.

"The police and marine patrol keep coming by, wanting to talk to him."

"Thanks. Better get Mac out of here, then." She meant to say it under her breath, but Nancy caught it.

"That'd be a good idea."

58

STEVEN BECKER

STORM SURGE

The Mediterranean Sea

JOHN HEARD THE RUMBLE OF THE ENGINES, THEN THE DECK started to vibrate. Rising from the single berth, he looked out the sealed porthole to see they were moving away from land. He paced the small cabin. It was all he had done since being taken aboard. Far from a brig, the cabin was well appointed, but it was nevertheless a jail. The door was locked from the outside and the porthole was sealed. He had been kept alone and, though he had asked, was unaware of where they were holding Faith, and if she was even here.

He had tried to remain vigilant throughout his captivity, waiting for a mistake that might lead to his freedom. None had presented itself, or at least none that he had noticed. Part of that was due to the bottle of pills on the table by the berth. With his leg pounding like a jackhammer, he'd taken several. Now that they were underway, he sat on the berth, reached over, and unscrewed the cap. Pouring two tablets into his palm, he thought about taking a third. Deciding against it, he swallowed the pills dry. He wasn't going anywhere for the immediate future, although his experience told him that opportunities weren't scheduled.

Twice he had checked his wound. There were no signs of infection, and it appeared to be healing well. When his captors had brought his latest meal, he had asked for clean dressings. Surprisingly they had complied, leaving him to think that Longino wanted him alive. He rose again, this time trying to loosen up the stiffness in his joints. If and when the time came, he would need to be ready. Walking around the room, John worked the bum appendage, testing how far he could push himself before the leg failed. The opioids helped mitigate the pain, though he realized there was a fine line between being mobile and clearheaded.

With land slipping away, he knew this might be his last chance. He would have to manufacture his escape. The guards had just changed as well, which would give him some extra time if he was successful. All things considered, his body was feeling pretty good right now, and there might not be a better time. Believing they were planning on keeping him alive mitigated the risk.

John banged on the door to attract the attention of the guard he expected was camped in the passageway. He'd been able to sneak a look earlier when they had delivered his food, and had seen a chair positioned halfway between two cabins. He assumed Faith was in the other room.

There was a sudden movement outside the door. The pain pills delayed his reaction, so he was slow to step back as it opened. His position put him closer to the guard than either would have liked.

"What?"

John didn't have an answer to that question. Glancing down the hall to buy some time, he noticed the chair was empty. The guard was alone. With the sight of land slipping away, he acted on impulse and, leaning forward, head-butted the guard.

Surprised by the attack, the guard staggered back. Adrenaline surged through John's body, temporarily blunting the dulling effect of the pills. John instinctively stepped forward. Seeing the holstered weapon on his opponent's right hip, John reached his hand underneath the man's right arm, grabbed a hand and spun it behind the man's back. By the time the guard regained his senses, John had him disarmed.

Before setting out to find Faith, he pushed the man into his cabin, shut the door to mute any noise, then slammed the butt of the pistol into the man's skull. He dropped to the floor. John quickly went to work.

Anything that even resembled a weapon had been removed from the room. The only things not bolted down were the sheets and towels. Grabbing a washcloth from the bathroom, John stuffed it into the man's mouth and, using the top bedsheet, tightly rolled the inert figure like a mummy. To secure the man, John rolled the second sheet in the same manner and lashed it around the man's torso. His captive was just coming to when John tied the knot behind him. The effect was a double-layered straight jacket. The man's face turned red as he fought against the bonds. John watched him struggle for a minute to ensure he couldn't escape, and left the room.

Finding Fatih was now his priority. After that he would figure it out as he went. It was too much of a risk to call out to her. Knocking on the cabin doors was not preferable, either. He had the element of surprise and moving to the next door he tested the knob. The door opened to an empty cabin. The two doors across the passageway yielded the same result.

John wondered if she was being held in another part of the ship, or maybe she wasn't aboard at all. Passing the guard's chair, there was one door remaining. Checking the corridor, he moved toward it and slid the locking mechanism away from the jamb. His search of the other rooms had only taken a few minutes, he could only hope it wouldn't cost more than that.

He knocked lightly as he cracked the door open.

"Faith?"

"John?" She threw her arms around him.

"No time for that. We've got to go," John said, hoping she wasn't going to ask what his plan was. They had several things going for them: surprise and darkness, which John figured would descend over the Mediterranean Sea in the next hour or so. Attempting escape with no knowledge of the ship's layout or how many people were aboard was not the smartest thing he had done. Backtracking from the thoughts of doom and gloom, he reviewed what he knew as he led Faith down the passageway.

He did have some knowledge. The guards, for one. There were three that he recognized, probably meaning they worked in eight-hour shifts. He cursed himself for not working out their schedule, but guessed they checked in every two or three hours. He looked down at his watch. Using the smaller number, and figuring it had been fifteen minutes since he rendered the guard unconscious, John estimated they had an hour and a half comfort zone. That would be six o'clock, about the time the sun set.

John also knew enough about the yacht to figure out where the exit was. Though the ship had many decks he had not seen, he was aware of which level they currently were on, and the location of the tender dock. Hopefully, that would be enough. On arrival, they had been hurried through the lower level, but it has been hard to miss the collection of water toys—including the submersible. He also knew from the direction of the shadows across his room that they were heading north and that meant the Straits of Messina, not a body of water to navigate with a Jet Ski or small, open boat. That left the submarine.

Before he worried about their method of transport, they had to reach the lower decks. Not wanting to risk the elevator, he pulled open a steel door, which opened onto a stairwell. They quickly descended two levels before he stopped. He put a finger to his lips. Together they waited, the only sound their individual heartbeats. After a minute John whispered, "What do you remember about the level we were brought in on?"

"I'm fine, thank you, and same for the rescue," Faith whispered.

John knew he had been abrupt, but his mind was on escape, not niceties. "Please. We don't have much time."

"We've been at sea for four hours with one stop about half-way. My guess from the airplane traffic I saw that it was Catania."

John tried to hide his shock. She had more situational awareness than he did. Blaming it on the drugs, he added to her summary. "We've got an hour, maybe a few minutes more, until they figure out we escaped."

"I'm not sure how many levels the ship has," she said, moving to the doorway.

To the side was a schematic of the ship mounted in a glass frame. Ignoring the irony of a Mafia boss having a safety plan, John studied the drawing. "Looks like two levels down from here."

Silence was more important than speed, so they descended carefully. Reaching the door they assumed was to the tender deck, John pulled the guard's Sig Sauer out of his waistband and signaled for Faith to stand back. Slowly, he cracked the door. The deck was pitch dark, the only illumination coming from small LED lights on the equipment. Straight ahead, to the side of where he thought the retractable door was, a brighter glow came from what he guessed was the control panel for the submersible.

John started toward the lights, but stopped when he felt a hand on his arm.

"The door's going to set off an alarm," Faith said.

"No worries there. Smile for the cameras," John said, pointing to a security camera mounted over the door. The flashing red light told him it was active. Disabling it would be easy enough, and possibly ignored, written off as a malfunction. Things constantly broke on well-maintained boats, even one this expensive. Glancing around, he noticed several more cameras. Taking out the one was not worth the trouble.

John took off toward the control panel, counting down the seconds until they had company. Figuring the steel door would open in less than a minute, the time it would take security to descend into the bowels of the ship, he reached the closed hatch and stared at the panel. Many of his contemporaries, including Faith's father, had retired, in part because of the transfer of assets from human, to computers and drones. John had bucked the trend and at least tried to stay current with the new technologies. He could deal with most systems, but when he found himself staring at a complicated computer screen, he felt inadequate.

Faith nudged him aside, and pressed several icons on the touch screen. John left her to it, keeping his pistol aimed at the steel door, which he expected would be opened any second now. A motor started to whine above and he felt a slight breeze as the hatch cracked open.

"Good job. Now, can you get that submersible in the water?"

"You want to take the submarine?" she asked.

John remained silent. This was no time for debate. Taking the submersible had several advantages over the surface craft, especially if, as he suspected, they were in the Straits. The yacht had many features above and beyond comparable craft, but it was no Navy destroyer. Lacking depth charges, the submersible could escape, whereas surface craft could be seen on radar and pursued. On their way across the harbor, he had studied the ship as best he could and hadn't seen a deck-mounted gun aboard. That didn't mean they didn't have one. He remembered how Mac Travis's friend Jesse McDermitt had weaponized his Rampage sportfisher. The mount for the fighting chair doubled as a stand for a fifty caliber M2 machine gun.

With the access door completely open, light flooded the deck. Now that he could see, John moved over to the submersible and, with one hand still holding the pistol on the door, released the tie-downs with his other. A cable with a large hook attached to a welded ring on the hull led to the boom of a small crane fixed to the deck adjacent to the sub. A thick electrical cable was attached to the port side. He released the twist-lock and discarded the charging cable, then moved to the side and stared at the crane.

Relief swept over him. The controls were common to heavy equipment. "Come on. I've got this."

Do we need to extend the dock?" Faith asked.

With the tender door almost open, John studied the controls trying to figure out how to launch the craft. He had been lost in thought for a second and missed when the steel door behind them opened. He didn't miss the gunshots as they ricocheted off the steel supports.

Two men stood by the door. The one firing was focused on Faith. The other scanned the room. John wanted to call out and reassure Faith, but stayed silent. The men knew he was in the room, but not where. Using the precious advantage, he slid away from the submersible and, using the crane for cover, took careful aim and fired two shots at the man.

One dropped, giving Faith the few seconds she needed to reach him. They were together now, but a third figure stood in the doorway.

"Longino," Faith muttered.

The mob boss held what looked like an AK-47. A flurry of bullets flowed from the muzzle. Hidden behind the bulk of the crane, nothing hit them, but a red fluid was pooling on the deck around them.

"He hit a hydraulic line. We need plan B." The line appeared to be critical to launching the submersible, and from the quantity of fluid spreading around them, John knew the shot had disabled the entire unit.

He fired twice, cursing himself for not checking the magazine when he had taken the weapon from the man in his room. There was only so much he could blame on the narcotics. His game needed to improve. The Sig Sauer 229 was not his preferred weapon, but he could tell by the length of the grip that it held an extended ten-round magazine. Minus the four shots that he'd taken, leaving him six remaining plus one in the chamber—if it had been full.

Having switched his rifle from automatic to manual, Longino continued to spray bullets across the deck, this time in two- and three-shot groupings. At his current rate of fire, he could pin them here indefinitely. Sending one shot toward the steel door to put Longino in a defensive position, John fired a second, taking the opportunity to peer out from behind the boom. Longino was alone.

59

STEVEN BECKER

STORM
SURGE

Catania, Sicily

MAKO HAD TRAVELED ENOUGH TO FIND THE SIGN BEHIND THE
baristas funny:

> *Heaven is where the police are British, the chefs Italian, the
> mechanics German, the lovers French, and it's all organized by the
> Swiss. Hell is where the police are German, the chefs are British, the
> mechanics French, and it is all organized by the Italians.*

Standing in what passed in Italy for a line, he couldn't have
said it better himself. Finally, he worked his way to the counter
and grabbed his order. Taking the coffees to the gate, he tried to
relax. At least TJ was going to be all right. That was a bright spot,
the only one they had. He approached the floor-to-ceiling
window and handed Saba her latte.

"Anything from Alicia?" Saba asked, as she popped the lid
and checked the brew.

Mako sipped his Americano, and glanced at the screen.
"Nothing."

Alicia's call in the dead of night had appeared to be good news though, as it often did, her timing sucked. Mako and Saba, realizing there was nothing they could do until they landed in Rome, had let off some steam. Mako had been wary when Saba suggested they share a room. Having to calculate whether she was planning something other than the obvious, or was truly interested in him, had left him in a dilemma. A bottle of champagne delivered to their room had eased his worries and eased the way for some welcome horizontal activity.

Alicia's phone call informing them that the ship appeared to be circling in a search pattern had put a halt to all activity in room 218 of the Palace Catania.

He was hopeful the yacht's actions were an indication that his father and Faith were alive and had escaped. The advantage of flying, which allowed him and Saba to reach Rome before the ship arrived in port, detracted from their ability to help his father.

When the attendant at the gate called for the flight to board, Saba started for the gate, but Mako reached out and stopped her. "Watch the show. It's not worth the fight."

Instead of the semi-orderly boarding procedure they were used to, the Italians made a mad dash for the gate. Mako and Saba drank their coffee and watched. Under different circumstances they might have laughed. When the crowd finally thinned out, they presented their boarding passes and walked down the jetway.

The flight was uneventful, offering them a brief, welcome respite to enjoy each other's company. While on the plane they were helpless to do anything; the underlying tension of that helplessness cast a shadow over them.

Before the wheels touched down, they both jumped into action, and turned on the phones they already held in their hands.

Mako's phone dinged first. Saba looked over at him. "Alicia?"
He nodded.

Saba's phone countered with multiple blips, claiming her attention. Mako texted Alicia, who got right back to him. He didn't know whether to be relieved or not.

Saba saw him set the phone upside down on his leg. "Problem?"

"The ship has turned back to Syracuse."

"That makes no sense."

"Could be a number of reasons. Mechanical failure ... "

Saba cut him off. "Or maybe they escaped."

Mako didn't want to get his hopes up, and turned back to the phone. By the time the plane had taxied to the gate, they were both up to date, though Mako was still unsure what to think or do about his father.

Saba must have read his mind. "You've got to trust him."

Mako tried to switch gears. "So, it's off to the Vatican."

"If it were that easy," Saba said.

With an abrupt bump the plane stopped at the jetway. The aisles immediately filled as the other passengers fished their luggage from the overhead bins. Despite knowing that it would accomplish nothing, Mako stood and joined them. Any action at this point would help him feel useful.

It was a fight all the way to the airport exit where, once they stepped outside, Mako started toward the cab stand. Saba stopped him.

"I've got a car and driver," she said.

Mako realized he had been so absorbed in his own world he had no idea what all the texts Saba that sent and received were about. "Hello, secrecy?"

"I've got resources, might as well make use of them."

"So long as they don't step on our toes."

Saba nodded, sliding into the backseat.

"Rome," he said to the driver, who raised his eyebrows, looking at them in the rearview mirror wanting for a more specific destination. Now that they were here, Mako realized he hadn't thought any of this through. He didn't have a destination —or a plan. "The Vatican," he told the driver, and settled back for the ride.

"Wait, we can't just walk in there," Saba said.

"We'll blend in with the tourists." Mako reached for her hand. "Newlyweds. No one will question us."

"Besides wondering what we're doing in the Vatican when we should be somewhere else." Saba winked.

"We can do that as well."

"Hold onto that last thought. I have an idea, though." Saba faced forward, trying to get the driver's attention. His eyes met hers in the rearview mirror, leaving no doubt he had been listening. She let it go.

"The Pantheon."

60

STORM SURGE

The Mediterranean Sea

"WE'VE GOT TO LOCATE THE OTHER SHOOTER," JOHN WHISPERED to Faith.

Several more shots pinged the steel boom, causing them to lower their bodies behind the machinery. John knew it was just a matter of time before Longino's man was in position. Facing two men with superior firepower was bad enough. Not knowing the location of the second shooter made it worse, as did the fact that his friend's daughter was beside him.

"There or there." Faith motioned to two locations.

John turned to study the areas. Something moved by one. "How can you tell?"

"Shooting lanes. I grew up with video games," Faith replied.

"Well, what's he going to do now?" John asked, trying to make light of their situation.

"If they work as a team, they're going to alternate fire and move in on our position."

Just as she said it a shot pinged the engine housing just inches away from John's head, coming from behind them. The man was in position now, and not worried about revealing his location. The machinery, which had provided adequate cover when both men were near the stairway, now left them vulnerable to the second shooter. "We've got to move."

It was a calculated risk. Although Longino had the deadlier weapon, he likely lacked the experience of the thug. The problem was there was no way to prove John's theory without testing it, and that meant exposing himself. Studying the deck, John thought Faith's shooting-lane strategy might work in their favor, provided he was correct.

"Cover me," John said, handing Faith the Sig Sauer. "Five shots left."

As he rose, she took aim and fired. The shot hit the door jamb, forcing Longino back inside the stairwell.

"Four."

Another shot struck behind them. It was closer than the first, indicating the shooter had found a better angle. "Don't forget our friend back there."

Knowing that Faith was competent with a firearm eased John's anxiety as he dashed across the deck and dove behind one of the jet skis. Several shots followed his progress, but they were too late.

Longino was still in the stairwell, but with the shooter somewhere behind him and aware of his position, there was nothing he could do about either man. John glanced over at Faith. She had shifted into a small space between the engine and the carriage to which the crane was mounted. It was a perfect hiding spot for one person.

John took a deep breath, released it, and ran for the door. Two shots echoed behind him. There was no sign of the bullets striking nearby and he started to worry about Faith, but he was too exposed to help her. The best thing he could do for both of them was to take out Longino.

Going up against an automatic weapon was not something to be taken lightly. Even if the man holding it was inexperienced, the odds were heavily in the shooter's favor. John looked around for a weapon, something to balance the scales. Several steps away was a workbench. Next to it, secured with two eyehooks embedded in the wall, was a mechanics tool chest.

John looked over at Faith again. A movement behind her caught his eye. "Faith!" he yelled to alert her. She turned a second too late. The man lunged forward, pinning the Sig Sauer against the boom housing. A second later the sound of metal on metal rang out as the pistol dropped to the steel deck.

There was only one thing to do. If the man had Faith, John needed Longino. The sounds of a skirmish across the room gave him confidence that the shooter was distracted. He quickly slid over to the toolbox and opened the top drawer. An assortment of wrenches were laid out by size. Reaching for the largest, he moved back to the door. The eighteen-inch-long wrench would be adequate to take down Longino, but there was still the problem of the gun.

"Don't move. I've got her," the man yelled from across the room.

John had to take another risk that if the man was going to kill Faith he would have done so already. Reaching back toward the chest, he opened the same drawer and removed one of the smaller wrenches. John moved the larger wrench to his left hand and, twirling the smaller wrench in his right to get a feel for the weight and balance, he reached for the doorknob.

John had no choice. Though he badly wanted the weight and reach of the larger wrench, he knew it was the wrong weapon. By the time he could find and strike Longino, John's body would be riddled with bullet holes. Setting the larger wrench down, he reached for the doorknob again, turning it quickly, and pulled the door open. His peripheral vision caught movement behind him. He was committed now with only a half-inch wrench for a weapon—or tool.

Lunging forward, to get inside the reach of the weapon, John anticipated where Longino's hands would be. Not expecting the attack, the man jumped back in surprise. Instinctively, Longino recoiled slightly. At the same time, he brought the gun up. Expecting John to go for the gun, Longino's finger started to squeeze the trigger. In the millisecond before the trigger activated the firing pin, John jammed the small wrench into the trigger guard. It stuck. Longino tried to fire again, which lodged the wrench in even more.

With the weapon disabled, John slammed the foot of his good leg into Longino's instep. John knew Longino would lean forward in pain, and when he did, John yanked the AK from his hands. Taking it by the barrel, he slammed the butt into Longino's head.

"I still have the girl," the other man called out from across the deck. "Let me go and I'll release her."

Nothing would be gained from a gunfight with Faith in the middle. John glanced down at Longino's body on the deck beneath him. A large pool of blood was spreading from the head wound, causing John to take several steps back. Leaning down, John didn't see a need to check for a pulse; instead he checked Longino's weapon.

"I'll do what I have to," the man called out.

John figured he had heard the loud click as he reseated the magazine and chambered a round. "I got no gripe against you," John called back. "Release her. We'll be taking that boat there. You can stay with the ship."

"I got some issues with staying."

John didn't care. The man would likely be cannon fodder once Longino's associates found out what had happened. When your only job is to protect your boss and he's killed, unemployment is your last worry. "Let her go. We'll take the boat and be on our way."

"Suit yourself, but I need some assurances."

John thought about his situation for a few seconds, deciding they were just wasting time. It was at least a half hour and probably longer since he had caught the glimpse of land passing by his porthole. Glancing at the open door, he estimated the ship was cruising in the neighborhood of thirty knots. That meant if they were heading out to sea, they would be at least fifteen miles offshore. With no idea of the range of the small boat strapped into a cradle behind him, it was time to go.

"What do you need?" With renewed urgency, John decided this negotiation was a waste of time. He moved away from the steel door where Longino lay. "Leave her there. The way to the door is clear."

"Clear, so you can shoot me."

John looked down at the rifle. Ejecting the magazine and clearing the chamber, he tossed it toward the open door. It skidded to a stop just inches before falling into the depths. "There's your assurances. Let's get this done. Your turn."

He heard Faith scream and instantly regretted disarming himself. Reaching for his pistol, he came up empty. Recalling Faith had had it, he saw it lying on the deck. Seconds later a second pistol tossed by the henchman joined it.

"I'm okay," Faith called out.

At the same time, John heard the sound of hard-soled shoes echo off the steel deck. The man looked over his shoulder as he reached the door, yanked it open, and disappeared. John ran to Faith.

"Easy. You sure you're not hurt?"

Faith rose unassisted and brushed herself off. "I'm good. Let's get out of here."

"I'm with you there." John went to the small boat, leaned

over the gunwale, and scanned the console. "Key's in it." Standing back, he realized starting the boat wasn't going to be the problem. Moving it into the water was. Glancing back across the deck, he saw that the crane used to lower the submersible was equidistant between the submarine and boat. It was used for both, and now, with the hydraulics disabled by the gunshot, was of no use.

"The jet skis," Faith said.

John glanced over at her, realizing the pair as positioned to allow them to slide off their cradles onto the retractable dock. From there they were easily pushed into the water. "You know what to do with them?" He had no idea, always thinking of them as the mosquitoes of the boat world.

"Yeah, it's easy." She released the cable on the bow used to haul the machine from the water and shoved it off the cradle. The wheels attached to the supports rolled beneath it. A second later, Faith stood beside it on the dock, doing her best to hold it in place as the ship plowed through the chop.

"Come on."

John repeated the procedure on the other craft. A few minutes later, after waiting for a lull in the waves, the jet skis were in the water. John looked over at her. Faith nodded that she was ready, and they started their engines. It took John less than a minute to get the hang of the controls, enough time to round the stern of the ship.

John was getting anxious about the range of the jet skis, but once they were fully around the yacht, he could see land only a few miles away. With a sigh of relief, he realized the ship must have been running parallel to the coast.

Faith had spotted what looked like a small town ahead and turned toward it. A second later, John accelerated to avoid the rooster tail sent back at him as she took off. He followed her toward land.

61

STEVEN BECKER

STORM
SURGE

Rome

SABA BROWSED THE AISLES OF THE SMALL RELIGIOUS GOODS SHOP, looking for a nun's habit that she could live with. While she shopped Mako got used to the idea of impersonating a priest. Frankly, he was surprised when the religious store by the Pantheon hadn't been struck by lightning when he snapped the collar in place. With an occasional apprehensive glance at the ceiling to make sure it was not about to cave in on him, he checked himself in the mirror. Black was his color, and he was surprised how well the the suit fit him.

A minute later, he emerged from the dressing room, and found Saba still searching for her disguise. The store owner hovered over her, a stream of Italian questions coming from her lips. In between diatribes, she shot nasty looks at Mako, who couldn't understand any of it. It wasn't hard to figure out what upset her. The woman was torn between making a sale, and knowing neither of them had anything to do with the clergy.

The old woman went into another tirade as Mako moved ahead of Saba, pulling the occasional dress from the rack. "Sister, this would look sweet on you," he joked, hoping the store-keeper didn't understand English.

Finally, Saba took two frocks into the dressing room. Mako decided to wait outside while she tried them on rather than be left alone with the woman. The street was busy with tourists flocking to the Pantheon. The ancient building was rumored to be the longest continuously operated church in existence. It had started as an old Roman temple, then co-opted, as many of their other sites were, by the Catholic Church. If the ancient structures were not suitable for conversion, they were built in front of, or around, or over, and pillaged of their stone and furnishings. Of all these buildings, the Pantheon's unique domed roof, oculus, and state of preservation make it a must-see.

People nodded to Mako as they passed. It took a few minutes for Mako to realize that the passersby were not being friendly so much as paying tribute to his calling.

In this case it truly was the clothes that made the man.

Mako had started to engage the people, nodding back at them, when Saba emerged from the store. She had chosen well, down to the sensible shoes. Checking their reflection in the storefront window, she nodded.

"Well, Father? Shall we go see the pope?"

Mako's laugh was interrupted by his phone. Alicia was back. Accepting the call, he moved into the alcove by the door. He could see the woman on the other side of the glass give him a stern look, but he ignored her, needing the privacy.

"John and Faith are safe," Alicia stated.

"Great news." Mako turned to Saba and told her.

"And Longino is dead."

"Go, John Storm. That's one down. Now we need to nail Maldonado to the proverbial cross."

Mako guided Saba toward the waiting car. Once they were in, she asked the driver to take them to Vatican City.

62

STORM
SURGE

Vatican City

"LOOKING GOOD, SISTER," MAKO COULDN'T HELP HIMSELF.

Saba smacked his thigh, glancing in the rearview mirror to see if the driver was watching, which, of course, he was. Looking at Mako, she opened her eyes wide and slid them toward the driver. Mako understood the gesture and settled back into his seat.

His relief after hearing that his father and Faith were all right was palpable, added to that the elimination of Burga and Longino, and he was giddy. Maldonado still remained, though, and that thought brought him back to earth.

"It'll be easy enough to get in, but then what?" Mako asked.

"I'm working on that. The clothes should allow us entry to most of the areas, but the individual buildings are secure."

"We want to corner him like a rat. If he's out in public, he can use his position against us." Mako was confident there was enough security present that the cry of a bishop would be instantly heeded.

"You're right about that. The best we can do for now is to get close. We'll find a way in."

It sounded all too much like one of his plans. Mako looked down at the Tiber as they crossed a bridge. With the Interpol driver searching for any scraps of information he could gather, Mako decided to text Alicia instead of call.

He was relieved to hear that TJ, barring some scarring, was going to make a complete recovery. Then the telltale dots appeared in a bubble, telling him that Alicia was typing something. While he waited, he realized that the injuries to TJ and the loss of the boat could be laid at his feet. Or, glancing at the green-eyed woman sitting next to him, her's. The revelation steeled him to recover the journal and complete the contract.

"Maldonado is not going to give up the journal without a fight," Saba said. "We should be ready."

Mako thought it might not be a bad idea to deviate a little from his usual lack of planning and figure out how to deal with the bishop before they met him. "For a guarantee of protection, he might. He's got to know he's hit the glass ceiling in the Church. Some of this is going to get out. Maybe we can craft it and turn him into an ally."

"We can't let the Church slither out of this unscathed. It'd be too easy to cover for them by glossing over Longino's involvement, saying that the Mafia were the ones who replaced the paintings with forgeries." She stared out the window.

"Easy is good," Mako said.

"They have to pay for what they've done."

Mako wanted to look in her eyes and see where she was coming from, but she remained facing away. He'd sensed before that she had an ulterior motive with Maldonado. He expected that possession of the journal would end this for him, but not for her. The problem was he didn't know how to achieve his goal and make Saba happy.

A few minutes later, before Mako had made a decision, the driver pulled to the side of the street. After crossing the river on Ponte Vittorio Emanuel II, the driver had taken a left. Ahead was the Egyptian obelisk planted in the center of St. Peter's Square.

"It'll be easier on foot from here," the driver said.

Stepping out of the car, Mako and Saba started to walk toward the square, which was actually in the shape of an ellipse. Before they reached the square itself, Saba moved to the outside of the northern colonnades, and turned right into a narrow alley between two long rectangular buildings. Passing underneath a narrow walkway, they reached the front of the half-round entrance to the Institute of Works for Religion, otherwise known as the Vatican bank.

The lobby was accessible to the public, but Saba steered Mako toward the side of the building.

"You know your way around pretty well," Mako said.

Saba didn't reply.

Mako left it at that. Whatever local knowledge she had was to their advantage. He had already noticed several groups of uniformed Swiss Guards, and knew there were countless other plain clothes security teams as well.

"Act natural," Saba whispered as they approached the side door.

Mako could see the security keypad to the side. They would not be able to get in without a code or badge. "Now what?"

"Be patient. This is where blending in with the locals will pay off."

No sooner had she said it than the door opened. Saba stepped quickly toward it, holding it open for the older priest to exit. He nodded to them, and moved away.

"See."

Mako wasn't about to give her accolades for getting in a door, but they were inside now. "I suppose you know where his office is?"

Saba didn't answer. She started down the corridor, stopping at an ornate door near the end. The name on the small brass sign to the side said: The Most Revered Bishop Albert Maldonado. "Okay, you've gotten us this far."

Saba turned the handle and entered the waiting room. Mako walked in behind her. Antique furniture was set on an oriental rug, covering most of a highly polished stone floor. At a small desk near a pair of wooden doors sat a very attractive woman.

"Father, Sister, can I help you?"

"Thank you. We are here to see the bishop."

"May I ask if you have an appointment?"

"Please tell him that Sister Saba is here."

The woman turned, gave her a strange look, and picked up the handset of an old-style phone. She depressed one of the keys and waited. Mako's heart was in his stomach. Despite the disguise, he felt naked. Fearing metal detectors, they had come unarmed. Maldonado's response to the call would dictate how this went.

"The bishop will be happy to see you."

Just as she finished, the right-hand door opened. Maldonado stood in the doorway, gesturing Mako and Saba inside. "Please hold my calls." He closed the door behind them and quickly went to his desk.

"Nice outfits." He sat down, reached into a drawer, and pulled out a pistol. "Just to make sure everyone plays nice."

To this point, things had gone much better than Mako would have guessed. They had gained access to the bishop's office without any trouble, but the cold steel in the prelate's hand told him it might not remain that way.

"You have the journal?" Mako asked.

Maldonado, keeping his right hand on the pistol, used his

left to open another drawer in his desk. He withdrew a manila envelope, from which he unceremoniously dumped Caravaggio's journal on his desk. "The old boy's as much trouble dead as he was alive."

"What do you intend to do with it?" Mako asked. Wondering why he was doing all the talking, he glanced over at Saba. Her focus was on Maldonado, not the journal. "May I?"

Maldonado nodded.

Mako picked up the old book and flipped through a few pages. He'd handled it enough to know it was authentic. Setting it back down on the desk, he looked at the bishop, waiting for an answer to his question. Instead, Maldonado waved the gun in his direction, motioning them to move away from the desk.

Mako and Saba stepped back as the bishop rose. He picked up the journal and moved to a painting that Mako thought looked eerily like a Caravaggio, since now that he had seen a few he recognized the painter's style. Swinging the painting forward on a concealed hinge, it silently moved away from the wall, revealing a safe. Maldonado pressed his thumb on an illuminated pad, and the safe door opened. With a smug look on his face, Maldonado placed the journal inside, and before Mako could react, started to close the door.

Saba was more alert, and lunged forward. Maldonado lost his balance. Reaching out to regain his footing, his gun hand smashed into a side table, upending it in the process. The sound of glass breaking reverberated off the stone floor as a vase containing some fresh-cut flowers shattered. A second later they could hear the bishop's secretary ask if everything was alright.

Saba had the pistol trained on him before Maldonado had climbed to his knees. With the weapon pointed at his head, she nodded toward the door.

A pregnant pause followed, finally broken as Maldonado called out that he was all right. Mako stared at the pair, who's eyes were locked onto each other. Glancing back to the safe, Mako reached for the journal.

"Go ahead, take it. If it goes public, the forgery in the Church of Saint Lucia has been replaced. There is nothing there to harm us," Maldonado said.

"Then we'll need something else," Saba said. "Let's take a walk over to the Sistine Chapel, shall we?"

"I'm good here," Mako said, grasping the journal.

"Not so fast. You can have it when I'm done with him, but until then, we're together," Saba said. The barrel of the pistol reinforced her order.

One glance at her told Mako she was not going to be talked down from this ledge. To him, it was a suicide mission to try to escort the bishop across St. Peter's Square, enter the Sistine Chapel, and make it to the basement without alerting security. Glancing from the gun to her face, he saw the look of a martyr. "Okay." Mako raised his hands, but not before sliding the journal into a large pocket in his jacket.

"Not so fast." Saba held out her hand. "You can have it when we're finished here." She waited while Mako handed the journal to her, then slipped it into her bag. "Bishop, you first. Mako on the other side." Saba moved toward the double doors. "Go ahead."

Maldonado walked out of the office first. "There's been a bit of an accident, can you have someone clean it up?" he asked the secretary. "We'll be back shortly."

With Maldonado slightly in front, Mako and Saba walked side by side down the corridor. They reached the exit door without incident, and were soon outside. To Mako's surprise, Maldonado headed into a courtyard, avoiding the square. He moved swiftly, almost as if he had a purpose.

They walked through another building and entered an enclosed courtyard containing several sculptures that had been converted to a parking lot. Passing through, they ended up at a discreet-looking door with two Swiss Guards standing beside it. One nodded to Maldonado, who returned the gesture. Mako was surprised when the uniformed guard opened the door. If the bishop was to sound an alarm, this would have been the time. Instead, it felt like he was playing along with Saba. They found themselves in a small room with an elevator. The cab was waiting, and Maldonado stepped in with Saba and Mako behind him.

Dropping several floors, the doors opened onto a subterranean warehouse.

They passed another guard, and entered the rows of heavy shelving. Some areas were glass-enclosed, others open. Mako followed Maldonado toward the rear, where he stepped into a side aisle and spread out his hands.

"I'm assuming this is what you wanted to see?"

Instead of looking around, Saba took out her phone and started to take a video. "Why don't you give us a tour?"

Her request startled Maldonado, who had expected a different kind of confrontation. Pausing for a long second, he held out his hands. "What is it you want to see so badly?"

"Your collection of counterfeit art," Saba said, calmly.

She had the bishop cornered now, and he knew it. Instead of just wanting to see, or even take some form of proof that the Church had been swapping out the classics with forgeries, she was going to record it. The damage that a video, showing the collection in the basement of the hallowed cathedral, could do would be devastating.

Maldonado slowly moved toward a long cylinder similar to the one they had seen him with at the Church of Santa Lucia. Removing it from the rack, he feinted like he was going to dislodge the end and extract the painting. Instead, he wound up like a batter, and swung the six-foot-long tube at Saba.

She was caught off-guard and ducked. Maldonado had swung with enough force to knock an entire rack full of art to the floor.

"I don't know what you're aiming for here, but can we go now?" Mako asked.

Footsteps could be heard running toward them as the dust settled. Saba pulled Mako into the next row, shielding them as two of the Swiss Guards ran past. The swing had taken Maldonado to the ground, and he brushed off the guards' attempts to help him, telling them instead that the priest and nun who had accompanied him needed to be detained.

Saba was looking around the corner, holding her phone in front of her, recording the entire scene.

"You going to video them shooting you? We're in a freakin' sovereign country here. They can do what they want to us."

"I've got just about enough," she said, panning the phone around the shelves. "One more thing and we're out of here."

Mako recognized more of the names on the labels of the tubes and boxes than he wanted to admit. "Can we move this along?" He watched Saba as she browsed the lower shelf of one of the racks.

The sound of footsteps could be heard running toward them. Maldonado's voice rose above the commotion as he directed the search. Mako looked for another way out besides the elevator. "There!" He grabbed her hand and pulled her down the aisle toward a steel door. "Stairs."

"Wait." Saba shrugged off his hand, continuing to scan the contents of the shelf in front of them.

Mako peered around the corner. "We don't have time for a shopping trip."

Saba continued her search, finally selecting a small box. Mako, who had been peering over her shoulder, was distracted and failed to see the label on the box. Hearing footsteps approaching, he moved immediately toward the stairs, fifty feet away. Glancing behind him, he saw their pursuers were gaining. It was going to be close. Accelerating, he grabbed hold of the end shelving unit, pushed it to the ground, and slid around the corner. Twenty feet.

A glance back showed Saba as she reached down and picked up a three-foot-long tube from the ground. She was moving toward him with the tube tucked under her arm.

They reached the stairs. Mako's hand was on the doorknob when it pushed open, knocking him backwards into Saba. A second later, as they struggled to their feet, they found themselves staring into the barrels of a half-dozen guns. Several more men joined the circle, which parted as Bishop Maldonado stepped into the center.

"What are we to do with you?" His question was directed at Saba.

"My people know where I am. Sovereign nation or not, we need to walk out of here."

"I have no intention of hurting you, though your boyfriend is a little more expendable." Maldonado's gaze flashed at Mako. He held out his hand.

Saba handed him the tube.

"Nice try. The journal."

Saba reached into her bag and extracted Caravaggio's journal.

There was something in the way she acted that made Mako glance at her. Even with the guns held on them, she was being uncharacteristically cooperative. The look he got in return was not what he expected. Her eyes told him they weren't defeated. Yet.

Live to fight another day was more than a practical mantra. This battle might have been lost, but there was something about Saba's expression that told him they might still win the war.

Maldonado signaled for the guards to lower their weapons. "Before I provide you an escort to the gates, I'll need your phones."

Mako had hoped the bishop would have forgotten the video that Saba had recorded. Saba reached into her purse, pulled out hers, and handed it to the bishop. Again, Mako got the feeling that she wasn't done.

"Might be a good idea to let me call my driver first."

Maldonado returned her phone. "No tricks. He can meet you at the Castel Sant'Angelo."

If there was some kind of hidden signal in her conversation, Mako couldn't discern it. Saba disconnected the call and handed the phone back to Maldonado.

He turned to one of his men. "Take them out on the Passetto di Borgo."

Mako remembered the route from their visit with Juliet. The half-mile walkway connected the fortress with the Vatican. It was a not-so-secret, secret, but an easy way to get Mako and Saba out of the Holy See without being seen.

Exiting the dimly lit Sistine Chapel, Mako squinted into the sunlight. He still had no idea what Saba was up to, and for the time being was happy enough being escorted, alive and uninjured, from Vatican City. Once across the border, he would have more options.

They were led into one of the buildings they had passed through earlier, up a short flight of stairs, and into the passageway.

The walkway that several popes had used to flee invading or mutinous armies felt like a walk of shame to Mako. The journal was gone, as was any chance of vengeance against Maldonado. As long as he remained inside the walls of the Vatican, there was little that could be done.

About three-quarters of the way to Castel Sant'Angelo, their escort suddenly stopped. Mako and Saba sensed they were free and started a slow jog, then an all-out sprint to the doors ahead. Barging in, they found themselves inside the cylindrical structure.

Saba had a smug look on her face. "You look like you won," Mako panted. "He's got the journal and your phone."

"The video is in the cloud, and...." She reached into her bag and pulled out the box she had taken from the bottom shelf. She handed it to him.

Counterfeits and forgeries made Mako's head spin as he took it from her and saw the label: Caravaggio. Something about the feel of it told him this was the original journal.

"How did you know?"

"Let's get out of here first. I can still feel his slimy eyes on me." Saba started toward the double doors leading to freedom.

EPILOGUE

STEVEN BECKER

STORM
SURGE

Key Largo, Florida

SITTING AROUND THE WAR ROOM MAKO, SABA, JOHN, AND FAITH watched the monitors on the large wall. Most were set to different news stations, but the theme was the same: art.

Bishop Maldonado had been confronted and arrested while trying to authenticate the *Nativity with Saint Francis and Saint Lawrence* using the forged journal. He was currently in jail.

"You need a journal to keep the journals straight," Mako said. Caravaggio himself would have been proud of the bishop's ploy. After "proving" the journal was authentic by confirming the *Burial of Santa Lucia* as the original, Maldonado had moved on to his real play.

By changing the journal entry for the *Nativity with Saint Francis and Saint Lawrence* to suit the forgery, Maldonado planned to pocket over two hundred million dollars. Longino's involvement made it difficult to believe he had been working for the Church and not himself, but the Holy See had had stranger bedfellows before. The forged journal had itself been a work of art.

Maldonado's ego had undone him. By taking Saba down into the vault below the Sistine Chapel, she had seen the box, and suspected the real journal was within.

The screens on the wall in front of them showed the result. The bishop had taken the fall, but the video Saba had recorded in the vault had gone viral. Groups of protesters were gathered outside every museum that housed a Caravaggio. From the Louvre in Paris to the small churches in Sicily, the art world had been stood on its head.

One of the doors opened, letting in the harsh Florida sunlight that, though filtered by the living room, was still strong enough to wash out the screens.

The group turned toward the couple standing there. Alicia entered with TJ beside her, using a cane for support. She walked him to the captain's chair, where he made himself as comfortable as his bandages allowed.

"Good to have you back," Mako said.

"Guys, this is TJ." Alicia motioned to Saba and Faith, introducing them in turn. The greetings were heartfelt, and it seemed like even though the women had known each other and the Storms for less than a week that real bonds had formed.

"Looks like we succeeded," TJ said after scanning the screens.

"We lost the contract—and the boat," Alicia said.

"There are rewards for whistleblowers," Saba said. "I've taken the liberty of applying for them in your names. That should help."

Mako knew it wasn't going to be enough to cover the lost contract and replace the boat. As long as it did the latter, he would be happy.

Working from his chair, TJ cleared two of the screens and, punching commands into his keyboard, posted several pictures of sportfishers.

"Which one do y'all like?" He paused. "I spoke to the insurance people at the hospital. As unlikely as it is, we're covered."

The relief that spread through the room was palpable. "Go big, dude," Mako said, causing a ripple of good-hearted laughter. One at a time, the screens showing the news were co-opted by pictures and specs for boats.

They laughed and shopped until dinner. It always felt like a bit of a letdown to Mako after a job ended. This felt different and he had to know if the feeling was shared. When they rose to leave the room, Mako reached his hand across to Saba and, feeling her grasp it back, smiled.

John brushed by him, with an unmistakable look telling him to be careful, but Mako brushed it off. Some things would never change—he just hoped *someone* could.

ABOUT THE AUTHOR

Always looking for a new location or adventure to write about, Steven Becker can usually be found on or near the water. He splits his time between Tampa and the Florida Keys - paddling, sailing, diving, fishing or exploring.

Find out more by visiting www.stevenbeckerauthor.com or contact me directly at booksbybecker@gmail.com.

facebook.com/stevenbecker.books

instagram.com/stevenbeckerauthor

**Get my starter library First Bite for Free!
when you sign up for my newsletter**

http://eepurl.com/-obDj

First Bite contains the first book in several of Steven Becker's series:

Get them now (http://eepurl.com/-obDj)

Mac Travis Adventures: The Wood's Series

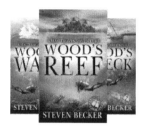

It's easy to become invisible in the Florida Keys. Mac Travis is laying low: Fishing, Diving and doing enough salvage work to pay his bills. Staying under the radar is another matter altogether. An action-packed thriller series featuring plenty of boating, SCUBA diving, fishing and flavored with a generous dose of Conch Republic counterculture.

Check Out The Series Here

★★★★★ *Becker is one of those, unfortunately too rare, writers who very obviously knows and can make you feel, even smell, the places he writes about. If you love the Keys, or if you just want to escape there for a few enjoyable hours, get any of the Mac Travis books - and a strong drink*

★★★★★ *This is a terrific series with outstanding details of Florida, especially the Keys. I can imagine myself riding alone with Mac through every turn. Whether it's out on a boat or on an island....I'm there*

Kurt Hunter Mysteries: The Backwater Series

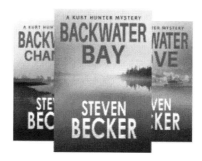

Biscayne Bay is a pristine wildness on top of the Florida Keys. It is also a stones throw from Miami and an area notorious for smuggling. If there's nefarious activity in the park, special agent Kurt Hunter is sure to stumble across it as he patrols the backwaters of Miami.

Check it out the series here

★★★★★ *This series is one of my favorites. Steven Becker is a genius when it comes to weaving a plot and local color with great characters. It's like dessert, I eat it first*

★★★★★ *Great latest and greatest in the series or as a stand alone. I don't want to give up the plot. The characters are more "fleshed out" and have become "real." A truly believable story in and about Florida and Floridians.*

Tides of Fortune

What do you do when you're labeled a pirate in the nineteenth century Caribbean

Follow the adventures of young Captain Van Doren as he and his crew try to avoid the hangman's noose. With their unique mix of skills, Nick and company roam the waters of the Caribbean looking for a safe haven to spend their wealth. But, the call "Sail on the horizon" often changes the best laid plans.

Check out the series here

★★★★★ *This is a great book for those who like me enjoy "factional" books. This is a book that has characters that actually existed and took place in a real place(s). So even though it isn't a true story, it certainly could be. Steven Becker is a terrific writer and it certainly shows in this book of action of piracy, treasure hunting,ship racing etc*

The Storm Series

Meet contract agents John and Mako Storm. The father and son duo are as incompatible as water and oil, but necessity often forces them to work together. This thriller series has plenty of international locations, action, and adventure.

Check out the series here

★ ★ ★ ★ ★ *Steven Becker's best book written to date. Great plot and very believable characters. The action is non-stop and the book is hard to put down. Enough plot twists exist for an exciting read. I highly recommend this great action thriller.*

★ ★ ★ ★ ★ *A thriller of mega proportions! Plenty of action on the high seas and in the Caribbean islands. The characters ran from high tech to divers to agents in the field. If you are looking for an adrenaline rush by all means get Steven Beckers new E Book*

The Will Service Series

If you can build it, sail it, dive it, and fish it—what's left. Will Service: carpenter, sailor, and fishing guide can do all that. But trouble seems to find him and it takes all his skill and more to extricate himself from it.

Check out the series here

★★★★★ *I am a sucker for anything that reminds me of the great John D. MacDonald and Travis McGee. I really enjoyed this book. I hope the new Will Service adventure is out soon, and I hope Will is living on a boat. It sounds as if he will be. I am now an official Will Service fan. Now, Steven Becker needs to ignore everything else and get to work on the next Will Service novel*

★★★★★ *If you like Cussler you will like Becker! A great read and an action packed thrill ride through the Florida Keys!*